Simon Ings is twenty-five years old and lives in London. He has had short stories published in several genre magazines, including *Interzone*, *Omni* and *New Worlds*.

HOT HEAD

Simon Ings

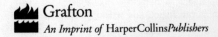

Grafton
An Imprint of HarperCollins*Publishers*

Grafton
An Imprint of HarperCollins*Publishers*
77–85 Fulham Palace Road,
Hammersmith, London W6 8JB

A Grafton Original 1992
9 8 7 6 5 4 3 2 1

A catalogue record for this book
is available from the British Library

ISBN 0 586 21496 8

Set in Caledonia and Avant Garde

Printed in Great Britain by
HarperCollinsManufacturing Glasgow

for Julie

Forty years I waited for you to come do my head in.
I love you massively!

– **NEWSPAPER VALENTINE, 1989**

ONE

The Tower Upright

If there was ever a universal culture on this planet, then it came in a cardboard box and on the side were stamped the words: made in Japan.

This culture might once have been called, with some justification, 'the West', but in the post-war period its economic influence was so vast, and its cultural heritage so etiolated, that no single name could embrace its intellectual glories, its catastrophic mundanities, its cherished and deadly contradictions. Even the most hostile actions undertaken or contemplated against this culture were but a renunciation of it, and implicit in each renunciation was the expectation of that alien, necessary culture continuing to survive and create.

This is the story of a woman born to Muslim parents; her cultural inheritance was drawn in part from her elders, from the old ways of her repudiative culture, and partly – from the age of six she was brought up in 'the West' – from the aggressive modernity of a newly unified Europe.

The flaw – the expectation of others continuing to

create, to be – sits at the heart of a repudiation, and this is as true for Malise Arnim (this name was given her when her father brought her to Europe) as it was for the particular Muslim society into which she was born.

So while this appears to be a story about a Muslim woman, it is in fact about a Western woman; and vice versa. Repudiations were nested within her, contradictory and subtle, and if at times during this story she seems immensely strong, or weak – or simply strange – then some of that will be a consequence of those forces within her, breaching no argument yet fatally undermined, opposed and yet dependent. Worlds within, not admitting of each other.

In Fundamentalism, Malise Arnim's elders thought they had found a way to consider themselves inviolate of Western influence. No longer did they follow the rich and contemptuous descendants of their colonial rulers. For a while the flaw in their argument was hidden. The repudiated West produced, in return for oil, goods the Islamic states themselves did not produce. Equipment, journals, textbooks: these goods were not associated with learning, effort or culture. They were barter goods – just one more natural resource.

Only when the Muslim world ran out of oil, and the West, gripped by recession, ceased to generate the communications, transport and arms by which the Muslim nations were governed, did those Fundamentalist states, riven from their revenue, wake to their predicament. They had, in the long Indian summer after the Iranian revolution, believed that all existing institutions were un-Islamic, and they had undone them one by one until – state after state found that this was so – only the army could rule. Military juntas have their own, irreligious prerogatives: Iranian forces overran Azerbaijan barely ten years into its new-found independence.

Soviet forces contained the action but they and their fellow Europeans were jittery and unhelpful at the conference table. There was a nuclear crisis: the Herzegovinian civil war was into its fourth month, and the States had just smuggled eight lightships through EC peacekeeping lines to rebel Finnish nationals.

The States itself, a month before, had been politically skewed by the Hispanic Lobby's bloodless *coup d'état*. No one knew who was in power, or why, or whether the lightships were a remnant of curtailed policy, or an omen of things to come.

At the age of six Malise fled with her father from Azerbaijan; they settled in the north of Italy, just outside Urbino.

When they first came to Italy, Malise's father tried to find work in Tarquinia, but all they had were factory jobs, and anyway, the oil was running dry; the factories were closing. The townsfolk wanted no more refugees.

He worked for a time in a seafood restaurant by the coast, and Malise followed him around while he waited on tables. Once an American man at a corner table asked her name, then said, 'Tell your father I'll have the *Bacalhau Portuguese* and a litre of red. Can you do that?'

He had haunted eyes. She wondered if he was Lobby, selling arms for oil. Because of her father's Francophilia, she was fast becoming a child of the United Europe: the thought of guns made her sick.

'Yes sir.'

'You live here?' he asked, smiling, when the food was brought to him.

She nodded.

'Is it a good place?'

She shrugged.

He stopped smiling. 'Do you know why I'm here?'

She didn't say anything. Lobby men were dangerous. It said so on the news.

'They're sending us back. Hysteria, mind, but they're sending us all back.'

It was the first time she'd seen an American. Boats came and took them away. Only the rich could afford a sea crossing, a lonely port, a new set of papers. The rest flew on the government ticket, into Washington and Dallas and New York. Malise had seen pictures of them on TV, being driven from the planes in trucks.

He ate some more then said, 'It must be strange living here.'

'I like the sea.'

'Surely it's a horrible place?'

'It's beautiful.'

He looked at her as if she was alien. 'But all those dead things –'

'They're interesting,' she said, and smiled, to show him how interesting they really were to her. She hated him, and because she hated him she wasn't going to let him see her hurt. It upset her to see dead things washed up along the coast, even while it fascinated her to pick apart their corpses with lengths of driftwood.

She hated the American because the States poured effluent into the seas and killed the things that lived there. She did not know that this was a recent development – that the States had not always been like that, that it had in fact pioneered the environmental cause that was so much part of her as a European.

(The United Europe into which Malise was being initiated was, like any young state, economical with the truth.)

The American sighed and put down his fork. 'Well, you live here, I don't. How strange, that it should all be so normal to you, so – nice.' He laughed.

It was not a laugh she ever wanted to hear again.

'Do you want anything else?'

'Ice cream. Liquorice, if you've got it.'

'Yes, sir.'

He was still laughing when she left his table.

Her father was looking out of the door, wondering where the custom had gone. She thought, how can people get in, if he stands blocking the door like that?

She brought the American his ice cream. He was in a jovial mood but there was panic behind his eyes. 'Kid, I like you. You want a present? Here.' He took off his watch and handed it to her. She didn't take it, so he put it on the table. It was a Rolex.

'Nice, eh? Go on, take it, before your father sees. I don't want anything for it. No favour, nothing. It's yours. What use is it to me? I don't need it. I can get another. There are lots of watches in America. Thousands of watches, and I can afford all of them. If I had any money. Only customs is going to take all my money, when I'm home. It'll be taken from me at the airport. With my clothes and my contact lenses and my crowns and false teeth. It's very safe, you see. America is a very safe place now, and it plays for safety. If you send us back, it doesn't know who it's letting in, does it? A quick debriefing might be enough, but then it might not. They use ice water. Hoses. Rubber hoses.'

'Get out.' The proprietor of the restaurant was standing behind the American's chair. He was very big. 'Pay and get out.'

When he left Malise giggled. The American had frightened her and it was good to see him go.

Every day Malise went to the beach. She sat in the sand and played with the dead things there till the wardens shouted at her to go away. It's poisonous, they said. It's dangerous to play here. She ignored their advice till one day she walked down to the surf and there was a line of seals – not dead, but dying. Vomiting worms.

Her father tried to explain it to her. Yes, he said, there are still walruses, and seals, and belugas. More every spring. Things are getting better. The EC and the Soviets and the Pacific Rim are making it better. It just takes a long time.

He gave her some pictures of the animals in the sea – animals she had known only as bleached bones till then. Dolphins, beluga whales, porpoises. Victims of the previous century's pollutants. They were beautiful, especially the dolphins.

One day she asked her father, 'Are there still dolphins?' He shook his head. 'No,' he replied. 'No dolphins. Not any more.'

They moved to Urbino. The thing she most remembered about their first day was the pottery market. The bright baked-earth colours glistened like mica; they tore at her eyes. The day before a fierce wind had blown dirt over the roads, and the dirt had formed drifts, making the way to their house very difficult and tiring. The dust was thick under their feet, deadening their footsteps. By the road was a wooden hut with a Coke sign nailed to its roof. Aquamarine paint had peeled from it like a snake skin – great metre-wide tatters of it clung to the leeward wall. Nearby a man and two women were clearing a patch of land. The man manoeuvred a mechanical cutter through bracken and weeds. The women, dressed in baggy black dresses and wide brimmed hats, raked away the leavings with home-made rakes.

Above them, halfway up a gentle slope, stood the ruin that was to be their home.

'You see?' said her father. 'That's our life now. A pioneering life!'

Malise started to cry.

Malise was too young to understand the contradictions upon which her new homeland was founded. Europe was the fastest growing economic state in the new world, and yet it was beset by agricultural crises: seasonal holes in the ozone layer over the Mediterranean, soil erosion, mutations in species genetically engineered for pest-control. It had the most highly trained working popula-tion in the world, yet huge influxes of refugees from Africa and the once oil-rich states of the Middle East were a perpetual threat to its economic stability. Its cultural influence had outstripped that of the United States, and yet it was in the middle of a violent crisis of federal identity.

Since the 2000 drought and the Oil Drain, European

governments had had to learn to deal with mass immigration as a given, not a 'problem'. Since the turn of the century Europe had become the focus of the largest movement of world populations on record. The starving masses of Africa and Arabia saw in Europe their only hope of survival. In the space of a decade, Europe's demography was changed out of all recognition. Europe now was neither predominantly Caucasian, nor Christian.

Europe had once been the hub of the old Universal Culture: the main distribution point for brown cartons stamped with famous names: Grundig, General Electric, Yamaha, Peugeot, Toshiba. Now popular demand led it to attempt something new, something more sustainable.

These popular pressures were as much religious and cultural as they were environmental. Europe's indigenous population had since the late nineteen sixties become intellectually concerned with environmental issues. African migrants from outworked and desertified rural areas brought a more than intellectual sense of immediacy to the long-running debate. Some thirty years before, the fall of east European Marxism had driven socialist opinion under the wing of the environmental lobby; the newly-emerged African left-wing intellectual caucus, therefore, found in environmental issues their natural political agenda within the European state.

The influence of Islam was also significant. The great self-betrayal of Fundamentalism had been to suppose that the *jame towhidi*, the 'society of believers', was the given state of things; that when post-Mohammedan forms of political organization were swept away, the *jame towhidi* would be left. Intellectualism had been killed off, and in its place had come not the society of believers, but a cargo-cult culture, bartering its natural wealth in return for alien learning and foreign skills. Droughts, the Oil Drain and subsequent wars had destroyed the Fundamentalists' precarious parody of statehood; now Europeanized Muslims, brought up among Westerners, educated in Western universities, repudiated the *jame towhidi*. At the heart of that repudiation, and for a Muslim it is a great and terrible one, there lay of course a flaw; it was assumed that an ideal society must be possible for the *jame towhidi* not to be it.

The very romanticism of the indigenous environmentalist movement drew the Islamic caucus to espouse its policies. They drew away from the *jame towhidi* only to seek heaven on earth.

For many years, Europe would find itself trapped between a rock and a hard place: neither a bastion of the old culture nor yet a champion of the new. Its environmental projects floundered even as its oil-built multinationals crashed. It was the richest state on earth and its economy was littered with big, unmarked graves.

When Malise was seven she contracted epiglottitis. She could not speak. Then a complication set in, a minor infection she hadn't the strength to resist, and she went deaf. There was no question of permanent damage, but how do you explain this to a scared seven year old?

This loss of speech and hearing, however brief, was, she decided later, the worst thing that could ever have happened to her; certainly, it changed the course of her life, shaping her in ways she could never wholly map, let alone redeem.

Malise had always been a talkative child, very much in love with her own voice, and her father had encouraged this. (He often said how he loved the noise children made; he loved children and this was one of the few qualities which endeared him to his indigenous Italian neighbours.) Now that sound itself was snatched from her, a sense of isolation stole upon the girl, far greater and more terrible than the circumstances of her illness really justified. She was at that age where the self becomes distinct from the objects around it. Recently everything had seemed alien to her, and her being unable to talk and to name the things she saw was the most frightening thing imaginable. Because everything seemed alien, nothing could comfort her. Her father, who did his best, seemed terrible and threatening.

She often woke up in the night because of the fever. Her father heard her tossing and turning on the bed, and he came in and picked her out from the sodden sheets to hold her and comfort her. She kicked and bit him. He put it down to her frustration and the fever and tried not to be too angry. The little bit of anger he did display terrified his daughter so much that afterwards she hid from him whenever she could, seeking relief and comfort solely from within herself. Here, in the realm of her imagination, the terrors were at least hers; they were not the world's.

Then one night, one of these terrors took on a life of its own. It was a nightmare. She knew it was different from the other dreams the very first time she experienced it. It visited her, night after night. It would not go away. It would not be controlled. Now, of course, not even the inside of her head was safe.

In the dream, Malise found herself walking along a

footpath by the sea. The iodine stench of seaweed filled her nostrils and refreshed her. To her right, the water span little spirals of reflected sunlight over its undulating surface. To her left there was a wood – strangely succulent, blue-green and brooding. The path curved along a narrow headland. A woman was selling ice cream from the open window of a chalet. There were benches, looking out to sea, and some yards further on, there was a steep hill made of cracked concrete. At its top stood a castle. The castle had many thin black towers.

A strange whispering hung in the air when she looked at it. It was not any language she knew or recognized. It was like all languages, run into each other, a semantic haze which distorted the air and made the highest tops of the castle's towers shiver against the sun, like the legs of an upturned insect. On the highest tower there was a woman sitting on a kind of balcony.

The woman was very beautiful. In order to see her properly, Malise had to bend her head back. But when she looked up, she saw that there was something in the sky – a tiny blot; the woman on the balcony was staring at it, too, and she was talking to it, very quietly at first, and then, as the little blot grew bigger, and heavier, she spoke more loudly, until at last she was shouting. The blot got bigger, heavier, terrible, monstrous.

The woman on the balustrade put her hands to her head and started screaming.

'STOP!' she cried.

STOP MAKE IT STOP MAKE IT STOP MAKE IT STOP MAKE IT STOP . . .

Then Malise would wake up, choking.

Her hearing returned. Her throat took longer to heal. It stung for hours afterwards if she spoke above a whisper. She did not talk if she did not have to. By then, of course, she had grown used to the dream and so she did not, in the end, tell her father about it. The opportunity to share her burden of fear with him was past.

The dream was her first secret. Now, she would be hidden from him.

Two years went by. The crisis in Herzegovina passed. The Brazilian petroleum nut crop failed. There was a civil war in the United States, and the Hispanic Lobby were overthrown. Democracy was restored. Canadian soldiers patrolled the polling stations in sensitive areas to ensure a free election. A new president came to power on a Public Transport pledge. Some generals met in a shack somewhere on the outskirts of Vegas and shot each other. They bequeathed a bizarre political inheritance, and not all of it was undone. Brazil remained part of the Union. The depopulated states of Iowa, Minnesota and the Dakotas were evacuated to make way for a nature reserve.

Meanwhile in Europe the first faltering steps were taken to establish Heaven on Earth.

There is a dictum – untrue, but widely held – that societies shape themselves to suit their technology. The West had held to this dictum and had eventually strung themselves up by it: on oil, ran their argument, depends our universal culture; and sure enough one day there was no more oil.

The new Islam had rejected the dictum, but had found nothing to put in its place. You can have technology without society, they found, but not a society without technology.

Not surprisingly, given the tendency in people to fill

any intellectual vacuum bequeathed them, it was a predominantly Muslim team of engineers who developed the world's first working Von Neumann machine. It was five foot high by three foot wide by six foot long; it lived for six months and built two copies of itself before breaking down. Neither of its 'children' worked, but then, nobody had seriously expected them to. These were, after all, pioneer experiments. The technology available to the team was not yet equal to their vision; they were the Charles Babbages of their day.

Of what did their vision consist? For the spokesperson of that team, Von Neumann machines – machines that eat and breed – 'will enable advanced human societies to be guided by the balances and checks of an unspoilt natural evironment.' Von Neumanns would, he said, act like a buffer or interface between the human and the natural worlds. Behind the scientist lay the Islamic visionary.

Had his computer science not been so revolutionary, he would have been dismissed as a crank. History has shown that he was not in fact a crank. He was a genius.

His name was Maulana Suryadi.

A German company who in the oil-rich days had funded the revolutionary space shuttle HOTOL bought its way into Suryadi's project. It dedicated half its working capital to the development of self-generating and self-sustaining machinery. HOTOL's philosophy was more practical that Suryadi's, more obviously valid. These machines were, it claimed, the way forward in a world that could no longer tolerate waste.

Suryadi, his best work over and ill at ease in a corporate environment, retired to England. He became an Imam, and spent his last years presenting radio programmes in Sylheti, wedding the technological advances of the European state to a new, more rigorous vision of a resurgent Islam.

The development of Von Neumann machines signalled the birth of a new universal culture. It developed so fast, it seemed to many observers that it must have stepped fully formed from out of its creator's brain. One minute, Suryadi and his co-workers were picking apart the mangled intestines of their first prototype; in the next, HOTOL's Von Neumanns were mining the moon and gathering rare elements from the Jovian atmosphere.

The new technology did not of course appear from nowhere. It had to be worked at and developed, like anything else. Because it was a reproductive technology, however, the scale of its advances underwent a more than geometric progression. The designers found that once the principles of their construction were established, Von Neumann machines were, by and large, able to solve their own problems as they appeared.

The spokespeople of HOTOL GmbH had told the truth: their new Universal Culture would not ever easily run out of resources. The technology on which the new culture was based was *alive*; it had its own ecosystem and no longer depended upon precious raw material. Theoretically, it could renew itself out of its own scrap forever.

The new universal culture, in short, came in a cardboard box, stamped 'HOTOL' – you only ever had to buy one of it, and it would last for ever.

*   *   *

There is a limit to how fast people can assimilate change. You could, glancing through a newspaper at this time, persuade yourself that Heaven on Earth was just around the corner, and so ignore the many and terrible difficulties in the world. On the other hand you could, if you were either old and cynical, or simply too young to comprehend the scale of events, ignore the larger, rightfully optimistic picture, and worry yourself sick over the details.

This is what Malise and her father did. As far as they were concerned, stuck on their derelict farm in the middle of nowhere, life was just one damned thing after another.

These are the events by which they measured their days:

Azerbaijani rebels formally ceded to Iran.

The refugee problem equilibrated throughout the EC. The Germans elected their first Turkish-born chancellor. In Britain, the National Front condemned necklace burnings and lost half their seats at the subsequent election.

Soviet and French peace-keeping troops quelled a week-long street battle between Shi'ites and Catholics in Madrid.

The EC soil conservation and renewal programme was a success.

The sea got better.

Someone genetically engineered a dolphin. But it was orange, and kept sinking.

The Emperor Reversed

Malise and her father lived in the east wing of the derelict villa. Many buildings like this were scattered across the Marches, empty and useless since the 2000 drought damaged their olive groves and vines.

The villas were linked by dusty roads. In the fields, the grapes and the olives were growing again. Unhusbanded and sickly, they were at least alive. Things are getting better, her father told her. Indonesian scientists are putting the ozone layer back together by a patented process. One day Europe will make good wine again.

Malise had never tasted wine. Nor, as far as she knew, had her father. It was just one of the things he said these days, to convince the people of the neighbourhood that he respected their ways and their weaknesses. He would try out phrases on Malise, and then she would hear them over again in the grocer's, or the coffee shop. Let's hope there's some good wine soon. It is a good thing for women, the Pope's decree last Friday. Next year a woman Pope, eh? Of course, it didn't always work. He got a black eye for that last remark, and Malise had gone crazy and had broken nearly everything in the shop, just to get at the man who had hit her father.

Although she was too young to understand all the reasons, she realized that her father was not well liked by his neighbours in Urbino. She asked her father why they couldn't have gone to Britain instead, which was at least Muslim now.

Malise's father just shook his head and smiled. 'It's not a safe place,' he said. 'Not safe at all.'

They were sitting on rocks on the southern edge of Lake Garda, just outside Desenzano. The water was off-white. Blue wave-shadow banded it like interference. A line of clotted cloud lay between it and the cobalt sky. Behind the headland, the sun was dying.

Malise shucked her blouse and pants and went swimming in the lake. Her father sat on the rocks, watching schools of tiny silver fish patrol the shallows. He was smiling to himself, a smile Malise recognized and which dismayed her. She stayed out in the water longer than she wanted to, hoping the smile would go away.

She watched him, and waved to him, but he did not see her. He lifted her blouse to his face and kissed it. The smile just kept on getting more and more fixed onto his face. At last Malise gave up the unequal struggle and swam back to shore.

He would, she knew, now tell her about her mother.

She sat on the rock, and while she let the evening air dry her, her father talked to her in the low, level voice he used whenever he mentioned his dead wife. Normally he would stare at her when he talked like this, because in certain lights, he said, Malise looked so much like her mother. This time, of course, he didn't stare. He couldn't; Malise was, after all, naked. He did not realize that Malise had learned, perhaps only half-consciously, to manipulate him in this way. Whenever it seemed likely that the subject of Malise's mother would arise, Malise would contrive, by some provocative gesture, to embarrass her father into silence, or at least into not staring at her so intently.

In fact Malise and her father had begun, without ever admitting or perhaps even realizing it, to play a sophisticated, almost sexual game with each other. This meant that the sexual connection Malise's father made between his lost wife and his daughter was strengthened and given substance. This troubled him, but he knew from his reading that in the West, these incestuous feelings need not shame him. He need only exert a healthy self-discipline, and these feelings, these quite natural feelings, would eventually become dilute.

The lesson Malise drew from all this was simple, and not at all sexual. She discovered that it was possible to exert force on someone by indirect means. People, she found, were an accumulation of balances. If you want to move something easily, you should first unbalance it. This is as true for people as it is for objects.

It was a precocious piece of reasoning for so young a girl, but not as remarkable as it might at first seem. Suryadi's new mathematics had rapidly seeped into the educational system, and its presiding image of checks and balances had already been firmly rooted in the young Malise at school.

Malise's only memory of her mother was of being dropped from a height of five feet onto a concrete pavement, and then of being soaked to the skin with a warm, black liquid that smelled of urine and rust. Because the memory was a vague and terrible one, she was never sure whether it was real or not. When eventually her father told her how her mother had been shot in the back while nursing her, Malise realized that her memory was accurate, at least in most details. The black fluid must of course have been red: her mother's blood. But Malise could hardly tell her father, who was still so obviously wrapped up in love and grief, that her only memory of his wife was of her death. This, then, became her second secret. By now, being hidden from her father seemed perfectly normal and natural.

Malise's father was describing how her mother got angry. 'First she'd click her tongue in annoyance, and not say anything for a little while, and you had about thirty seconds to back off before she'd strike!' He laughed, uneasily, and skimmed a pebble into the lake. It sank without bouncing. 'It was like a little alarm-bell. *Click* – "You have thirty seconds." Afterwards there was always this tone of self-deprecation in her voice; not apology, so much as regret, "Sorry, but you cut the wrong wire."'

'What did you argue about?'

Malise's father shrugged. 'Politics.'

'Was she very political?'

'Very.'

'And you?'

Malise's father stood up, handed her her blouse. 'Get dressed.'

Their home in the Marches was dilapidated and neglected, but Malise, though she was at first appalled by the dereliction of the place, soon found she preferred it to Tarquinia; the coast, she remembered, had seemed to consist solely of sickly fields and dirty kitchens, sea holly and broken pavements, and she was glad to be rid of it.

One weekend her father, as a treat, took her on an outing to what he called 'a secret place' – it turned out merely to be some other part of the coast. Still, Malise thought, glumly, as she looked around her, at least there aren't any dead things on the beach – she was grateful for that, at least. Memories of how she used to pick apart all those corpses nauseated her now.

'Soon there won't be any need to be afraid of the sea,' said her father, and he put his arm round her shoulder and squeezed her. 'It'll be back to rights very soon. Come on!'

They played on the rocks and eventually Malise cheered up. Recently, her father had taken to playing with her more often. It pleased and surprised her. She wished he'd been more like this when she was younger. Now, when he played tag with her or hid from her and jumped out to shock her, she was flattered, yes, but also a bit put out, that he should think her young enough for those games.

He tired before she did.

'You win,' he said.

He said, 'Now for the surprise.' He led her along the coast a little way to the mouth of a cave. 'Shall we explore?' he said.

It was a wonderful surprise. She loved hiding places. She hugged him and rushed inside. She gagged immediately, came stumbling out. 'Dad . . .'

The smell hit him, now. 'Christ,' he said.

The smell was foul and chemical; like rotten meat stirred up in typewriter correction fluid.

'Something's dead in there,' said Malise.

'Yes,' said her father.

He said, 'It wasn't like that when I first came here. It's a tidal cave. The sea comes in here. Something must have come in to die.'

'You said nothing died in the sea any more.'

Malise's father laughed. He meant to comfort her but to Malise it sounded like he was laughing at some dreadful trick he'd played on her. 'Everything dies, sweetheart.'

She pushed herself away from him. 'Liar!'

She was thinking of her room, the postcards her father had bought her, the little plastic dolphins she'd hung above her bed. They were beautiful creatures, but God had come too late for them.

She ran back to the beach road.

'Everything dies, sweetheart!'

Her father's library held a strange conglomeration of leather-bound books he had inherited from his father and cheap paperbacks with the acid so sharp in the paper it tickled her nose. He worked hard in their new home and now he bought new paperbacks all the time, many of them in English, which he'd learned as his second language in the Soviet-financed school.

He let her read anything she wanted. 'You're in the West now,' he said, and she wondered what he meant, since the phrase had little meaning for her generation. 'In the West, girls do what they want, think what they want. You can be anything. You can be president.' Then he laughed, and Malise wondered at the laugh, because there was no humour in it.

He showed her books and some of them were beautiful. She was entranced by the mathematical elegance of the ancient Islamic masters. The tapestries of medieval Europe also fascinated her, particularly those in the Musée Cluny.

Again, Malise's taste in art was precocious but not as surprising as it might seem. The notion of patterns made up of themselves, repeated over and over according to some simple rule of combination, was far from new to her; she was drawn to the rigid geometries of the great Islamic artists more by a sense of recognition than by anything else. Her interest in medieval art was less easily explained. Certainly her father's books influenced her; then there was her school library, which had one or two books of plates, which she came across more or less by accident. But exposure to something does not explain a liking for it. The most one can say is that its iconography haunted Malise's dreams: the lady in the high tower, the lone figure wandering beneath its battlements, woods, witches and grails – some part of the Muslim girl's heart was rooted in this alien landscape. Her love of the pictures was but the first manifestation of its glamour.

Europe has its own myths, magic, and character. Malise, an alien there, would spend the rest of her life attempting to penetrate its secrets while at the same time running away from them.

Sometimes her father talked to her about her taste in pictures as if he were telling her off, or at least trying very hard not to.

'You have no sense of perspective,' he complained once, coming into her bedroom just as she'd finished undressing, so she had to dash into bed to hide herself from him.

In his hand he held the book from the Musée Cluny.

He waved it at her. 'You see,' he said, sitting at the foot of her bed, 'these pictures are just flat units placed in space. Perspective's just used to place each object, it doesn't inform the way the object's depicted.' Then he went out and brought her back two books. One was of work by Atkinson Grimshaw, and one was by Stanley Spencer.

More than ever before, Malise wanted to go live in England.

A week later, Malise's father hit her. They had been playing. He had lost and he had hit her. He had done it without thinking, the way her schoolfriends did some-times and because of that she couldn't, somehow, feel as angry or as hurt as she thought she should. Instead, she felt dirty and confused. She wondered: would it happen again? Was it how things were going to be, now? It was as if playing games with her had let him off the hook, so that he didn't have to be adult.

Malise knew she wasn't supposed to interrupt him when he was working, but she had to talk to him.

She opened the study door. 'Dad?'

He grunted. He was hunched over the desk, drawing a toy. It was how he made his living now, as a draughts-man for a toy company.

'Please,' she prompted.

'Later.' He didn't turn, but she could see his face was flushed. Was he angry? Angry with her? She clenched her fist against the side of her head, where he'd hit her. The skin was bruised but not broken. Her head ached, but she couldn't tell him about that. Not unless he looked at her.

She moved closer to him, looked at the drawing, and

the writing below the design. 'That's a nice name,' she said.

'Thank you,' he sighed. He reached out and touched her, gently, on the neck. His face looked very strange, almost frightening. He had been crying, and now he was trying to restrain his tears. This made him look belligerent, the way a little boy looks angry if something has upset him.

Malise shivered. There was nothing grown up about him at all.

He continued to spend a lot of his time with her. He hardly let her out of his sight. They played lots of games. They played hide and seek in the ruined villas, and when he was so close she had to bolt from him he came charging up behind her with a great roar and she'd stop and turn and watch him, watch the great cloud of white choking dust at his feet billow up behind him, high up above the hedges. His whole skin was white. He looked very young and savage.

He had not always been a toymaker, but Malise could not remember what he had done before, and he would not tell her. Something with chemicals and aircraft. These days he played with his toys for hours, enraptured by the simplicity and elegance of his craft. He could get quite jealous of his toys, and, if she was playing with him, he sometimes snatched them away from her before he remembered himself.

When he did this, Malise would stare at him, amazed rather than angry, and he would blush and laugh and hand back the toy and go back to work. Sometimes he was lovely, yes, but at other times, Malise decided, he was like a child – a troublesome older brother, cocksure, sarcastic, always in the way; and sometimes, which was worse, a younger brother – blind with need and want, brutish as a young animal.

Seven of Cups
Upright

In the mornings Malise made breakfast for her father.

He scowled. 'Eggs? *Again?*'

'They're good for you,' Malise replied.

'So's castor oil.'

'Don't tempt me.'

He put his head in his hands. 'What did I do to deserve a dietician for a daughter?'

'They teach us about it in school.'

'Is nothing sacred?'

'Your egg's getting cold.'

'Toast?'

'Not until you've started your egg.'

One day when they were exploring an abandoned outbuilding Malise sneaked down to the cellar and found a case of Sangiovese. On very special days they drank a bottle of wine together. It felt deliciously wicked. On these days it felt good to have a father who was more like a brother.

One day a shadow passed by the window while they were drinking and Malise looked up to see Farzad, ducking below the window sill. Her father leaped up and found the boy waiting at the front door, as if he hadn't been by the window or seen anything. Malise stayed out of the way, listening to her father rage but not able to make out the words.

Farzad had come to give them a message. His father wasn't able to give Malise a lift to school the next morning. Malise was driven to school in Urbino by their neighbours – two dour brothers who had escaped Iraqi persecution only to impose the same regime in miniature (it seemed to her) upon the eldest's own son. Malise used to go round and ask if she could play with Farzad and the brothers told her he was ill, or asleep, or busy at work, and then finally they told her father that they didn't want any Western girl bothering their son, but that if she still needed a lift into school, that was all right. They kept a dog, which her father for some reason of his own called Schwarzkopf. They brought it round sometimes when they came to complain about the bonfires her father lit as part of his attempt to get some of the fields working again. The dog growled continually and slobbered on the carpet. There was a stain on the cream rug to the left of the settee where the dog habitually sat. It was big, ugly, stupid, scarred and utterly vicious and sometimes she thought, that is how the son will be. Dogs grow up quicker, that's all; the dog's got there first.

Her father hated them all. He crossed his legs in front of them. He told her, 'Walk behind little Farzad past the school gates to please them, and when they drive off give him a swift kick in the backside from me.'

Malise enjoyed school, especially art and mathematics. Her father mulled the words over in his mouth. Because she was good at both subjects her father called her his little flower of Islam. In the attic room of the house he had built up a library celebrating an older, finer, livelier culture which went under the name of Islam, and he liked to think that in his daughter had been fashioned all the creative qualities of a belief and a way of life whose reactionary form he had tried, and failed, to tolerate.

He taught her to respect deeds over beliefs. The cultures he described to her from his books seemed utterly cut off from the modern terrors which haunted them, and she was never able to bridge the gulf between the two. In her eyes, she wasn't Islamic. She repudiated Islam. She had no religion. She was outside time. She belonged to the mythic realm of her father's library.

The first rains came. They turned the streams mud-brown and wrecked many of her father's amateurish improvements around their home. He was so angry and frustrated that he hit her again, twice. Malise went to school and her face was all bruised. The teachers were solicitous. They asked her what the matter was. She told them she'd got into fights with other children, but she could see that they didn't believe her.

'Dad,' she said in the morning, 'I can't go to school.'

'Go to school.'

'But my face –'

'Go to school!'

So she went to school, and after assembly one day she was taken aside by her maths teacher. 'Come with me,' she said. Malise followed her. They talked for a time. When her maths teacher, who also taught civics to the older pupils, started to ask her questions about her father, she refused to answer.

The next day her maths teacher drew her aside after assembly again and told her to see the school doctor.

She wasn't given any choice about it. It was almost as if she'd done something wrong. The doctor was a man with a high bony forehead and fingers that were too long. He closed the door behind her and told her to undress and there was something in his voice which made her say, 'No.'

He stared at her. He was genuinely surprised that she had refused him. But she had had practice. There were many times she'd wished she'd kept saying no, but then, you weren't supposed to do that. If you were a child you weren't supposed to refuse.

'Is there something you don't want me to see?' the doctor said, and he sat in his leather chair by the window and the light glinted off his spectacles, so that his eyes were like two white-hot coals.

'Yes,' said Malise. 'There is something I don't want you to see.'

'Do you want to tell me about it?'

'I piss with it.'

The doctor wrote something on his blotter. 'That's not something I expect to hear from a girl your age.'

Malise stared at the floor.

'Well?'

'I'm sorry.'

'This is –' he laughed uncomfortably. 'This is just a routine examination.'

'Then where's the chaperone?'

'Chaperone?'

'I'm a Muslim girl,' said Malise. 'I need a Muslim chaperone.'

'But your teacher said she didn't think – well, yes, I'm sorry. There seems to be some mistake.'

He knew she was lying, because she wore her hair short, and uncovered. She never wore a scarf even in a climate where many Westerners had adopted desert garb to protect them from the sun. But he had no choice but fetch a chaperone, and while he was hunting her out Malise fled the surgery.

She walked all the way home. When she got there her feet were covered in blisters because it was a long way and that morning she'd gone off to school in new shoes. She found her father in her room. He was doing terrible things to her toys.

His upraised fist descended. Metal flashed, a savage downward stroke.

The hammer missed its mark, and thudded into the carpet, clipping the toy, which scudded across the floor towards her. Malise snatched it up instinctively. It was the one she'd watched him draw the first time he'd hit her. The plastic was crazed in one place, but it was still intact.

He turned to her. Sweat sparked on the bony crescent of his forehead. 'I'm so sorry,' he whispered, and he covered his face. 'I'm so sorry.'

His hands were bleeding where he'd hit them with the hammer.

He never hit her again. He woke up screaming in the night instead.

Eventually he told her about his nightmares, about how they weren't so much nightmares as memories. He told her about his old job, and how the aeroplanes he'd made chemicals for had been warplanes and how the chemicals were poisons. He told her how he had given evidence to a military committee against a colleague who, it turned out later, had been his wife's lover. He had, he said, been tipped off about the government's intention to kill his radical wife the day before it happened. He had warned her at the last minute, but it was too late. They had shot her trying to escape. When they handed Malise back to her father she was covered in blood.

It was a kind of warning.

'To start with,' he explained, one evening while they were waiting for the heating system to shut itself off, 'I believed I was doing right. It was a job. I had superiors, and employees, and I was promoted, and reprimanded if I came in late, and it was – normal. Just a normal thing to do. It was only a technical job. Not to do with people.' He shuddered. 'But the terrible part is, some part of me *knew* what I was doing. There was a part of me – a horribly violent part. It enjoyed what I was doing. I used to think that I had got rid of that part of me and now –' He glanced at her bruised face. 'I'm frightened,' he said.

He said, 'I think you should be frightened too.'

One evening Malise's father took her to Pesaro to see a magic show; it was one in a long sequence of clumsy, apologetic gestures.

The acts were slick and colourful and clever. Malise ate pistachio and liquorice ice cream and didn't notice when it dribbled down her best dress. She was entranced.

The opening act of the second half was different to the others. This man had no fanfare, no glittering assistants, no music to accompany his trick. He was short and plump and he wore thick, round spectacles. He walked with a stoop and acknowledged the crowd's applause with a diffident little nod. He waited for the auditorium to fall silent.

Malise could feel the tension around her. This man is known, she thought to herself. The murmurs persisted. People shuffled in their seats and readied themselves for him. He does not need music, she thought.

The magician introduced himself and asked for a volunteer to come out on stage.

A thin, prematurely balding man hesitated then stepped forward to scattered applause. Behind the magician, a stagehand brought on two wooden chairs and a sheaf of white writing paper.

The magician placed the chairs so that he and the volunteer were seated facing each other. He picked up the sheaf of papers, and rolled the top sheet into a ball about half the size again of his fist. He then told the volunteer that he was about to make the large, loose ball of paper disappear before his eyes.

The volunteer laughed and the audience joined in. They knew there was to be some catch to what had been claimed. The magician acknowledged the audience and spent a little time bantering with his volunteer, and while he did so, he tossed the ball from hand to hand. Then he stopped. He laid his left hand on the gangling man's knee. Watch carefully, he said. The audience will know, but they will not help you to know. You must find out for yourself.

The audience heard and understood.

The magician juggled the ball in his hands, then flicked it over the man's left shoulder. The audience laughed at the silliness of it, but the volunteer was bemused. He had not seen the ball of paper fly over his shoulder.

Malise shuffled on her seat. That's crazy, she thought. That can't be right.

The trick was performed again. And Malise noticed something. The magician threw the ball with his right hand to his left and tapped it over the man's shoulder, but as he did so his right hand would jiggle and slant, and the young man's eyes were directed to the wrong place, the moment the paper ball 'disappeared'.

Another ball. Another.

The young man was sweating. The laughter of the audience gave way to applause. Another. Another. Crumpled paper flew past the volunteer to the left and the right, but always his eyes were distracted by some flick or gesture or shake of the magician's free hand.

The magician stopped a moment and wiped his forehead with a handkerchief. He offered it to the young man. The volunteer grinned and accepted it gratefully and it came to Malise then that they had come to an understanding. There was something aggressive and knowing about their smiles. They are duelling, she realized. They are playing an ancient and honourable game together.

The magician began again. Another.

Another.

The young man leaned forward, but that only made it easier for the magician to lead his sight away. The young man tried keeping one hand in check then glancing quickly at the other, but still the stillness and sudden flicker of his eyes was drawn in by the jiggling movements of the magician. At last the paper was gone, and the magician leaned forward and whispered to the volunteer.

The young man turned round and saw the crumpled paper behind his chair. Something extraordinary happened. The audience did not laugh. The audience did not breathe a word.

They know, too, Malise said. They know they are honoured to have seen this.

The balding, gangling young man turned back to the magician and clapped. For a while his was the only applause. Then, as a body, the audience stood and cheered.

The magician turned to acknowledge them, and his glasses sparkled like jewels.

Afterwards her father asked her what she thought of the show and he was surprised that she chose the simple act as her favourite. He had been worried that by giving away the secrets of his magic the performer would have bored or disappointed Malise.

Malise kept her peace. She stared along the coast road and her mind was full of patterns and balances.

Magic works, she thought. Magic does not come from outside the world – it is all around us, if only we knew how to look. It is not a *thing*. It is simply the way the world weaves itself before our eyes. We obey the weave; we look in the right directions and the world seems solid.

Turn your head suddenly, she thought, and you will catch the world out: you will catch it performing magic.

So she turned her head suddenly.

She saw a street, a cheap hotel, a red neon sign – 'Durma Aqui'. On a top floor balcony, there was a woman leaning over the iron railing, looking up into the sky. On the pavement, by the door of the hotel, a young girl stood looking up at her.

Malise choked so much she thought she was going to pass out.

''s nothing,' she said, pushing her father away. She hawked and spat. 'Piece of pistachio nut,' she said.

It was four months before Malise Arnim could face going back to the park.

Little had changed. Black men squatted by the lakeside walks as they always had, hawking pots of unguents, blocks of hashish and cotton bags of aromatic spices. They lit joss sticks around their goods-laden rugs and a fragile tide of sweetness billowed in the foul night air. The tips of the incense sticks shivered in the breeze like ruby fireflies. Boys wandered up and down the path, selling cans of German fruit beer from trays hung from slings around their necks. The Muslims ran Britain now, a theocratic junta was in power, but here at least the beer sellers weren't afraid of the mullahs.

London was a freeport, governed by a shipping cartel who paid taxes to the central government in Leeds and hired their own police force from the academies in Glasgow and Reading. Islamic jurisdiction stopped short of the M25. In this way the beleaguered and much-criticized Muslim government of Great Britain generated much of its revenue. London acted also as a sop and potential bolt-hole for nervous natives, who, twenty years into religious rule, still feared a Shi'ite-style crackdown.

Britain was the unlooked-for and unexpected birth-place of the Islamic renaissance. The refugees who had flooded Britain from war zones in Azerbaijan and Bangladesh when Malise was a girl had found in Imam Maulana Suryadi's mildly Ba'athist teachings, in his television programmes and chat shows and radio talks, a uniquely welcoming introduction to Islamic life and co-existence in the West. In ten years those bland words of comfort and homely wisdom had bred a revolution. Suryadi's movement, with its federalist sympathies, was increasingly at loggerheads with Britain's States-friendly government. When the country's political affinities polarized around racial issues, a bloodbath ensued. A revolutionary junta, its legitimacy weighed in the blood of a million impoverished Pakistani and Irani refugees and their Western liberal allies, took control of England and Wales. Its political complexion at first yawed wildly as the contradictions of the time and Suryadi's own teachings came to light; it was said that it had sent whipping vans into the streets of Manchester even as it enforced EC legislation on the rights of homosexuals. No wonder, then, that the natives were restless, that they had demanded their old capital for themselves – a place where they could feel secure in their Western future, and a port to carry them away at the first sign of a crackdown.

Malise stopped and lit a cigarette. She closed her eyes and sensed the vital parts of her body drumming a slow, tidal fugue within her. For a second it submerged her awareness of the struts supporting her bird-boned body against Home's crushing pull. While she smoked she glanced over the goods laid out on old rugs – belts, gloves and ornate purses, jewellery made of wood and beads threaded on wire, knives with hand-carved handles.

A servomotor on her shoulder whined unsteadily. Some days before she had buckled that part of her exoskeleton, stumbling on some steps. She shook the rod to which the motor was attached, unjamming it. It beeped its thanks. In the dusk, the lights of the camp fires blotted out surrounding detail, turning the park black and textureless, like a sea of oil.

This was a good place for the homeless to camp, well away from tall buildings – Moonwolf's favourite target. The sky cleared; the moon, thirty degrees above the horizon, cast a cold sheen over distant buildings. To her right the truncated Telecom Tower gleamed as though it were wet.

No one knew what Moonwolf was when it first hit. Some said it was a semisentient mining utility gone rogue during the Brightening. Others said it was an alien artefact, sent by hidden beings who feared the human race. There was a time when such questions did not concern Malise. She had had her own explanations. Now she wondered what its purpose had been. To destroy everything in sight? Or to stay alive in the face of a perceived threat? Perhaps it just wanted to play.

She wondered, could it reason? Could it age? Could it accept the defeat that awaited it? The irony was painful – she and her fellows had sacrificed so much to win, but now the time had come it didn't feel like winning. There was no pleasure in the destruction of Moonwolf. Only a sour taste – a sense of futility.

Malise studied the smashed tower. A rod, railgunned from the lunar surface and sent crashing and flaring through Home's atmosphere, had passed through the communications tower with the ease of a bullet through a squash. Twisted gantries bearing rough slabs of stressed concrete reached out from the side of the tower along the line of the strike, defying gravity like the gush of innards in a comic book illustration. Another stream of contorted metals had succumbed to gravity and bled down the side of the block.

The jumbled shapes took on strange symmetries in her eyes. They hinted at something she could not reach, could not quite remember.

It was not like last time. It had been later then, much darker, and apart from the whores and their clients she had been alone on the path. She had looked across the water, turning a head heavier than the one she now owned, its now empty ops cavity filled with the datafat and delicate Dutch nano-mechanics of her former profession. And she had watched helplessly as two figures left the cover of bushes and seized a man in a white raincoat.

They had frog-marched him to the edge of the lake, and while one of them held his face under the water, the other pulled his jeans down. They waited till his legs were still and when he was dead they had raped him.

A thermal image had flickered into life behind Malise's eyes; the corpse cooled and faded into the lake: yellow-blue, green-blue, turquoise-blue. A police-woman, her helmet a forest of scopes and communications equipment – cheap, outdated equivalents of the things inside Malise's head – had passed her, had noticed the gravity support skeleton fastened tight around her limbs, and the intense way she stared into the blackness.

She followed Malise's gaze, then laid hold of the seemingly fragile struts strapped round the ex-spacewoman's jacket. Malise turned in surprise, and the policewoman arrested her.

Malise had tried to bargain. Evidence from the equipment in her head in return for silence.

Karen Gaynor, the arresting officer, shook her head. 'I'm sorry, Arnim. The rules are strict. Datafat down-well needs more licences than a Belt digger.'

'How much are the licences?'

'Are you a government?'

Malise bowed her head.

Gaynor leaned forward. 'Listen, let's save time. No deals. Is that clear?'

Malise sat back in her chair and half-shrugged. Gaynor took it for an answer.

'What kind of 'fat you got in there?' she asked.

Malise didn't reply. She was listening to the click and pip of a dozen busy terminals, the swish of pneumatic doors, muted conversation in English and Gujarati and the riffle of fanfold paper. She gazed at the floor. Grey tiling – slightly soft, shiny but impossible to slip on. There was a cigarette butt by the left front leg of her chair. She dislodged it with her heel and kicked it under the desk.

Gaynor grew tired of the wait. 'We have people can examine you and tell us. You want that?'

'Combat grade.'

'What?'

Malise looked up at Gaynor. 'In my head. It's *Dayus Ram*. Combat grade.'

Gaynor's eyes widened. 'Arnim. Shit. I thought I recognized you.'

'Break it to the men I don't sign body parts.'

'You're the one gave Moonwolf its name, right?'

The muscles in Malise's face tightened. 'Skip it.'

Gaynor held up her hands in a placating gesture. 'Anything you say, ma'am, but I'll tell you for free, war hero or not, you can't keep your toys while you're down-well. If you were Marie Czynski herself, I'd be saying the same.' She tapped the side of her head to indicate the datafat and nanomechanisms inside Malise's skull. 'This isn't just some tight-arsed *fatwah*. Our law facilitates an international peace-keeping directive, Haag-administered within the EC. You heard of Haag?'

Malise stayed silent for a time. She'd heard of Haag. 'Get on with it,' she snapped.

Gaynor looked at her computer screen where their conversation was being textualized. The interpretation was smooth – a couple of highlighted phonetic spellings here and there, but otherwise readable. She said, 'How long were you standing at the lakeside before I came along?'

'A few seconds.' Malise was facing the screen but her eyes were focused on a different place.

'You told me they grabbed him and took him to the edge of the lake and they –'

Malise closed her eyes tight shut.

'Okay,' Gaynor soothed. 'What I'm saying is, all that took longer than a few seconds. Right?'

Malise shrugged.

'So how long were you standing there?'

'Maybe a minute.'

Gaynor glanced at the screen, pulled a what-the-hell face and leaned forward towards Malise, blocking her line of sight. 'You little fuck,' she whispered, 'why didn't you hail someone?'

Malise looked straight at Gaynor for the first time. 'You people weren't on my frequency.'

'Crap,' said Gaynor.

Malise smiled – a tense, brittle imitation of the real thing. 'Okay.'

'You could have tuned in. If my helmet can do it then your toys can.'

Toys. The word played taunting echoes round Malise's head. 'Sure.' She hunched her shoulders. There was anger in her eyes.

'Why didn't you save him?'

'Maybe I didn't want to.'

Gaynor looked at her a long while. 'With the things in your head you could have spoken to us while concealing both your ID and location. You could have reported the incident easily enough and not got involved. So what was the reason for . . .'

'I didn't think that fast,' Malise said. She wanted the interrogation to finish, and didn't really care what conclusions Gaynor drew from her words. She rubbed her face, frustrated by her tiredness. She had to wake up but the coffee wasn't helping. Anger would do it – the adrenalin might spark the slush in her head to come up with some kind of plan. She *wanted* to be angry, but dread at what they would do to her dampened her responses. Being falsely accused now – of cold-bloodedness, or voyeurism, or even complicity – might kindle her anger and warm her. But of course, being angry she'd only get herself into more trouble.

Gaynor told the monitor to close up. The system picked on her words. A 'save' icon blinked centre-screen. Gaynor tapped in a phone-number, picked up the handset for privacy and started speaking.

Malise realized she was through to HOTOL. Something stirred in her at last – not anger, but desperation. She leaned towards the terminal and hit a letter key, cutting the connection. 'Listen to me,' she pleaded.

Gaynor paused a moment, undecided, then dropped the handset onto the table and pushed her chair away from the desk. 'I'm listening.'

'They're not toys.'

'What?'

'The things in my head. You call HOTOL to take my 'fat away, and you're blinding me as surely as if you mashed my eyes in with a nightstick.'

Gaynor folded her arms, waiting for the pitch.

Malise's heart beat faster. The policewoman didn't understand. How could she? How could anyone? 'With this gear in my head I see colours you never dreamed of. There must be a use for me down-well. Maybe some government project. Maybe a military research station. *Something.* I can't let myself be blinded.'

'You haven't a choice.'

Malise grabbed Gaynor's knee and squeezed it hard, '*Help me.*' When she realized what she'd done she let go like Gaynor's flesh was on fire. It had been a stupid, clumsy gesture and she could not afford to do this wrong. Silently she cursed herself.

'Does this look like a job centre?' Gaynor said, but the expected irony was missing from her voice.

Malise's heart pounded. Somehow her gauche plea had made Gaynor uncertain. The words she needed spilled out of her without her having to think about them. 'How much of your time will it take? Well?'

At last Gaynor nodded, acknowledging the rightness of it. 'Give me two days.'

'Right.'

'You'll owe me.'

'Anything.'

Malise spent the intervening time on her sculpture. She assembled her FizzyArt kit in the living room opposite the futon, which rolled up into a settee on a black-stained base. By the window there was a feedback tank which tended twelve tropical fish. She wished now that she'd never bought the tank. Why keep living things if you don't get to tend them yourself? She remembered the plastic dolphins, hung above her bed when she was little. She shuddered and shook her head as if to free herself from the memory.

The room held no other furniture. There was no carpet – just dark polish over bare boards. On the walls were photographic blowups of London Docklands, the way they were in the nineteen seventies. They were pictures of buildings, not people. There were no people in them anywhere. The ceiling light was the kind that varied its hue as well as its strength. She set it low and blue-green when she worked on her sculpture.

She'd been crafting the figure for a long while and, as her analyst had promised, it was like a friend to her. She'd even named it.

Amy.

Its arms were too long for its frame and ended in many-jointed hands two feet from wrist to finger tip. The fingers themselves were nail-less and flattened. Ridges of downy blonde hair ran up inside each arm. Spines grew in the arm-pits.

Its neck was fifteen inches long. Its jaw resembled two scythes sheathed in parchment. The blades were warped and tied tip to tip at the chin by a knot of pulp and yellow teeth. Its nose was a purple membraneous flap.

Its eyes were huge bloodshed whites, each pricked by a black dot. Its hair was a grey halo. Malise examined its legs; the bones were visible through loose, varicose flesh.

Malise ran her fingers through her cropped hair and 'saved' Amy. Then she swapped cards in the drive of the machine and called up her other sculpture.

A nest of black insect limbs bloomed from a white hemisphere. Blue filaments webbed the off-white surface of the ball, like cracks in old porcelain.

The limbs were angular and precise, and while their postures were grotesque the individual structures were smooth and functional-looking, and reminded her more of pumping equipment, or old steam engines.

Technically Malise had never left HOTOL's employ and this had, against all likelihood, worked to her advantage. When she'd arrived down-well her ostensible superior at HOTOL, a maverick violin-playing archivist called Schoemann, had helped her keep her 'fat. He had misassigned her records to keep the Brussels office ignorant of what she'd done.

And he made her a promise. 'Any time you want to go back, Malise,' he had said to her about a fortnight after her descent. He prised the vodka bottle out of her tight-gripped fingers. 'Any time.' She made him a promise, too – not to drink. Seeing an analyst called Dempsey was part of that promise.

Sadly, Dempsey was full of shit.

For a start she had given Malise the sculpting package. She said it was to 'help objectify things'. Malise felt foolish and angry, riding the subway back to Archway with the FizzyArt box tucked under her arm. As if this was all she needed!

Not that it wasn't a neat toy.

One evening when she was bored with Amy and had nothing better to do, she played absently with the FizzyArt projector, to see what else it could do. Before she knew it this was the result: black spines, cracked eggshell. It had sprung out of nowhere; it didn't feel as if she'd made it at all. She showed the sculpture to Dempsey. Dempsey said it was a displacement activity, a device her subconscious mind had invented to deceive them. She made Malise feel obscurely guilty.

And yet Malise felt sure this eerie object contained some strange half-knowledge, some sense of 'rightness', of awareness behind a veil of forgetfulness – a solution –

The phone rang. Malise picked it up off the floor and turned to the window.

Gaynor was there. Malise thumbed a return picture. A 'send' icon blinked bottom-left on the pane.

'You want the bad news or the bad news?' said Gaynor.

'No jokes,' Malise pleaded.

'Only one company allowed to run 'fat – R&D outfit, name of Dreyfuss. A lot of ex-astros work there. They go in nine A.M., jack in for thirty minutes, spend the rest of the day writing about it, and at five P.M. they put their 'fat back on the shelves and go home. That's the nearest you'll get to legal use here. You want it, I've got a contact number.'

Malise looked at the floor. 'You know,' she said softly, 'that's shit.'

Gaynor shrugged. 'It's law.'

Five days later, two polite grey-suited men called at Malise's apartment. They carried suitcases full of headgear and keyboards and trailing wires. They offered her pills and her own easy chair, called up images of the murder from inside her skull and displayed them on a membrane screen for her to see. 'Joachim Kennedy,' the Haag agent said. 'His name. Pretty.'

The other was an Indian datafat expert hired to take the information from her head. He blushed and averted his eyes from the images of the killing.

A week later some more men knocked at her door.

They stripped her skull.

She stood across the street from the office block, watching light play across its blue glass fascia. Now and again the street cleared of bicycles and electric trucks and she noticed her reflection in the office frontage – diminutive, stalk-limbed, black, as though the glass were swallowing up the light. She waited a while, going over in her mind what to say and how to behave. It took a long time and she grew tired of pacing up and down. She sat up against the foundation stone of the building opposite the HOTOL office to rest her aching legs. She wanted to be angry, but it was as if they had taken the anger out of her along with their equipment. An hour went by. There was no emotion to dredge. Just the beginnings of an aching bitterness. It took another hour for her to admit to herself that she couldn't face going in. Then, just as she got up to leave, Schoemann came out the building.

He spotted her and came over. Even from across the street he could see there was something wrong. He took hold of her hands and she said, 'They took my eyes.'

Schoemann hailed a rickshaw and took her home to his flat in Highgate.

The hallway was papered in huge gallery-quality Holbein blow-ups. The doors leading off it were spray-painted silver. The laboratory ceiling was plastered with handbills and music posters. Schoemann's futon was hidden from the rest of the living room by a Japanese wood and paper screen. There was a hippy-style top hat gathering dust on the top of the record shelves. Most of the records were vinyl. The player was a studio-grade laser transcopier linked to four speakers suspended on wires from the ceiling and stabilized by floor-mounted guy lines. The desk was bashed and scratched and a book had been wedged under the leg with the missing foot. It was solid wood – mahogany. An early typewriter with 'Underwood' still visible in gold leaf on the front had been jerry-rigged to feed data to a plasma monitor, parked behind a bakelite phone held together in places with micropore bandage. The holes in the phone's dialling ring had been worn oval.

On the floor were a pair of gloves and wrap-around shades wired to a white box the size and shape of a telephone handset. Schoemann told Malise to slip the gear on while he went to fix them something to eat.

The gloves responded to movement. The glasses focused pictures on the wearer's retina. It was a good simulation. EC combat craft from Cuban bases against Sikorsky gunships. Dogfights over the rotting wreckage of the Brazilian rainforest.

'Here.'

It was a spinach curry, slow-cooked since early that morning. 'All flavour, no vitamins,' Schoemann remarked, as he handed Malise a bowl of raita.

Afterwards he said, 'I can't do anything for you now.'

'No more eyes?'

Schoemann shook his head. 'No more eyes. It's as I said at the beginning.'

Outside: screams in the street. Angry obscenities.

They looked at each other, got up from the table and went to the window. A man was tugging at a woman, and the woman was beating at his arm. They were pulling each other in opposite directions and shouting filth at each other.

'Drunk,' Schoemann said, and left the window, 'Might as well leave them to yell it off.'

Malise stayed put by the window.

'He's tugging, not punching, it'll be okay.' When Malise still didn't move he came back and laid a hand on Malise's arm. It was shaking. 'Relax.'

Malise couldn't hear him. Her unblinking eyes dripped tears.

Schoemann shook her. But Malise was seven months and half a solar system away, seeing but not seeing, hearing but not hearing, reliving the reason for her being here, down-well, a cripple and blinded.

She is riding a seventeen thousand ton ball of concrete around the radiation shell of Jupiter. The gas giant looms above her. She can just make out a smudge of pink – the Great Red Spot, fading as it grows old.

The concrete ball is hollow. The space inside is metal

lined. It's been flung from its tight equitorial orbit well within the radiation shell by a skyhook two thousand kilometres tip to tip. Neither artefact is of human design.

Something has sprayed a big red blotch on the side of the concrete egg. Beneath it, the metal shell is uneven, indicating a hatch, or a scope – or a weapon.

Malise alone is there to greet it. The war with Moonwolf, the rogue lunar Von Neumann, is too fierce – it consumes too much human power and concern. Only two astronauts could be spared to investigate what a loyal, half-forgotten dumbhead ordnance probe round Jupiter has noticed.

One astronaut was assigned to the skyhook, one – Malise – to the egg.

Like all astronauts she fears this place. The Jovian system is unimaginably vast, and so its size excuses mysteries. But that is not the whole story.

Some twenty years before, it was seeded with technologies which, closer to home, birthed Moonwolf.

The machines were human-built – commercial explorative and mapmaking verybrights made cheap and produceable en masse by advances in high temperature superconduction and organic processor design.

No-one told the verybrights about Von Neumann but in two years they figured the dynamics out for themselves. They began to eat, and to breed. They built copies of themselves in Von Neumann's classic mould, and they began to think, and turned their eyes to the skies, and to the blue-green home from which they came, and which believed it still directed their actions.

Perhaps they laughed.

The machines on the moon made their declaration of independence clearly known from the outset; the Jovian machines simply fell silent. People call the conjectural

Jovian entity the Massive, in tacit acknowledgement that the numerous machines exploring that system have probably, like their Lunar cousins, developed some kind of single identity.

There is evidence for this, albeit conjectural.

Think, for a moment, of all the astronauts lost here, all the research stations that have vanished, all the vehicles lost without trace. Think of Marie Czynski, the first freelance pilot in the Jovian system. She was lost ten years ago. Stolen, they say, by something inhuman. How else to make sense of her last words, seconds before comms blackout?

They say that on her birthday her face thrusts itself, huge and smiling, three hundred miles from ear to ear, from every White Oval on Jupiter. Those who've seen it say she mouths that same sentence, over and over.

She says: 'The clouds are full of babies' fingers!'

To aid her in her mission, Malise has with her some drones, monitors and gash-built peripherals which she controls via the datafat in her skull. She pictures an icon and a menuscape meshes over her vision. She whispers her choice of equipment and the mesh fills with data, graphics and statistics.

In the safety and comfort of her ops couch, Malise can run several drones at once. It is a trick of mind and datafat she has trained long and hard to master, in the fight against Moonwolf. She'd employ that trick here and send a drone to the craft first, only no-one makes the right kind of equipment and the stop-gaps they've put together for her are unreliable.

She drives the demolition laser out from the shadow of the ship as if it's a part of her and guides it towards the eggshell. She unfurls its limbs.

Two insectile legs curl towards her, their jack-hammer spines exuding cyanoacrylate adhesive.

A dumbhead buried just above her left eyeball hears her whisper instructions to the laser, closes off her image-intensifier and tells her faceplate to fog.

She squeezes a mental trigger and the laser fires. Incandescent gases rush from light-smelted rock. Through her gloves Malise feels the push of acceleration as plasma billows from the excavation.

The laser releases the eggshell, spins itself about and returns to the ship.

Malise clambers over to the fresh tunnel. A thermal overlay tells her its glassy sides are blood heat and cooling rapidly. She manoeuvres her awkward bulk in line with the opening and uses an ice axe to tug herself inside.

A large black handle is set in the middle of the circular hatch, undamaged by the laser blast. Malise pulls it. Orange frost oozes from the pressure collars.

She pulls herself into the room and shuts the outer door. Gas blows through a grilled vent, moistening the plastic walls and misting her heated visor. She opens the inner hatch.

Something moves at the edge of sight, grips her arms, draws her from the lock and sends her tumbling. Malise scrabbles for handholds and turns in to face the room.

An attenuated hand reaches towards her. A nail-less powder-pink digit taps her visor. She blows out and droplets of phlegm spark like static on her face. Her skull monad brings cross wires down over her vision, fills her ears with distances and dimensions to describe what her terror-struck eyes are perceiving.

The thing she will call Amy has her surrounded.

The hand retracts. The arm cantilevers and the thing

laps at its finger. Its proboscidic tongue writhes and taps globules of spittle down a veinous purple throat.

Malise's legs kick, a foetal convulsion. She tumbles head over heels and her gloved hand finds the edge of the air lock. She swings herself inside and vomits into her helmet. She inhales and chokes on cooling bile. She tenses her throat against another spasm and whirls round to close the hatch door. Through the brown-streaked plate, she sees an elongated foot sweep towards her head.

She has time to close her eyes. It hits her and her face-plate snaps. Vomit and blood and screams gush out. The rest is a fever dream.

Schoemann shook her. She came back to her senses. She looked into Schoemann's eyes.

'You all right now?'

'I'm fine,' Malise replied, shakily.

'Is – is that what happened by the lake?' Schoemann asked her.

'You've got yourself an answer.' His guess was right but Malise didn't want to talk.

'So what –'

'Don't.'

It was as if a wall had sprung up between them. Something about her eyes, the set of her mouth, the way she looked away from him almost as if she were ashamed, stopped Schoemann from pushing the questions he wanted to ask; something about his silence, his acceptance of her unwillingness to talk, convinced Malise she should stay silent.

They wanted to talk but there was nothing they could

talk about. They tried to talk about nothing but neither of them could think of anything.

In the end Schoemann hailed a rickshaw to take her home.

Riding home, she was filled by the misery and terror of her blinding. It did not leave her, not that night, nor the night after.

For four months she fought it.

Now, in the park again, with the lake and the tower and the fires around her, she knew the battle was lost. It would be part of her for ever. This miswired nerve. This painful stump.

At the entrance to the zoo two men loaded wicker crates into a van. Bird calls from inside the tiny cages washed over the sounds of a drunk screaming, a barrel organ, Krishnas tubbing drums and bells, and a choir.

The monkey houses were closest. Malise elbowed her way into a crowd of Japanese refugees and looked in at the cage. Inside, a topless woman in Geisha trappings moved in stylized anguish around a prone man whose face was hidden behind a fearsome warrior mask. Such corrupted No-plays were popular: crude and predictable fusions of martial arts and sexual acrobatics. This one had just begun.

'One florin.'

A fierced-moustached man pushed a bucket into her stomach.

Malise shrugged and pushed the man away, but the easy manoeuvre was checked by the slow responses of her gravity cage. He pushed the bucket hard against her midriff again and caught the pelvic strut of her cage. 'Florin.'

Malise sighed and took from her pocket the small silver hexagon the man demanded. She dropped it onto the edge of the bucket. It rolled away into the crowd. He turned to follow the coin, and she walked away.

From the bottom of a shallow slope lined with spice-sellers and fiddlers came raucous screaming. There was a dog-fight in the penguin pool. Three men on step-ladders called the odds with idiots' gesticulations. The crowd waved fists and papers. Icy lamp-light glistened on their wet chins.

The unlit tunnel running between the two halves of the zoo stank of urine. Near the entrance stood a pot-bellied man in a torn suit. She handed him a handful of coins and he opened the door for her.

She entered as the lights blew out. Strobed ricochets of blue and pink turned colourless, curled into themselves, yellow to sepia to black in the chrome edging of the bar, in the chains, straps and bangles of the dancers. A new beat took over; fast and thundering and strangely syncopated.

Malise came here often. She liked its old-world, 'Western' feel.

She bought a coffee and set it down on a free table. Pastel graphics played a design around the ring of the cup — green tangents, turquoise radials, and kanji etched in ruby. She smiled to herself. Twenties kitsch.

She scanned the dance-floor. Behind the dancers there was a stage. A sheet covered the back wall and behind it many flash-units were shooting blue-white flares at random across the raised area and into the room. In the centre of the stage stood the life-size figure of a woman in a long-veiled bridal gown. Her hands and face were wrapped in gauze.

When a flash-unit fired her silhouette jumped into life – blind-spot black, quick and vital, a figure of Death. A flash from another part of the white screen, and the figure's shape jumped again and changed. Watch long enough and you saw the silhouette move to a strange sea-rhythm of its own.

Malise's grip was tight round the scalding cup as she brought it to her lips. Her mouth tasted of oil and acid. She rubbed at her eyes.

The music changed: something snappier, a reggae riff over tripletime.

Another blue flash pierced the air around her.

He stood blocking her line of sight. He was fat, in his late forties, like most of them here. She knew just from looking at him he was a relic. One of the old city hustlers; all cocaine and futures.

Moonwolf had crushed the cities and with them the old ways of getting rich. The ones who came here lived now for the style of the old ways, concealing their redundancy behind the sharpness of the image. This man, for instance, wore a white suit with wide lapels, heavily starched, like they could cut. Malise sighed. A fat shark. When he opened his mouth to speak, his mouth was red like a wound.

'Malise Arnim.' He sat down and touched the table. Colours mushroomed from his fingers and rippled across the polished surface towards her.

A pink-suited waiter stood a tall glass of something dark and fizzy next to her half-empty cup.

'Kentucky and Coke, right?' the stranger said.

Malise gave him an assessing smile. 'You're out of date. I don't drink.'

The man smiled back but it came out wrong, made him look like a sleaze.

'What is it you want?' Malise said.

He leaned forward. His eyes widened a little and he glanced quickly to his left, in case the two old ladies on the opposite table were listening. Malise's heart sank: it was another goddamn pitch. 'I need a hot-head,' he said. He brought out a packet of cigarettes and offered one to her. She shook her head. 'Name's Cowley. Been doing a bit of research, begging your pardon. You headed an assault team against Moonwolf.'

Malise nodded. 'You read the faxes.'

'I get the impression they weren't happy at you jumping down-well last year.'

Malise thought about it. 'You're some kind of journalist, yes?'

He laughed. 'I don't want your memories, Arnim, I want your eyes.'

'Meaning?'

'Meaning I can get datafat for you. Cheap.'

The man was a clown. Had to be. Months ago she had checked out Gaynor's story about Dreyfuss and the licences. It was all true. 'That so,' she said to Cowley, and tried to keep the irony out of her voice.

'I want you to put it in your head then perform how I say.'

'Nah.' Malise swirled an ice cube round in the untouched liquor before her.

'You know p-casting?'

She looked up at him, thought a moment and said, 'In-head cartoon simulation. Ersatz datafat experience. They use semibrights to make the shows. They can't record live action because they can't make artificial recorders good enough. 'Fatwired people can do the job, but the hardware's been thin on the ground. Till now.'

Cowley's eyes widened, 'How did –' He glanced around him. She'd made him nervous.

'Hands up,' she said, 'I've got you surrounded.' Then she smiled to calm him. 'Relax. No traps. But what other reason would there be to 'fatwire me than have me – "perform"? You want to record what it's like, right?'

She'd wound the man up by talking so casually. To him the idea was secret, dangerous, hot. The laws were strict, the 'fat hard to acquire. To her his plan seemed as crude and naïve as a kid's toilet game.

'I've got eyes for you, Arnim,' Cowley said. His voice shook a little. He was eager and afraid. 'All you have to do is what comes naturally.'

Malise shrugged. 'My body's my own.'

'Then you don't get the kit.'

Malise couldn't help but nod. However she might fool around with him, if she wanted the kit it would be on his terms. If he was stupid, he'd be tenacious, and stick to his asking price. If he was smart he'd know renewed sight was easily worth the price he was asking.

She thought about it. 'What kind of datafat you got?'

'*Dayus Ram* combat issue.'

He was a clown after all. She laughed out loud.

Cowley leaned forward. 'Recorded experience, customized sense data, colours you don't normally see, that's what I'm selling. Think of its street value! That kind of demand doesn't go unsupplied. The units are there, if you know where to look, if you move in the right circles. You're not the first soldier to down-well, right?'

Malise nodded. In spite of herself she was interested. 'Okay,' she said, half disgusted with herself, 'what's the flipside?'

'A show a week. Porn p-cast. Six hours' work.'

'And what do I get?'

His mouth twitched, like he was going to leer back some smart-ass reply, then he caught himself and said, 'Use of the 'fat. Full time, for as long as we need you. It's safer in your head than under my mattress.'

'And if I send you a postcard from São Paulo?'

Cowley shrugged. 'I wouldn't advise it.'

'Messy?'

'You find it difficult enough to walk as it is.'

'Charming.'

'Not my department.' Cowley gave her his number. 'Think about it, all right?'

The p-casting studio was set up in a windowless room on the top floor of a Kennington bingo hall. In the taxi to the studio Malise watched TV. A science programme was demonstrating new remote surveillance gear. She leaned forward when they mentioned Dreyfuss and showed a kind of biological drone system – wired dogs and human operators wearing 'fat behind their eyes. Malise whistled softly. What kind of licences did they need to play with datafat like *that*? More to the point, maybe there would soon be a way to earn her eyes without dropping her pants every week. Then she could tell Cowley to shove his hardware where it hurt.

Malise entered the foyer.

An Indian man Malise recognized came out through

a door marked 'Stalls'. He hesitated, treated her to a toothy smile and scuttled out into the street.

'This her?' The stranger with Cowley was thin, wire-strung and round shouldered like a cyclist. Pale hair was slicked back with dressing cream. There were food stains on his jeans.

'Come on inside,' Cowley said to Malise. 'Garry here wants to meet you.'

There was an antique computer console on a bare desk, a green tin locker, an easy chair and a wilted house plant on the window sill. Cowley unplugged the computer and put it on the floor. 'You sit on that, love,' he said to her, and gestured to the desk.

She went over to the easy chair instead, but Cowley caught her by the arm and led her away. 'That's for Garry. Garry, sit down, get comfortable.'

Malise sat on the desk.

'This is Garry. This is who you'll be acting with. He's 'fatwired, too.'

Malise ran IDs and drew a blank. Whatever it was in Garry's head (and the cursors told her there was something) it wasn't a HOTOL unit.

The phone rang. Cowley answered it.

She looked hard at Garry. He seemed familiar but she couldn't place him. She ran a profile search. It was the nature of the datafat in her skull to be able to access parts of her mind to which she herself had no immediate access. With it in, she never forgot a face.

'You want a drink, first, Malise?' Garry said.

From a plastic bag behind him he brought out a bottle of Stolichnaya. He produced a paper cup and filled it half full.

Cowley turned his back to them and talked whispers into the phone.

So what was the secret? She subvocalized and a cursor flashed. The phone conversation was now being recorded.

Garry came over and held the vodka under her nose. 'Come on, love, drink up.'

'I don't drink,' Malise said.

'Just a sip, come on, just a sip.' He tipped the cup till the vodka ran down her shirt and made a stain between her breasts. She grabbed for his hand but he dodged out the way and laughed. 'Hey, relax, love. No offence.'

Her datafat recognized him. She nearly fell off the desk.

When Cowley was done Malise said, 'Hey, any chance I can see what p-cast booths look like?'

Cowley didn't seem to hear her.

'Hello, Mr Pimp, show me the booths, will you?'

'What?' He looked at her like she was a ghost. 'Oh, sorry, honey, I can't do that. They're in use. Privacy. Get me?'

'Will some day.'

Cowley stared at her then laughed. It was a false, cold sound. 'Hey! I *like* that.' He stroked her under her chin. His hand was trembling. 'Look, why don't you freshen up? I've got some business with Garry.'

She took his tense little smile as a warning and left. In the bathroom she played the other half of Cowley's phone conversation, snooped by the sensors buried behind her nose.

They were going to kill her.

Preparing the virus was easy. The hard part was launching it before Garry murdered her. He fucked her so it hurt, and her eyes flowed with data and tears.

'Bend over,' he said. His face was flushed and sheened with sweat. He'd taken something, cocaine or acid or some meaner cocktail, to help him do what he'd been told to do, what the man from HOTOL had told him to do. She would stop him, blind him, crash his primitive 'fat by transmitting a code that would white out his vision. If she lived that long.

He hit her and repeated his order. She bent over. She was weak without her skeleton, fragile. She did as he said, and hoped he got kicks enough not to kill her yet.

He made to fist her.

She entered the menuscape. A phosphorescent blue field set against a blood-pulse sky. Hovering just before her was the tree-like icon of her virus. She hadn't written her weapon so much as sculpted it from existing viral artillery; this quick-to-understand symbolic landscape gave her a visual representation of what it could do. It looked right.

'Now,' he said, and gripped her arm so it sang with pain, 'eat me.'

She patched in comms, sucked him, felt his hands slide round her neck, and fired. And it went wrong.

The virus *changed*, mutated before her eyes, and now it didn't look right. Not right at all.

A slender jawbone scythed through the crimson clouds . . . a shin bone wheeled beneath it. Two white balls – peeled eyes with little black points for pupils – spun themselves out of the air. A halo of soft grey threads spooled out of the red sky. Spine-ridged arms flung themselves out of the ground either side of her in a shower of black petals. Feet high as mountains thundered over the plain towards her. The world turned and her 'fat closed down.

She kneeled up and fought against nausea. She tasted blood. There was something in her mouth. She spat it out.

Garry was screaming. He tore at his eyes, which was what she had planned. The red pool at his groin was a bonus.

She whispered for an icepack. Her hand went cold, nerve signals filtered and synthesized so as not to register pain. She stood up and took the blazing light bulb from its socket. Soon enough, Cowley came to see what the screams were for. An easy target. The scalding glass blew up in his face.

She fled the bingo hall. With no time to dress, let alone strap on her skeleton, she was arrested within the hour. She was given dirty looks, slacks and a shirt, and shown into an interrogation room. Her leg muscles felt as if they were hooked to the bone with razor wire. Turning from the hip was like being hit in the stomach. Detective Sergeant Karen Gaynor called the Kennedy homicide file up on her monitor.

'Have you heard of snuff?' Malise asked her as she scrolled through the reports.

'Like tobacco?'

'Like killing people on film. There.' Malise gestured to the monitor. 'These weren't the murderers.'

Gaynor called up the ID overlay. 'No, it was them.'

Malise brushed Gaynor's hands off the keyboard. 'Look at me. These were not the men I saw.'

Gaynor thought for a moment. 'You telling me your datafat screwed?'

'Jesus!' Malise stabbed the terminal's OFF button. 'Who, may I ask, did you have to fuck to get this job? *Those are not the right pictures.* I've never seen these men before in my life.'

'Markham said you agreed the faces were the ones you saw.'

'Who was he? The tall thin one?'

'Yeah, went with the Malay guy, name of Asiyani, to your flat.'

'Great. This morning I saw Asiyani walk out of an adult p-cast cinema.'

'So he likes an early fix –' She double-took. 'P-cast?'

Malise nodded. 'I've a new helping of 'fat in my head. I really don't know why I'm telling you, but anyway. This Cowley, he's a pornographer. He's picked up software which turns datafat plug-ins into pan-sense cameras. He got me the 'fat and we were going to make movies together. His cinema's in Kennington. Very private. Bingo hall with p-cast booths at the back. Asiyani's a client.

'Not long after we trip over each other in the lobby I say Hi to Cowley and some meat he wants me to perform with name of Garry, then Cowley gets a phone call. I run comms and record the conversation. Meanwhile I make small talk with Garry. He's 'fatwired too, but he's too tall for an astronaut and the unit he's running is mickey-mouse. He's from Dreyfuss maybe? So much for licences. Anyway, he seems familiar and finally I place him. He killed Joachim Kennedy. I go to freshen up – Cowley wants a quiet word with our sex murderer – and I replay the phone conversation. It's a Malay accent, telling Cowley I saw Joachim get his in Regent's Park and I'm most likely a police snoop. It sounds like Cowley, Garry and Asiyani set up Joachim's killing. Snuff, maybe?'

Malise took a long draught of coffee and went on:

'Sure looks like it, because they tried to pull the same stunt on me. Cowley was all sweetness and light from the time I got back from the bathroom and we dressed down for the occasion, then he pissed off and Garry tried to kill me. He was running his p-casting software at the time. Snuff, right?' Malise tapped the side of the console. 'Asiyani must have altered the data he took from my head. He substituted different faces for the ones I saw.'

'But Markham saw the faces and he didn't mention any switch.'

Malise let out an hysterical scream which was only half-pretence. Her nerves were shot, she was sore as hell and could barely sit, and now shock was setting in. She folded her arms to stop herself shivering and stared hard at Gaynor's reflection in the monitor to keep her mind from splicing her vision with images of Garry. 'All your policeman cared about was my confirmation. You must know how easy it is to confuse faces.'

'So what you want me to do? Arrest Garry? Cowley? That's easy. Give me a description.'

'And Asiyani.'

'You haven't given me enough to go on.'

Anger and frustration whited out her sight. 'Then *frame* the fucker. Blame some GBH on him. There's Garry lying in a pool of his own blood back at the bingo hall —'

Gaynor put her hands over her face. 'Do I really want to hear this?'

'That's why I need a cell for the night. Cowley will be looking for me. Look, before you move on Asiyani, call Schoemann. He's a friend of mine, a data super for HOTOL London. If Asiyani's left any incriminating information on HOTOL files – like the original faces, right? – Schoemann will be able to hack it, but he'll need to know before you move in case Asiyani lets a virus loose and wipes the system.'

Gaynor blinked. 'Anything else?'

Malise rubbed her shins and winced. 'Yes, get Schoemann to bring me another skeleton before I pop a tendon.'

She awoke in her cell to the sound of the coffee maker in the
hall grinding beans. She sat up. A man walked in, turned on
the light and handed her a little plastic cup of espresso. He
hadn't shaved, his hair was a mess and his face was slick
with sweat.

'Hey, Schoemann,' Malise said. Her voice was shaky
from sleep. 'You look like shit.'

'Get dressed.'

Malise blinked.

'Come on!' Schoemann pulled the covers down off the
narrow iron bed. 'We're moving.'

'Gaynor . . .'

'She's down in the lobby.' He pulled her up by her arm.

Memories of Garry burst across her vision with appalling, eidetic clarity. 'Don't fucking touch me!'

Schoemann let go.

'Just piss off and let me dress,' Malise breathed. She put
her shirt on. Schoemann went out and came back with a
skeleton. He helped her strap it on. By some miracle her
legs felt fine – a little weak, maybe, but nothing the
skeleton couldn't handle. They took the lift to the lobby.
Gaynor joined them by the duty desk. She was in uniform,
a pistol at her belt and a scope helmet tucked under her
arm.

The car was Schoemann's – French, pre-century, with a
smashed headlight.

'What's the rush?' Malise said.

The motor turned. They pulled away with a chalk-on-
glass squeal of tyres. Kingsway was empty. Schoemann

hammered his foot home repeatedly. The acceleration pressed Malise into the seat. Then, as they coasted into a sickening sweep around Bush House, he said: 'Ever heard of Walter?'

'Walter who?'

Waterloo Bridge was badly potted; the car swung and tyre rubber squealed against the left-hand kerb.

'I put suckers into Dr Asiyani's system. Asiyani's that little guy took the pictures out your head. He's a HOTOL employee on secondment to Dreyfuss. It's some kind of subsidiary of HOTOL's R&D installation in the Belt, name of C-Ledge.'

'Just keep your eyes on what's left of the road,' Malise muttered through gritted teeth.

'Minute goes by, I meet Walter. Walter's a systems phage I helped write for the company years back. It shat on me.'

Gaynor leaned forward and yelled into Malise's ear: 'They redphoned the station. They wanted us to bust a data thief. Guess who.' Malise glanced at Schoemann. 'I warned him.' Gaynor laughed, an explosive sound in Malise's ear. 'You've never heard anyone drop a receiver so fast.'

'Who fucked your clearance, Schoemann?'

'I don't know, but it's not possible for anyone under the rank of senior exec to alter clearance gates in an installed programme. Whoever protected Asiyani's files, it wasn't Asiyani. Some very important people did him that favour, and they must have a reason.'

'What now?'

Schoemann pointed to a black plastic rectangle jammed at an angle into the CD rack by his left knee. 'That's running tonight's systems data against public records –

registrations, maps. If there's a weak-point in the Dreyfuss caretaking, we get its physical location.'

'So will whoever's got the same toy,' Malise said.

He tapped the box with affection and narrowly missed a truck. 'This is the only one works to full efficiency. A year ago I figured I needed some life insurance, so I added some lies to the patent. We got six free hours.'

'We?'

'Gaynor tells me Asiyani's trying to get you killed. That doesn't make you curious?'

'You curious, too?' Malise asked the policewoman.

'Nah. Medal-hungry. Either you two breach Dreyfuss security and dirt spills out like Schoemann says or you're pride of place on my bust sheet.'

An amber LED lit up on the black box. Paper curled from its underside. Schoemann stopped the car, tore the paper from the machine and read it.

'Bingo,' he said.

The park separating Asiyani's new house from the main road was a landscaped strip of spray-sown grass, interrupted by clumps of sickly trees, stagnant streams and metal high-backed benches. To the right lay match-wood bedsits and to the left, a light industrial complex.

A wide path of broken, sunken brick bisected the park. They followed it to its end.

Number four Reveley Walk stood in darkness. It was cheaply built, and the gloom made it seem impermanent, as if its walls were flats in some huge theatre.

Malise's heart beat fast; she was obscurely afraid that it might fold up and vanish at Dr Asiyani's command, and with it all trace of the brutish, ritualistic killing in the park.

According to Schoemann's black box Dr Asiyani was moving home. A safe-cable from his old address had been decoupled two days before. Twenty hours later a Dreyfuss Corporation laboratory a mile away had registered a new safe-cable. It led here.

Malise looked in through the windows. The place seemed empty.

Gaynor went to work on the door.

It opened straight on to the living room. Against a partition wall stood a desk cluttered with computer gear. Schoemann sat at the keyboard. Once the boot programme had run he tapped instructions on screen.

'You hooked up?' Malise asked.

The screen flickered. 'It's a system I know,' he said.

'How long will it take?'

'An hour at the outside. If you want coffee the place is probably stocked for his arrival.'

Once Gaynor had been round the place and given it an all-clear Malise went into the kitchen, drew down the blind, went back and turned the light on. She searched the cupboards, brimful of packaged foods, for instant. It was there. She brought three cups through into the living room, sat one on the desk beside Schoemann and handed one to Gaynor who was sitting on the sofa near the stairs. She took hers with her upstairs. There were only two rooms: a bathroom and a double bedroom with two single beds.

Schoemann laughed.

She leaned over the banister. 'What is it?'

'Short cut,' he called up to her. 'He's replaced an entire safe-routine with a return punch.'

'Why?'

'Lazy. It's not that unusual.'

Malise descended the stairs.

'The bad news,' he went on, 'is I couldn't by-pass the user log to get the information ported.'

'So they know we're here?'

Schoemann plugged the phone jack into the back of the machine. 'Dumping will take thirty seconds.'

Something scratched the door. Malise started.

'Relax,' Gaynor said. Schoemann tapped in the e-mail number of Gaynor's office. 'It's been going on since you went upstairs. I used my helmet scopes; there's nothing there.'

Another scratch.

'I'll take a look,' Malise said and made for the door. She stopped short. There was something wrong. She called up comms but there was nothing but static. She called up heat-seek. There was a large, eye-aching blind spot in the middle of her vision. Something was jamming her perceptual software and doing it badly.

'Damn thing won't answer,' Schoemann said.

'Hurry up.'

Schoemann tried three times, then pulled the socket out of the coupler and plugged it into the handset, put the receiver to his ear.

The scratching on the door became persistent.

He tapped the receiver, listened again.

Something thumped the door. The blur behind Malise's eyes shimmered.

'Asiyani's not on the bloody phone,' Schoemann yelled. 'He's not connected!'

Malise went over, snatched the handset. Nothing.

'I'll dump it on card,' he said.

He sat back down at the desk, reached into a black file box and drew out a card at random. He fumbled it into the drive and started tapping. The door rattled on its hinges.

The disk whined.

'Come *on*,' Gaynor shouted. She drew her pistol and stepped towards the door.

'Let it finish,' Schoemann muttered.

The door frame shuddered.

Malise went and stood by the banister. Behind her she heard matchwood snap. Gaynor loosed two shots into the door. The concussion made Malise's ears pop and she fell back on the stairs. 'For Christ's sake –' she shouted as she scrambled back to her feet.

Schoemann ran to Malise. The door blew in. Gaynor stood her ground. Wood splinters buried themselves in the soft armour of her jacket. She levelled the gun at the opening. Something low and black rushed her, hit her in the belly with the force and speed of a car. Gaynor fell screaming to the floor. Malise caught a glimpse of white. Teeth, clamping the liquid black where Gaynor's guts were. Gaynor keened – a pure, fluty tone with nothing of pain and everything of death about it. Schoemann seized Malise and they scrambled up the stairs.

He dragged Malise into the double bedroom, pushed a dressing table in front of the door and leant up against it. Malise's legs gave out and she fell. From downstairs came the sound of shattered plastic. Schoemann propped one of the beds up against the door as well.

'They'll be here in a second,' Schoemann said.

'It's the dogs, right?'

'Like drones.'

'I know drones.'

'Take them. Do it now. Go under.'

Malise squeezed her eyes tight and patched every

combination of comms and drones utilities she knew. Nothing. 'I can't,' she whispered. There was nothing but static. There was nothing to get hold of.

'*Try.*'

They leaned back against the underside of the upturned bed, adding their meagre weight to the blockade.

Something hammered the stairs. Claws clicked on bathroom tile. Something hit the door. Malise fell forward in Schoemann's lap and the door shuddered under a second blow. A strong scent filled her head. Something savoury bloomed in her mouth. 'Schoemann,' she said thickly, 'there's . . .' Blood filled her mouth, grew tough, sprouted veins, bands of muscle, brittle bone.

It jammed itself between her teeth and exploded.

Malise awoke in a Faraday room. Foil covered the windows, the floor, the door. The metal lining of the room blinded her special senses to electromagnetic fields. No more stereo FM in her teeth. No breakfast time TV behind her eyes. No calls for help to passing police.

Light from a fly-specked fluorescent tube bounced harsh reflections off her tired eyes.

She'd been undressed. The eiderdown they'd thrown over her was greasy against her skin. She pushed it off and suffered as best she could the coldness of the room. A key turned in the lock. She stumbled to her feet. An old man opened the foil-lined door and came in. He was carrying a breakfast tray. He didn't say anything, just set the tray down and walked out. Again the sound of a key in the lock. She didn't reach the door in time to stop him and her throat stung like hell – she couldn't cry out. She sat back down on the smelly mattress and propped her chin on her fist. The coffee smelt terrible – harsh and badly brewed. There was some plastic-white bread, a piece of processed cheese wrapped in plastic film, a dollop of red fluorescent jam on the side of the plate, a knife with a smear of the jam on it and a knob of orange margarine on a saucer.

She ate and drank, not thinking, not daring to. Images of Gaynor kept slipping into her vision. She tried to shake them clear, to drown them in sweet jam and bad coffee. When she finished she examined the room. Foil was stretched across the window frame. Malise tore it aside and looked out. She was high up. Dirty, smeared towers pointed up through a sea of rubble and waste. Docklands – the old financial centre of the city.

She continued her examination of the room. A chrome door handle protruded from the foil plastered across the fitting. She tried it. The door was locked. She rapped at the door.

A rasping sound. The door was pushed open a little. She snatched the handle and swung the door wide. The man who had brought her meal stood a few feet back from the door.

'Hi,' she said.

He didn't smile.

'Can I come out?'

The man just shrugged. 'Might help if you had clothes.'

He went away. Malise stepped into the corridor. It was carpeted in a sickly, dirty purple. The material was worn threadbare down the centre.

'Here.'

He was behind her. Her clothes were in his hands. He dropped them at her feet.

'Where's my skeleton?' she said.

He shrugged.

'Why's that room Faraday-boxed?'

He bit his fingernail. 'Them's your clothes.'

She dressed. He watched her, unembarrassed and dead-eyed, like a eunuch two months from pension.

Her shirt had blood on it. Gaynor's. Nausea tightened her throat. She flung the shirt on the floor. 'Least you could do is wash the fucking thing.'

The old man shrugged. 'Not my department. Come on.'

She trod gingerly after him on shaking, unsupported legs. There didn't seem to be much else better to do. They took an elevator up to the top floor. How had a building this tall remained undamaged during Moonwolf strikes, she wondered. The lift doors opened. Malise stepped out.

The floor was open plan and full of expensive furniture. All the upholstery was pale leather or velvet, blue-white offset by soft pastel greys and pinks – all soft, sea-curved lines, no sharp angles anywhere. Hand printed silk curtains shivered in the air-conditioner breeze. The carpet was thick steel-blue shag.

The lift doors hissed shut behind her. Malise glanced back. The man had gone.

She walked through the furniture archipelago.

White silk brushed the arm of a *chaise-longue*. Malise double-took. White silk – sleeved round a white arm. Malise stared at the figure reclined upon the couch.

The flesh of her arms was the colour of bleached bone. She wore a sari, tightened by velcro fasteners to accentuate the generous curves of breast and hip. Her hair was a white dandelion clock, an even three inches over her pale skull. Her eyes were black pits, no iris visible: in each ivory orb a gaping hole.

The woman smiled a greeting and waved Malise to a seat opposite her. Malise sat back on it. Her feet didn't touch the ground. She moved forward, so as not to look small, so as not to be trapped by the furnishings if something bad came along.

They sat in silence for a time, each assessing the other, then the stranger laughed. 'You like my apartment?'

Malise looked about her. Every wall was a window on the outside. The whole shattered vista of the city lay around them, hot and vital. As they watched, strong winds blew cement dust into the air about the buildings, softening the outlines of the smashed landscape, reinterpreting the scene in impressionistic grey pastel, and the outside became distanced, like something taken from film or from memory.

Her voice was no more than a breath, a gentle, haunting hiss like water on a distant rock face. 'My name is Snow. I worked for C-Ledge. Do you know where that is?'

Malise nodded. Of course she didn't: C-Ledge was in the Belt. Beyond that she knew nothing. She wasn't supposed to. No-one was, not even all the people who flew there. It had started life some sixty years ago – a small AI research complex funded by HOTOL. When the war began against Moonwolf C-Ledge came into its own as the system's only big front-line R&D faculty next to the overstretched *Dayus Ram* torus. With status came a new building – an ambitious oneil, a gigantic rotating cylinder in space with parks and fields and small villages. In five years it had achieved virtual operational independence from the parent company. C-Ledge was a place where pure research met long-term investment; in return it handled work clients liked to call 'sensitive'. It was a secret place and with secrecy had come rumour. This woman might be lying, might never have worked in C-Ledge – but she looked the part.

'Worked,' Malise prompted. 'Past tense?'

Snow smiled again. Her expression was warm, but the empty black of her eyes made it seem carnivorous. 'I invented a new form of datafat. A radically advanced tissue. They thanked me, took away my samples and my data, and locked them at the back of a very big, very secure vault. If they have their way no-one will ever know of my invention.'

Snow looked down at her hand. Her nails were long and varnished white – all but two fingers on her right hand, and the thumb of her left. Snow saw Malise watching, closed her eyes and turned her head away a little – a show of modesty. She waited for her prompt.

'Go on.'

Again, the smile. 'Thank you.' She cocked her head. It was supposed to be a quizzical gesture, but to Malise it was as if she were judging the distance between them, like a predator.

'C-Ledge have invested a great deal of money in existing datafat technology,' Snow said. 'They are receiving a more than ample reward for their investment. Of course, the war helped. A lot of new developments were made – ways to augment dumbheads, ways to train obedience into verybrights and subvert rogue systems. Ways to brighten systems without having them eat you. C-Ledge acquired some great minds. We worked very hard. You and Nouronihar's other hotheads didn't just fly *Dayus Ram* 'ware against Moonwolf. You flew C-Ledge 'ware, too. More and more of it when *Dayus Ram*'s limitations were shown up. Did you know Nouronihar came and worked with us afterwards?'

Malise nodded. Nouronihar had designed *Dayus*

Ram's combat grade 'fat – the 'fat which she currently had installed.

'In other words,' Snow went on, 'C-Ledge are not interested at the moment in technological revolutions. They've *had* their revolution. Why rock the boat? Well, I guess I rocked it. What I've invented is as fundamental a leap as was the leap from silicon to 'fat.'

Malise tented her fingers before her mouth and nodded. She said: 'Meanwhile Joachim Kennedy's corpse got fucked up the arse in a park at three in the morning.'

Snow stared at Malise. 'Dreyfuss Corporation,' she said, choosing to ignore Malise's response, 'is a third-generation subsidiary of C-Ledge. Its division in this country is Dreyfuss Biologic Plc, whose recent investments have been underwritten by Schoenhause NV, a Belgian holding company whose sole apparent purpose is to guarantee the interests and assets of former fourth-generation HOTOL subsidiaries, most of whom are little more than shells – names by which financial assets are manoeuvred without exciting Monopolies watchdogs. Dreyfuss make expert systems for plant security. I smuggled a sample of my tissue out of C-Ledge and went to work for Dreyfuss Biologic. My status earned me *carte blanche* in the equipment I ordered and in the experiments and feasibility studies I carried out. My work continued. The dogs you saw are part of it. That's why you couldn't leash them. The two systems aren't directly compatible.'

'Tell me about Asiyani.'

Snow shrugged. 'Asiyani predicts that licensing laws for datafat down-well will soon be lifted. The Human Rights people in Den Haag have been making conciliatory noises for some time. The British government doesn't like it but it wants to distance itself from the old-guard Islamic caucus.

Asiyani believes my own success in obtaining those hard-to-get licences is the sign of some imminent political breakthrough. Asiyani has been working on possible applications for regular datafat should Haag's licensing restrictions be relaxed. Some of his applications are baroque. They have lives – and deaths – of their own.'

Snow stood up from the *chaise-longue* and went to the window. 'It is not my concern,' she said; her voice had an edge of anger in it. 'Asiyani will be arrested soon enough. He will go on trial, his actions will be made public and Dreyfuss Biologic will be visited by the Official Receiver, or whatever they call themselves these days. There will be no relaxation of the Haag code, and my work will be axed. The most significant work in the AI field since 'fat – axed, thanks to one man's murderous prurience and stupidity. We have different reasons for hating Asiyani, you more than most, but believe me, my reasons are strong enough. Do you think I *like* having to protect him?' She sighed and shrugged. 'He will be caught, one day, and because of that I must move my work, my smuggled tissue, and that is a delicate business. Until yesterday, I did not know how it could be done.'

She turned and faced Malise. 'Now, though, I have you. I want to install my new datafat in your skull. You and a dog I have prepared will then demonstrate the system to some buyers from the United States government. After you have performed these services, you may come work with me in the United States. Alternatively, your old datafat plug-in will be reinstalled and a sum representing six months' pay at your offered salary, two hundred thousand ECUs, will be paid to you in cash. It should just about be enough to enable you to live in hiding for a few years. In hiding: from the police, from HOTOL, from Den Haag . . .'

Snow came and sat beside Malise, reached over and took her hand. 'I hope instead you'll come with me.'

Malise shivered – Snow's flesh was cold. Snow looked into her eyes, and Malise saw that the dark pits in her eyes were in fact heavily tinted contact lenses.

Snow was photophobic.

'And if I say no – to all of it?' Malise said.

Snow leaned forward and kissed her on the jaw. Malise felt lipstick smear against her skin. Snow laughed softly in her ear. 'You won't.'

'Yeah?'

'Snow sent me.'

The boy sucked his teeth. 'Guess you'll do.' He undid the door chain and stepped aside. Malise entered the hall. Three rusted bikes were propped up against the left-hand wall.

The strut round Malise's left calf (Snow had given her back her skeleton) caught against a pedal and threatened to bring the machines toppling onto her.

'Watch what you're doing,' the boy sneered.

He pointed her to the kitchen. The floors were bare. Wallpaper hung in tatters on the walls. She dumped her rucksack on the yellow formica-topped table and looked round. The stove top was thick with grease. Dirty plates and pans had been stacked in the sink up to the level of the grey window sill. A yellow paper was stuck to the window with brown, peeling Sellotape. Light shone through it, and Malise read the message it displayed to the outside world – something about squatters' rights.

'This here's food.' The boy opened a cabinet. Processed bread, UHT milk, tins of dog food.

'Vegetables here.' He kicked the door of another cup-board. 'Your room's upstairs, first left. I'll take your bag. You do the washin' now.' He gestured at the sink.

Before she could respond he was gone from the room, and her bag with him. She went to the window and looked out.

Old, dumbly designed living blocks. Broken windows, graffiti, puddles and dogshit.

The sky was steel-grey, an even stratospheric cover – oppressive, claustrophobic.

Malise tried to open a window but it was stuck. The plates in the sink stank. She saw there was a used condom stuck to one of them.

The boy came in again. 'I said clean up.'

He took one step towards her. 'Go on.'

She turned back to the sink, took a fur-necked milk bottle from beside the draining board, broke its bottom off against the tap and turned, releasing the bottle with a gentle under-arm swing. It fell at his feet. He jumped away.

'Just cut the shit,' she said, evenly. She walked out, picking up the broken bottle, turned up the stairs and found her room. She put the bottle down, shucked the top half of her cage and her jacket, and went to the window again. It opened a little on dirt-clogged hinges. The air was hot and humid. She took off her top and bra, and ran a hand under her breasts to wipe off sweat. Her bag was dumped in a corner, beside some packages.

She opened them, A three-seasons sleeping bag still in its wrapping. A camping light. A pillow. Some porn: SM and leather. She wondered if they were an insult, or just some dumb gesture at intimacy. She heard the front door slam, and voices in the kitchen. She reached for her jacket and slipped it on, holding it closed over her breasts. Someone ran up the stairs, opened the door.

A different boy this time: tall, gangling, about twenty. He had a straggly beard which failed to conceal badly pock-marked skin and a hunted look. 'You're Snow's,' he said. He had a Belfast accent.

Malise nodded.

'Stuff okay?' He pointed to the corner of the room.

'Fine.'

He grinned. 'Good. Look, we eat out, Neil and me, Thursdays, but you stay in, right? Snow said you're not to go outside. There's food in the kitchen. Okay?'

'Am I going to see her at all?'

'Snow? Sure. She's coming round in the morning.' He turned. 'Come down and talk if you're lonely. Oh.' He turned back, reached into his pocket and threw a ball of silver to her. She stepped aside and let it drop.

''S okay,' he said. 'Blow. Present. Happy stay.'

'Bad cop, con cop.'

'Wha'?'

'Never mind. Thanks for the gear.'

He shrugged. 'Yeah, well . . .' He walked backwards out the room, closing the door as he went.

She knelt down and unwrapped the foil.

Cannabis. Cheap, cut with waste. She dropped the cube out the window. Let the rats trip.

A while later she went to the kitchen and made herself a coffee, then looked into the living room. It was empty. She went in, lay back against a beanbag and stared out through greasy, dropping-streaked windows at the sky. Behind her through the evening silence came a scrabbling sound.

Mice, maybe. Beetles.

*　　*　　*

The next morning they scrubbed down Malise's room with carbolic and bleach. As they worked the boy with the beard, whose name was Jarvy, said: 'Y'know, this sterile room business, it matters less than you think. There is no evidence an operating theatre's any safer than a good clean room. And masks! You know why they were first used? It was so surgeons didn't wipe their noses then have to rescrub. They're to stop snot getting in open wounds. That's all they're good for. Bacteria sail straight through them.'

Malise wiped stinging soap from her forehead and dropped her pad into the bucket beside her. 'Who told you this stuff?'

'Snow.'

'You know, Jarvy,' she said, 'you really give a girl confidence.'

Neil rubbed the sleep out his eyes. The carbolic did its work: he yelled and fled the room.

'Stupid fucker,' Jarvy said to himself.

'So what's with Laurel?' said Malise.

'Wha'?'

'You never seen those two men . . . ?'

'Oh.' Jarvy nodded. 'You mean me an' Neil? Is there a problem?'

'You're like kids on camp.'

'Yeah,' Jarvy laughed, 'a couple of freaks, I guess. Good though.'

'At what?'

Jarvy made scrabbling motions with his fingers.

Malise nodded. 'Might've guessed.'

Jarvy laughed good-humouredly. 'Snow don't understand everything about the Dreyfuss system. It wasn't just her who designed it. She's a biochemist, not an engineer. So we'll be recording trial data for her to give the buyers. Stuff they'll want to know before they buy the system and take her on their payroll.'

Malise shook her head. 'Sounds dumb to me. Why don't they ship her and the system over and worry about its value afterwards?'

'I dunno. Maybe they'd rather shit on someone else's lawn. She wouldn't be getting over there at all if it wasn't for the military angle, or that's what she tells me.' Jarvy dropped his soap into the bucket. Caustic droplets spattered Malise's cheek.

'She's really going through with this?' Malise asked, softly.

Jarvy shrugged. 'Well, it's what she was born for, she says.'

'They'll smother her. She'll never see the sun again. They'll wrap her up in red tape till she chokes.'

'That so.' Jarvy went back to scrubbing. The sun was shining, it caught in his hair, and along the line of his jaw. His mouth was set tight.

Snow arrived late that evening. She handed Malise the paper she'd promised, which had a short and confused crime report which mentioned Schoemann.

Jarvy and Neil carried a futon out the van and into the squat. Snow followed with a duvet and a bottle of wine.

'You travel in style,' Malise said.

Snow gave her a cool smile. 'You deserve it.'

Snow wanted her. There wasn't much tenderness, but her lust and technique were refreshing. It helped. It put a memory between her and Garry. When Snow got her breath back she lay on her front staring at Malise. She had taken her lenses out but Malise couldn't make out the colour of her eyes by candlelight. They bored into her – dark, mysterious, cooler than ever.

'Tell me about Schoemann,' Malise said.

Snow raised herself on her elbows. 'You don't rest, do you?'

Malise reached under her and stroked her breasts, feeling them swing against her hand. 'Would you rather we talked about Gaynor's stomach ache?'

Snow sat up sharply. Candlelight wove across her face. Her lips were sharp with anger. 'You pick your moments.'

'What do you expect me to do?' Malise kept her voice soft. 'Schoemann was my friend. Gaynor was going to nail the men who tried to kill me.'

Snow sighed, exasperated. 'Gaynor fired through the door without warning. My radio man had his eyes put out by splinters.'

'They used your monster to tear her guts out.'

'It was our only weapon.'

'They broke Schoemann's fingers.'

'His fingers got dislocated when they trussed him –'

'And beat him. Or don't you read the papers?'

Snow jerked forward then stopped herself, settled back on her haunches. Malise saw her left hand unclench and bury itself in the folds of the duvet. Malise shuddered. Not now. God, not now.

Snow's voice was little more than a whisper. 'So he got roughed up. Two months and he'll be back on the *Playgirl* cover playing the Stradivarius. Gaynor was a bad cop. Schoemann was unlucky. You know it. I know it. So why the game?'

Malise shrugged. 'Okay.' She lay back on the futon.

'Why the game?' Snow insisted. She slid forward and leant over Malise and ran the nail of her forefinger around Malise's right nipple. 'Tell me.'

Malise shivered. 'I want to know. Why are you so desperate to end up in prison?'

Snow pulled her hand away. 'Come again?'

'I want to know why you're doing it.'

'Prison?'

'Jarvy tells me you're going to work for the Yank military. If your tissue's so radical, they'll bleed all the information they can about it from you. They won't think of you as an employee. You'll be a resource, a valuable captive. They'll steal your work and keep it for themselves and when they're done with you they'll seal you up so no-one else gets to take advantage of what you've developed.'

Snow laughed. 'Thanks,' she said. 'But where I'm going is no prison. And if it is, it won't stay that way for long. You don't know half what I can do. The more I do for my employers, the more I'll do *with* them. In a year, perhaps two years, I will *be* the military.'

Malise thought about it; Snow watched her with deep black candle-sparked eyes.

How did it feel, Malise wondered, to hold a breakthrough in your hand? Could it make you overlook the obvious? Snow must know what would happen to her – she wasn't stupid.

No, not stupid: driven.

They made love again.

While Snow slept Malise lay awake, thinking. If Snow's datafat was as great an advance as Snow suggested, then it was a dangerous and powerful innovation – the kind you test on other people before you use it on yourself. How could she have been so irresponsible as to bring it Home? Malise stared at Snow.

What am I to her? she wondered. What are we all?

A vector?

A seed-bed?

Snow's hair was a thin white dandelion clock. Malise stroked her scalp, wondering what thoughts lay inside – what plans were being hatched there.

Her fingers found a line of raised tissue.

Malise's heart thundered. She felt the shape of it, traced it with a trembling finger.

It was a port. A datafat port.

That was how Snow had smuggled her tissue in: she was a hot-head.

Around four A.M. Malise awoke with an aching bladder. She slipped out from under the duvet and tottered stiffly to the bathroom.

Her legs ached. Her knee-joints had swollen. She shouldn't have knelt so long scrubbing the floor.

She eased herself down on the pan and pissed, looked round for tissue, and came up with a local newspaper. She tore a scrap off and wiped herself dry with a charity photospecial. She leaned up against the wall and staggered back to her feet. There was someone at the top of the stairs.

The figure shambled forward. The cherry-red coal of a lit cigarette hovered about at waist level, then rose to head height. In the glow Malise made out Neil. Cannabis scented the air between them.

'Need a slash,' he murmured, shakily. Malise got out his way. He leaned against the cistern and unfastened his trousers. Once he was done he turned and shambled back to the top of the stairs. He looked back at her and took a ragged breath. 'You know,' he said, 'you're pretty.'

Malise felt the night air on her skin. 'Thanks.'

'Legs kinda skinny though.'

'Up-well they're normal.'

'How do you fuck, with legs skinny like that?'

'Believe me,' she said, 'you don't want to know.'

Neil nodded. He turned away from her and staggered downstairs, leaning on the banister for support.

Minutes later Malise heard voices in the living room. Rhythmic grunting. A cry.

She wasn't sleepy any more. She went into the bedroom, put on her slacks and jacket. Snow didn't wake. Malise sat in the hall facing the bathroom. She thought over the past few weeks.

Snow wasn't the only one facing prison. But being on the wrong side of the law and in danger wasn't the worst of it – the worst was the stupidity of it all. How the hell had it happened? One false move and somehow she'd got tied up in espionage. Twice in as many days she'd been nearly killed. She shook her head and cursed quietly to herself. What was the point in trying to reason it? She was on a downward swing. She just had to be patient. She'd reach an upturn in the end. Either that or death. Neither were so bad as this constant waiting, this enforced passivity.

The door of the lavatory was still open, and first light greyed the window in the far wall.

For a while it remained a sharp, dark rectangle in a wall of black, then the texture of the patterned glass became visible. The outlines of the room, the doorway, and the wedge of bare board between it and where she was lying fuzzed into view. As the light strengthened, so the perspective grew more stable.

Malise watched the patterns grow and now and again she wiped at her eyes. Staring too hard, she lied to herself, wiping the tears off her fingers onto her fatigues.

Snow left around five thirty. Malise, Jarvy and Neil took breakfast together. Jarvy was quiet as usual. He had a bundle of printout and was flipping sheets over and back, intently following some difficult sequence. Neil was squirming round on his seat like Jarvy hadn't used enough jelly the night before. He kept staring at Malise. She stonewalled him.

'Jarvy,' she said. 'What's that you're reading?'

'Just checking out the leash.'

'The what?'

Jarvy lifted his gaze grudgingly from the page. 'Leash. What you'll hold the dog by. The command-link between you and it.'

'Oh. Who wrote it?'

'I did,' Jarvy replied, his face once more hidden behind printout.

'You good?' Malise said.

'Guess.'

'Jesus,' Neil muttered.

Jarvy glanced over the top of the paper stack. 'What's with you?'

'You never talk to me at breakfast. First time you open your mouth, it's to that bint.' He gestured savagely with his spoon. 'What's with you at breakfast?'

'I work mornings.'

'You always ignore me at breakfast.'

'I'm sorry.'

Neil threw his spoon into his cereal. Milk spattered the table. 'Fuck sorry,' he said. 'Just *fuck* sorry.'

A shadow moved past the window. Neil was at the door just as the bell went. 'I fucked your spacer squeeze,' he shouted. 'I fucked her up the arse. In your sterile fucking room.' Next they knew, Neil was staggering over to the sink with his hands between his legs and a look as if he was going to add colour to the washing up. Snow came in. She leaned over and kissed Malise on the mouth.

She had coffee with them, then sent Jarvy and Malise outside and down the ammonial steps of the flats to the car-park. They went over to Snow's van and Jarvy unlocked the back. 'How much can you lift?' he asked her.

'Try me.'

He pulled down a plastic-wrapped board and shuffled one end to Malise. Malise tested its weight. 'No problem.'

'Okay then, we'll take this up.'

Halfway up the first flight Malise's legs seized up. They put the board down to let her rest. The sun cast sharp shadows around them. Underneath the block everything more than a few feet away was sheer black, except where puddles caught the sun at oblique angles and cast it fierce and shimmering into their eyes.

'You okay?' Jarvy said, as though it was his fault she'd got tired.

'No problem. Just my legs ache from yesterday. Come on, it stinks out here.'

Neil's cheers echoed from the bathroom as they manoeuvred the board up the stairs and propped it against the door of the cleaned room. 'Hey, Snow!' he yelled. 'I can still get it up!'

'Scrub up,' said Snow.

'Bitch.'

Malise washed and shaved her head, and they laid her on the board.

'Go on, Snow, loosen her clothing some more,' Neil cackled.

'Just think doorbell, Neil,' Malise muttered.

'Hold still.' Snow tightened the brace around Malise's head and checked the straps connecting the brace to the board. The makeshift operating table was too short for Malise. Her ankles dangled and dug painfully over the bottom edge. Jarvy brought a cushion but it kept slipping off onto the floor.

Snow gave Malise acupuncture before unclipping the port in her head. There were adhesions beneath the skin and she had to scrape them free with a scalpel. Malise felt the blade chew across the bone of her skull and groaned.

Snow took a surgical hammer from the tray of instruments and peeled off its plastic shrink-wrapping. From where she lay Malise didn't get to see the chisel. A single, mild blow unloosed her skull catch. Snow put both hands to the side of Malise's head and lifted the port off. Malise watched her draw it away: a black rubber plate dripping pink-streaked juice, a HOTOL decal hotfoiled in its centre. Snow turned the plate as she put it out of sight below the bed. Malise glimpsed shaved skin.

Snow picked up something like a white anemone and tore off its bubblewrap. Tacky lubricant dripped onto Malise's shirt. She bent forward and placed the anemone in Malise's skull.

Malise's port was fitted with cusps where enzymes

consumed the lubricating oil, clearing the nodes of the 'fat package. It took a few minutes for electrical connections to fire between cusp and node.

Snow squeezed jelly round the rim of Malise's skull cover and slipped it back into place. 'Cigarette?'

'Christ, no!'

Snow laughed. She loosened the straps on Malise's head. 'Lie still, princess.'

Malise relaxed. She whispered the mantras of her old profession. Nothing. There was nothing yet. Relax. Take things slow. She took deep breaths and closed her eyes.

Picture yourself.

She felt her limbs weighed down by gravity too strong for them; her left leg was crooked a little, but her ankle still dangled awkwardly off the edge of the table. Her shoulders were at an angle, the line of them not quite perpendicular to the line of her spine. Her right hand lay palm uppermost. She felt the sun on its dry, sensitive centre. The tightness in the muscles of her neck made her head ache. She loosened them by concentration.

When she was as relaxed as she could get she tried to picture herself from a place on the ceiling. The image came out distorted. Her idea of her self was changing, warping, and expanding to fill the new spaces within her. Her homunculus was evolving in strange new directions – cancerous swellings and nightmare etiolations. I've killed myself, she thought, wildly. I've killed the human in me.

Snow, Jarvy and Neil came back in.

'You should be on-line now, Malise,' Snow said.

Jarvy and Neil crouched at the door and tore bubble-pack off fresh keyboards and loops of cable. Jarvy ushered Neil in and closed the door carefully. Snow loosened the strap across Malise's forehead then wired her skull up to the boys' machines. Malise tilted her head and watched Jarvy and Neil set up their equipment. They slipped on tinted strobe-glasses. Their faces suffused with preternatural brightness – sunlight from one angle and screen-glow from another wiped the expected shadows from their faces.

They were speaking a foreign language – rich in abstracts and acronyms and aggressive, energetic images. 'Ware talk.

She watched them out of the corner of her eye, and saw the concentration written on their faces. She listened hard to their strange conglomerate of medical diagnostics, near-obsolescent jargon and commonplaces used in senses lost to her. It made her feel ill to try and decode it. Panic welled in her mouth.

What was it they had put in her head, that they should use such strange languages in its presence? Unbidden, sacrificial metaphors filled the room. Their talk was incantation, their screens scented fires. Snow had buried ritual weapons deep inside her skull.

'On-line,' said Neil.

'On-line,' said Jarvy.

'On-line,' said Snow.

And, behind her eyes, something alien flexed itself.

Malise slept most of the day. Every once in a while Jarvy came up and wired her head and let her see on a monitor how the datafat link could be supervised. His fingers on her scalp were gentle and slow as he connected the electrodes. His fingers treated the keyboard the same, as if he were stroking the machine into doing what he wanted. It scared her and comforted her by turns.

The squat was his place, he said. With the money Snow was paying him he would split and get somewhere up in the Free North. Glasgow needed good 'ware people. It meant leaving Neil, and Neil was cut up about that.

'I kind of gathered,' Malise said.

'You don't trust him, do you?'

'Well put.'

Jarvy shrugged. 'I love him,' he said. His candour put Malise off-balance – she didn't know what to say but 'sorry', and she wasn't, so she said nothing.

The silence drew on. In the end Jarvy gave her a shy half-smile. 'Better get some more sleep. You look dozy.'

Malise nodded. Truth was, she was just about coming to for a while. Staying up since four had messed up her sleep pattern.

That night, three A.M. by her watch, the door to the flat opened and she heard Neil come in muttering curses. There was heavy scuffling in the hall and a clatter as a bike got knocked over. Malise sat up. Jarvy's voice. Neil's reply. More clatter. The living room door swung shut on their conversation. Malise lay back and drew the sleeping bag up round her shoulders.

An eyeball burst on her tongue and flooded her mouth with a sweet fragrance.

She woke shivering, forced herself to relax, slept again.

Dreamed.

Blood gushed from a slashed groin.

She woke, relaxed, slept.

Dreamed.

Bone cracked between her teeth and fat trickled down her throat.

Woke.

Slept.

Dreamed.

Snow nodded, sympathetic. 'I guess that's how a dog dreams,' she said.

'You mean I'm hooked up twenty-four hours a day?'

Snow turned to Jarvy. Jarvy shrugged. 'More likely when I was running tests on it early this morning I opened a few gates I didn't know were there.' He said to Malise: 'I'm sorry you had such a bad night.'

Malise shrugged. Shit, she thought. Her mouth felt furred. Her skin was all glued up.

'You want another coffee, Arnim?' Neil offered – a rare display of civility.

'She's had enough,' Snow told him. 'She needs sleep, not stimulants.'

'Thanks, Neil,' Malise said. 'Make it strong.'

Neil grinned maliciously at Snow and went into the kitchen.

Snow took no notice. 'Jarvy, the trial's tomorrow. You be ready.'

'Three more bench tests. Half an hour each.'

Malise went into the kitchen. Someone had got around to washing the plates at last. Neil had her coffee cooling to drinking temperature by the basin. He was battling with a primitive can opener and a tin of dog meat. 'Can I see the dog?' she said.

Neil looked up from the savaged can. 'Guess you should,' he said. 'When I get this done.'

'Here,' said Malise, and extended her hand.

He gestured her away with an impatient wave. 'I can open a tin, godfuckit.'

The dog was a Schnauser – a hunting dog bred for speed and strength. It was four feet tall at the shoulder. They were keeping it in a damp-walled utility room next to the lounge.

'Christ it's horrible,' Malise said. Jarvy followed them in and patted its neck. When it finished the dog licked the bowl clean. The bowl toppled over and skidded over to Malise's feet. She drew away as the great animal lumbered after it.

''S okay,' Jarvy assured her. 'It's still dozy from the op.'

Malise looked at the circle of crude stitching round its head. She grimaced, disgusted.

'That must hurt like hell.'

'Doesn't look like he's worried.'

'But later. What about infection?'

'Won't be a later. Not for him.'

'Oh?'

'Infection of the meninges. Been pretty hacked around. Rush job.'

'Christ.' All of a sudden the great dog didn't seem so fierce. It looked thin and lonely and it would die soon; Malise found herself drawing comparisons. 'How do you know all that?'

'Jarvy an' me scanned it,' said Neil. 'Got some new hardware downstairs. Diagnostics. Want to see it?'

Malise shook her head. 'Skip it.'

Neil looked from Jarvy to Malise then left the room muttering obscenities.

The Schnauser came over to her. She let it sniff her hand, and she wiped the mucus from its big wet nose over the fur of its back.

Jarvy left the two of them alone.

She knelt down and patted its neck. It moved forward and licked the corner of her mouth. The smell of rancid meat was overpowering but she didn't pull away.

Rush job.

Malise was luckier than the dog; there'd been no need to perform half-assed neurosurgery on her. Her skull already had a hole. She wasn't really human to begin with. Still – she touched the staples on the side of her head – she and the Schnauser weren't so different. Two halves in the same experiment.

She sat down. The dog came and laid its great head in her lap. Neil appeared in the doorway.

'Hey,' he said. 'You two gonna fuck? I got a camera . . .'

She wanted to get up and slam the door in Neil's face, but the pulsing weight of the dog leant up against her pinned her where she sat.

'You have weird dreams, baby,' Malise whispered, and the dog looked up at her; its look was like a reply.

For some reason she found herself crying again.

Jarvy hammered on the door and woke her up. 'Arnim? We're leaving.'

Malise hobbled to the bathroom. She threw water in her face and looked at herself in the fly-spotted mirror. Her face was covered in acne. Too much tinned food. Not enough exercise.

Her eyes sagged, giving her face a deathly cast. She

squeezed a pimple and wiped the pus away with a flannel.

The towel stank. She used her shirt to dry herself. She went back to her room and picked out her last clean top, her leather trousers and jacket. She picked up the skeleton and strapped it on.

'Malise?' It was Snow.

'Okay, okay.' Malise came out and descended the first step. Something caught in her gullet. She took another step and coughed to clear it but it pressed on her throat. A third step and she couldn't breathe. A fourth and she fell. Something disgusting filled her mouth. She came to a sprawling heap at the foot of the stairs.

She choked. Straight away Jarvy was beside her, his fingers in her mouth, checking for obstructions. He turned her over, picked her up from the waist and yanked her to him, forcing the air out of her so she could breathe again. She drew a ragged breath and sank to the floor. Neil knelt down at the top of the stairs so he could see them. 'She okay?'

Snow was beside her, checking for broken bones. Jarvy yelled, 'You been pissin' with my equipment?'

'Hey,' Neil laughed, nervously, 'just thought she'd like breakfast is all.' Jarvy stood up and ascended the stairs.

There was a lot of yelling, all of it Neil's. Malise struggled to speak. 'Relax, dear,' Snow whispered in her ear. 'Neil must have let you in on Rover's feeding time. Dogs bolt their food. How are you? Can you feel everything?'

Malise wiggled her toes, then lay still for a while, tensing and relaxing, sensing for damage, the way she'd been taught to. 'I check out,' she said at last.

Snow kissed her forehead. 'Lucky.'

Malise retched but there was nothing to bring up. 'Lucky,' she muttered through a mouthful of saliva. 'Great.'

The truck was decked out with the gear Jarvy and Neil would use to monitor the test. Terminals and trestles and two wooden folding chairs were propped up in a corner. There was a pile of rugs for the Schnauser to sleep on, and a dentist's chair for Malise.

There was no way to see where they were going because they rode in the back of the van. Snow drove, and she wasn't telling them their destination. The test would be observed, she said. Yank snoops would be watching, out of eyeshot. Snow didn't know whether they'd be there in person, or whether they would swallow their pride and install some Singapore-import surveillance around the test area.

Neil was sitting propped up against the wall of the van. Jarvy was asleep, his head on Neil's lap. Neil ran his hand through Jarvy's hair.

Malise could tell they were travelling south from the sounds outside the truck. Bicycle bells. The creak and clatter of rickshaws. Snow's horn and her voice, muffled by the tin walls, yelling for space to manoeuvre the awkward vehicle. The cries of street traders . . .

Six hundred years ago the streets here began losing the trades which had given them their names – Poultry, Bread Street, Shoe Lane – and became home instead to Britain's financial centres. When Moonwolf blew London apart new streets emerged from the rubble, and fresh names were given to them. Tincan. Thread Street. Horsemeat.

She remembered coming here at the busiest times,

when she first down-welled, to prove she could cope with the crowds, with the rush of bodies pushed up against her – to prove she wasn't a cripple.

The van rumbled and swayed as it crossed the pontoon bridge. This betrayed their location more precisely. Bridges over the Thames had been the first targets of Moonwolf's attack on London. Now more than twenty narrow pontoons were slung across the river. She'd been south only once, searching out a moving sculpture she'd heard was by Karel Shaw, an artist her father adored, and whose pictures had given her exhilarating nightmares as a child. When she got to where it was supposed to be she saw a line of children, hundreds long, bearing buckets of clay and debris out of a wide excavation where Campbell's Galleria once stood. The frame of the building had been cannibalized for a massive drainage project.

To her left rust-red plates dribbling river water held back the Thames – a fragile wall of metal held in place with huge steel buttresses. These were necklaced at intervals with shards of stressed concrete – remnants of the floors the buttresses had once supported.

To her right, women stripped to their waists in the summer heat attacked the remaining foundations with picks.

Then, on the other side of the mustard-bright channel, Malise saw the listing wreckage of Shaw's moving sculpture. She got to play on it and thought of her father a lot and was happy.

Now she wondered if it was still there, or whether it had been pulped and recycled along with the rest of the spoil.

The journey took two hours fifteen. The Schnauser

slept through it all. It seemed so docile, they must be doping its food.

When they arrived Jarvy wired her up, Snow roused the dog and took it for a walk. She was back in five minutes, puffing and red-faced and smiling.

'Christ,' she said, 'it's good to be out the crush.'

'Don't worry,' Malise said, 'where you'll be going there won't be any other people for miles around. Miles and miles and miles.'

Snow leaned over her. 'Malise, please don't make a scene. You're only saying those things because they're listening.'

'Hi there Uncle Sam. Keep burning the midnight oil.'

Snow shook her head. 'You sound like Neil.' She went out with the Schnauser.

'Ready?' Jarvy said.

Malise nodded.

'In your own time, then. Have fun.'

Malise closed her eyes and pictured an icon.

The new datafat package seized control inside her head and the world swelled round her. Malise closed her eyes, whined, staggered on too many legs, felt the bite of a collar round her neck, choked with the stench of everything around her, and fell over.

She got up.

She opened her eyes. The world was wide, wider than it had ever seemed with unaided human sight. Alien, too: monochrome, like the super-resolution combat 'scape she used to train on. Snow walked her across an expanse of grass. The world was big and clumsy and unsure of itself; it was shapeless and drowned her with sensation: baritone birdsong, the slow growl of the wind, the concussion of Snow's boots on the damp turf.

She smelt a distant dog turd and her mouth watered.

The world weaved in and out of her mind's focus then settled.

They were walking over a heath, a desolate place made strange and pregnant with sound, the weird parallactic procession of hawthorns that grew upon it, the superb black-on-white definition of its most distant features.

Malise strained at the leash and Snow tugged her back.

Her heart thundered with anger. Rage came upon her so suddenly she didn't know what had triggered it. Her head swam. Bloody images filled her sight; horrible, powerful – thrilling.

At last her rational mind caught up. Encephalins, she thought. The brain chemistry of emotion is the Schnauser's, not mine. This is how a dog feels rage. Snow had forgotten there was a human being in here – or perhaps she just didn't care. Maybe putting a leash on me gives her a kick, Malise thought, and it hurt her to think that, because going to bed with Snow had been good, the least manipulative thing done to her in days.

Snow knelt down and Malise tried to growl at her, only she couldn't get her throat muscles to work properly. Snow cocked her head and gave her a wry smile. She said something but pitch-shift made it unintelligible. Malise wondered if it was an apology. Snow unclipped the leash and kicked Malise gently in the flank. Malise took the hint and ran.

She barked with delight. It felt more like flying than running! Suddenly, gravity was no longer something she had to fight against. It was more a gentle, steadying line of force, holding her to the plain of the horizon, like the coils under a ground-effect rail.

She ran back to Snow and they played the fool together.

Fetch. Sheep herding. In a while Malise lost all sense of disorientation and clumsiness. She was the thing itself. If she could she would have laughed. The Yanks must be pissing themselves.

When the test was over Malise went on ahead of Snow to the road. From some indeterminate place above her there was a deep growling, like an aeroplane behind cloud. She stopped and looked up for it. By her right ear, a million flutes blew a single, clear harmonic. Beautiful. She turned her head and got a brief glimpse of the VW decal.

Her front leg went under the wheel, then her shoulder. The whole crushed mess got ripped off in a second, and already her flank was caught. The wheel ran down her back as surely as if her spine was a rail. Her skull splintered. Shards of bone blew out around her and pain and fluid bloomed from her eye. The wheel mashed her teeth into the tarmac and the fluting sound of protesting brakes rose up into her skull.

A flash of green.

The van assembled itself around her.

Jarvy was sitting white-faced at his console. Neil was on his back, laughing fit to choke.

They drove back to the squat. The drive was uncomfortable; Snow's anger made her driving erratic. Malise couldn't stop shivering. They parked and Snow opened the back of the van.

Malise was first to the door of the flat. She reached into her pocket for the key and the door swung open.

'Hi.' She was taller than Malise and twice as broad. She smiled. Her teeth were very even, very white. 'I'm Rea.'

Behind her Malise saw shadows shift in the hall. Figures moving into careful, tense positions. Snow was next on the balcony. Malise turned to her; her eyes spoke a warning.

Rea took a step back. Two men eased past her and out the door – black jackets bulged with the promise of weaponry. Snow just stood there, frozen. The last Malise saw of her, she was being frog-marched out of sight. Neil and Jarvy came up together just as Snow and the men were rounding the corner.

Neil shouted and tugged at one of them. He let go of Snow, turned and hit Neil so fast the boy never even got to raise his hands in defence. Jarvy stood watching, unemotional, his delicate hands clenching rhythmically. Neil staggered, turned with his hands covering his ruined face and leaned up against him.

'Jarvy,' the woman named Rea shouted, 'get that dickhead in here.' Jarvy ushered Neil towards the flat.

Neil pushed blindly past Rea, still covering his face with his hands. Malise heard his footsteps hammering the stairs. Rea shepherded Malise and Jarvy into the living room, where five more jackets were waiting. Some had weapons drawn – ugly, powerful handguns.

'Jarvy,' said Rea 'tell her what she needs to know then put her to bed.' She turned to Malise. 'Get some sleep. You'll be needing it.' She patted Malise's cheek with her gloved hand.

Up in her room, undressed and lying propped up on one elbow in her sleeping bag, Malise stared at Jarvy. He was swinging a gun round his fingers, like it was a toy. 'You're Stateside, right?' she said.

Jarvy nodded. 'Sorry to give you that line of bull about Neil and the North an' all.'

'Is Neil part of this, too?'

Jarvy spun the gun on his palm and caught it as it toppled. He didn't answer her. 'You know yet why you fucked up?' he said.

'Frequency shift. Nothing sounds like it should. I didn't hear the car – not to recognize it. Didn't your diagnostics tell you that?'

Jarvy took a pack of Gitanes from his top pocket. It was the first time she'd seen him smoke cigarettes. He offered her one. She took it.

'Yeah.' Jarvy blew out smoke and grimaced as if he found its flavour unpleasing. 'You can relax about your buddy. Snow's heading Stateside, and you'll be joining her just as soon as we get what we need from the Dreyfuss site.'

'What's that?'

Jarvy dragged on his cigarette. 'Another fucking dog. When you mushed up that Schnauser you mushed up the datafat in its head; the van went and pulped its skull.'

Malise swallowed hard. 'Tell me about it.'

'So we go in for some more.'

'Why can't Snow smuggle out another dog? She's done it once – why can't she do it again?'

Jarvy shook his head. 'The Dreyfuss site is crawling with Haag agents. It seems someone, not Snow, got caught abusing their datafat licence – there's something about a homicide investigation.'

Malise closed her eyes. 'Asiyani,' she said, her voice hollow.

'Snow told you about him?'

'It's through him that Snow found me.' Malise rubbed her eyes. 'Shit.' Joachim Kennedy's killing again –

it was all set to fuck her up a second time. 'So all the back doors are closed, I take it.'

Jarvy nodded, glumly. 'Not even Snow could guarantee to get the goods out while Haag are around.'

'And you?' Malise asked. 'Can you guarantee to get the goods?'

Jarvy snorted. 'We get *paid* to risk dumb stunts like this.'

'And just how easy will it be?'

Jarvy spread his hands. Search me. It was a gesture she hadn't seen him make before. 'Dreyfuss guard their plant with Dreyfuss dogs. They've bootstrapped their own plant security.' He shook his head and stubbed out the cigarette on the floor. 'It's got style, I'll hand it to 'em. And there's the Haag people to consider. We'll take casualties.'

Malise shook her head. 'I'm not your sort of soldier. Just get this goddamn trash out my head and let me go.' She sensed that she was trembling, that she couldn't control it.

He shook his head. 'You're precisely the kind of soldier we need. We need you to steal the dog. We need you to leash it. That way the operation goes smooth. Smoother, anyway. You won't be in danger. You'll be in the van, leashin' a dog, you'll run it back to the van and then we drive off.'

'When does this happen?'

'Tonight. There's a satellite footprinting the area now, getting us ground plans. We move out in three hours.'

'Neil, where is he?'

'He's okay.'

'Where's he gonna be?'

Jarvy turned great cow eyes on her.

Malise stared at him. Her heart began thundering before her mind caught up with the reasons. She thought of the Schnauser, of the operation, of the sheer cold speed of things. Neil – who loved Jarvy – who was – 'Why?' she breathed.

Softly: 'This is a delicate operation, Arnim.'

Malise shimmied out of her sleeping bag. She grabbed her jacket.

Jarvy caught the other sleeve. 'You never trusted him, Malise.'

Malise yanked the jacket away and stumbled to the door. Jarvy followed her. 'He could have been opposition!'

Malise twisted painfully on her unsupported hip and staggered downstairs, over to the room where they'd kept the Schnauser. She flung the door open.

The room was in darkness – orange city-light from the open window marked out Rea's silhouette. She was drinking from a hip flask. Malise felt for the light switch and pressed it down.

Neil was sitting on a wooden chair near the door. He was tied there with wire. His chest was misshapen. The crotch of his trousers was piss-dark.

Yellow rivulets coursed over his bare feet.

Rea drove Snow's truck. Malise travelled in the back with Jarvy and the rest of the team. They checked and rechecked their weapons – huge, unreal German automatic rifles – with nervous, irritable gestures. They wore matt black cycling helmets rigged with comms equipment. Jarvy sat up against the concertina door beside Malise and showed her some satellite pictures.

Malise studied them but all she could see was Neil's feet dripping, the puddle beneath the chair. 'Jarvy,' she said, 'you knew what was coming to your pal?'

'No.' He avoided her gaze, but she knew if he looked at her his eyes would be empty.

'Was he good in bed?'

Jarvy turned to her. His face was neutral as a grey sky. 'I gave you some maps. Learn them.'

The drive took about an hour. Malise guessed from the crack of glass and rubble under their wheels, and from the layout of the map, that they were somewhere in the derelict Square Five Mile.

The truck stopped and the engine died. The concertina door spun open and the jackets disembarked, leaving Jarvy and Malise alone together. Just before the door rattled shut again Malise caught a glimpse of a rubble-strewn square contained by broken tower-blocks. The structures were stark and simple in the moonlight, like they'd been airbrushed. A brick road led from the truck, and Malise recognized it from the satellite pictures Jarvy had run off for her. A one-bar firegate straddled the road some fifty yards away. Further down there were spindly trees and high-backed benches. Shattered streetlamps like giant rush stems bowed their heads over the road. There was a rise to the left, and Malise knew from the plans on her lap that the Dreyfuss production site was on the other side.

'Get in the chair,' Jarvy said.

She settled back in the padded black dentist's chair, blinked up her datafat and pictured an icon. When she was ready she let the 'fat override her optic nerves.

Little pink pyramids filled the dark blue emptiness

behind her eyes – compatible systems eager to hand-shake.

'What do you see?'

Malise shook her head. Figures shuttled in and out of her focus and they were badly wrong. Unless – 'Jarvy,' she said, unable to suppress the quaver in her voice.

'What is it?'

Malise swallowed. Her mouth was dry. 'Dreyfuss Corp – what they've made, what Snow's made I mean – it's big.'

There was silence for a time.

'What's big, Malise?' Jarvy's voice was patient and level.

She concentrated once more on the map. Her datafat was adamant. No errors. She couldn't even begin to realize the scale of what she was being shown. The thing around her was bigger than – than all the computational systems she had ever known barring –

'Jarvy?' she whispered, 'it's a goddamn Moonwolf, Jarvy.'

'Can you penetrate it?'

'Jarvy, you listening, it's –'

'I'm listening. I hear you. Hurry up.' There was fear in his voice.

'You want me to do this?' She was stalling, and the longer she held out the worse it got. Memories of Moonwolf flooded her. It was too big for her. It would kill her . . .

No. She forced down the panic. There was something wrong, there had to be. Nothing could be that powerful and exist in such a small space. How could a Moonwolf fit on a Docklands industrial site? It made no sense.

Snow's words came back to her, unbidden. A break-through. A big breakthrough. Oh *fuck*.

Jarvy said, 'If it's what you say it is we've no time. Go under. Do it. Do it now.'

She iconned instructions to her comms package and entered one of the pyramids.

Black. All around her. No sound.

No data.

There were no dimensions to this mathematical space.

It was empty. Nothing but raw processing space. Brain dead. Still-born.

A line on the horizon.

Brilliant, pure white. A carpet of light unrolls before her and turns blue. Above it a red sky mists into existence. It pulses once. The ground softens.

Malise moans with fear.

She hears the moan, feels the slickness of the plastic seat underneath her, hears Jarvy's breathing, and her own, the click of a data card as Jarvy plays with his machines – but before her eyes, and in her nostrils, lies a different place.

The scent – grass. She looks down. Blue grass. New mown.

She knows where she is now. A consensorium – a kind of interactive p-cast. They used them on the Dayus Ram *to train her for combat against Moonwolf.*

A breeze springs up, carrying a different odour, fetid and warm and strangely erotic.

Dogs.

A black pool bubbles out of the ground and spreads towards her. She floats towards it. Another pool appears to her left, and another. Could these features, the way they're arranged on the infinite-seeming plane, the scent of grass, the bloody clouds above, could all these things mean something? Are they part of a coding procedure? Can she key into a Dreyfuss dog only by somehow passing a test set in this environment?

The black, unreflective pool is close to her now, and its lack of feature unnerves her. Suddenly it stops expanding. It's about forty metres in diameter.

From the surface a sculpture rises — struts and bars bloom from the blind-spot blackness and coalesce to form simple geometric shapes. The shapes join and become more complex, turn to buildings, roads, lamps — some kind of light industrial estate. Belatedly, Malise recognizes in the sculpture a three-dimensional map of the Dreyfuss site.

And the other pools? Do they represent other extensions of the HOTOL empire? The set-up smells of something big, something wealthy and worth infiltrating.

She turns to look at the other pools.

Something as high as the world blocks her view.

She forgets training, tries to move hypothetical legs, tread hypothetical grass, turn and run across hypothetical space. She falls to the ground and her scream carries on the breeze.

She can't feel the chair any more, or hear Jarvy's keyboard.

She gets back on her feet and dizziness floods her. She sways, and her boots mash the grass beneath her. She listens to her screams. Have they any objective reality, she wonders, or are they just a wave peak, a fractal measure of terror?

The thing towers above her. Its topmost spines tear ragged holes in the clouds. Blood rains down. She blinks *against the salty downpour, tensing her throat against whatever passes for vomit in this place.*

It is incomprehensibly vast. To walk from the cracked-white porcelain base to the tip of its topmost spine would take years. It is too big to be believed – only she's seen it before.

In fact, she made it.

It's her FizzyArt sculpture.

Feet high as mountains thunder over the plain towards her. She feels the concussions, turns and looks up. A whorled toe grinds her into the earth.

Malise drew a ragged breath and stood up. Her legs bent the wrong way.

She looked around her. A grassy bank. Weeds, insects mating, the smell of shit.

She turned her head. Boots. Little ridges at the heel where the plastic has been cut from the mould, mud on the highly polished toes, black laces frayed in places, a heel worn down a few millimetres at the heel.

The rustle of stiff fabric. Serge, cotton, kevlar weave. Things in the pockets. Keys, pens, coins, slips of paper, maybe a cigarette packet.

A man in uniform knelt down and patted her head. He had calluses behind his fingers. His hand was well-muscled. It stank of soap. She took a few tentative steps forward. She was a dog – a Dreyfuss dog. She shook herself and stretched. No clumsiness, no hesitation, no sign of mental or bodily betrayal. She was in.

An impossibly low, mellow fluting came from the mouth of the man who had knelt beside her. It took her a moment to make out the words.

'How are you, boy, eh?'

She caught a whiff of oil. Oil and gunmetal. She looked at his belt. He wasn't armed. Behind him through the chainlink, someone in black eased forward out of the darkness.

Damn Rea! Why hadn't she thought of that? The Yanks' weapons stank strong enough for any dog this side of the complex to smell them and start baying.

The man's face fell. 'You're still leashed, right?'

Malise nodded her long, graceful dog's head.

The man wiped his face. 'Shit, you had me worried with all that staggering about. Sorry, mate.'

His hand spat blood. His cry bubbled to nothing as a gaming dart snicked his throat.

A muffled curse, the clank of metal on metal.

Malise turned. Rea and three jackets were at the fence, cutting the wire. It sparked. Alarms rang for two seconds then died. The silence gave Dreyfuss an edge – their dogs had keen hearing.

Shapes, huge and threatening, bounded into view behind her, black on charcoal, bobbing silhouettes against the paler grey of the Dreyfuss buildings. They must have had forewarning to be this close. The smell, of course. Rea's goddamn artillery.

The fence was open. Rea and another man donned insulating gloves and held the fence open for her. Malise bounded through the gap in the fence, over the rise (claws scoring stones and discarded Coke cans, crackling crisp packets and bits of old hypodermic), and towards the truck.

It wasn't there.

Gunfire shattered the urgent silence – an appalling concussion that scrambled her brain and pumped up her adrenalin to screeching point. She reached the avenue. The cheap brick powdered when she dug it with her claws. The air tasted filthy – saltpetre and burning rubber and droplets of roast diesel.

Another gunshot. Without really willing herself to run – the endorphins in her system were doing the work without her – she fled down the avenue at breakneck speed, past half-dead trees and strange shadows and fences with gates in them that led nowhere and abandoned fridges and drifts of crumpled newspaper, away from where the truck should have been, into the relative cover of the unlit parts of the city.

She was in the heart of the derelict park bordering the Dreyfuss site. She skittered to a halt on the gravel and listened for sounds of pursuit.

Nothing.

Why the change of plan?

Panic seeped through her.

Why anything?

She looked around. Ornate bridges were slung across mossy stone channels. To her left – a derelict fun park and a shit-rich sand pit.

For a moment she thought she knew the place.

For a moment it felt like a homecoming.

She never heard the shot.

Suddenly her eyes went mad. Statistics, trajectories, damage reports and crossbone icons skeltered through her optic nerves – urgent despatches from the datafat buried in the dog's shattered head.

Malise fell, bleeding and pissing all over the road.

She was dead.

In fact, she made it.

It's her FizzyArt sculpture.

Feet high as mountains thunder over the plain towards her. She feels the concussions, turns and looks up. A whorled toe grinds her into the earth.

'Jesus!'

Malise opened her eyes.

Jarvy was backed up against the wall of the truck. He had a machine pistol in his hand, levelled at her. His comms helmet lay at Malise's feet. Urgent voices were calling him.

'Jarvy?' she said. Her throat was raw. She coughed. Blood sparked on her tongue.

'You back?' The look of fear in his eyes unnerved her.

'I think I fucked up,' she confessed. 'There was nothing to leash, just – nightmares.'

Jarvy moved forward cautiously and snatched up his cycling helmet, twisted the throat mike round and recited his call sign. He said: 'Rea, sorry. Arnim just went batshit. No, I didn't. Something – yes. Out.' He turned to Malise. 'She told me to kill you,' he said.

His computers laughed at him.

He whipped round and stared at his monitor. 'What the fuck –' he muttered.

Malise drew in a ragged breath. She whispered to her datafat to show her what had filled Jarvy's screen. Gold kangi clicked into view. She pictured an icon, ran a cryptographics package. It took only a few seconds to decode the message before her eyes. She read it out to Jarvy. 'It's Snow's towerblock,' she said.

'Your 'fat's translating this?'

Malise nodded. 'It's a data-map reference. Snow's

home terminal's still got access to Dreyfuss' main system. I can web a dog from there.' But not if I'm dead, shithead.

Jarvy fingered the side of his helmet and spoke into the mike. He told Rea the news. He didn't mention Malise. He cut the connection and looked up at her with big, sad eyes. 'She says go to Snow's apartment,' he told her. 'Maybe we can throw them into confusion, sneak a dog out later.'

Malise remembered Schoemann's toy. She felt tired and empty. 'Who d'you think overran your system to give you that map?' she asked.

'Dreyfuss.' Jarvy snatched up the handful of photographs he had shown Malise. 'Who else? But you got a better idea? Here, show me the block.'

Malise pointed. Jarvy stared at it a few seconds, then dropped the pictures back on the floor. 'I got it,' he said.

He moved to the back of the truck and pressed a switch that sent the concertina door swinging up on its roller. Jarvy leaped down to the tarmac and turned to her. 'Close the door. The bottom button.' He pointed to the crude metal control box mounted on the wall of the van. 'I'm gonna wait here a while. If you open the door and I'm still here I'll blow your fucking head off.'

'Have a nice day,' Malise muttered and went to the box. Something huge and black steamrollered Jarvy into the road. Hands reached up from under the tailgate of the van and grabbed Malise by the ankles and yanked her to the floor of the van. She heard the engine turn and catch. A shadow engulfed her. She reached for the control box. Fingers clad in black driving gloves pressed the button for her. The door rattled down.

Malise's jaded gaze travelled over the gloved hand, to

the glistening chrome of a Seiko watch, a gold cufflink shaped like a dolphin, a shirt of sugar-pink silk, a green tweed jacket; a thin, lined face obscured behind throat mike and Rayban glasses.

'Hello,' he said. 'I am Detective Inspector Aert Carmiggelt of the Haag Feds.'

Malise flopped back to the floor and closed her eyes. 'And I,' she said, 'am fucked.'

TWO

The Papess
Upright

On her fifteenth birthday Malise came across a gipsy
wagon parked on a disused hill track about four miles
from home. At the bottom of the hill a young woman
washed clothes in a stream. She scrubbed them against a
stone which lay just beneath the surface of the water,
then beat them dry on the pebble shore. When she
arced the clothes over her head, spray rainbowed the
air.

Malise went down to meet the woman. She had dark
skin and hazel eyes with laughter lines around them –
lines Malise hadn't expected, for otherwise the woman
looked quite young – no more than two or three years
older than herself.

They talked a while about nothing then the gipsy
woman led her by the hand up the slope and they sat
together on the steps of her wagon.

Malise saw that beneath the dust, its wood panelling
was painted in strong primary colours. Strange designs
were patterned upon the cracked boards – doves and
mushrooms and flowers.

'Do you like them?' the young woman asked her. 'I painted them myself.'

'They're beautiful,' Malise replied, but she found them strange and frightening.

They drank tea together. The young woman brought out a tin of Gauloises and a small greaseproof envelope and mixed a little grass with the roasted shag from the tin. She pressed it into a clay pipe and lit it with a Zippo.

Malise saw that around her wrist she wore a bracelet of dull metal, like pewter, set with a large red carnelian. She watched for the stone to flash but it did not reflect the sunlight at all.

'You live round here?' the young woman asked.

Malise nodded. The woman offered her the pipe, but she shook her head. Smoking made her cough.

It seemed as if the flesh round the young woman's eyes crumpled a little more as she smoked. It gave her face a worn, bedroomish look. She said, 'I don't know this place. I've never been here before.'

'I like it,' said Malise, because she couldn't think what else to say.

'You see, I don't see most places more than once. I just spend a day or two in a place then I move on.'

'How come?'

She said, 'I'm the last gipsy.'

'What does that mean?' Malise didn't know much about gipsies.

'People have had it in for gipsies for a long time,' the young woman explained. 'Stalin, Hitler, even the Welfare! You should have seen them in the fifteenth century. Life and soul of the good folk of Europe. They brought the Tarot with them.'

For all her reticence, Malise liked this kind of talk – it

put her in mind of her father's library, its strange peoples and perspectives, its wild, melancholy stories. But she was younger than her years and a bit nervous; it took her a while to get up the courage to question the stranger. At last she said, 'Where've you come from?'

The woman shrugged. 'The south. I travel just a few miles each day. I couldn't tell you the name of where I slept yesterday. Do you like the wagon? My uncle makes them. Country crafts, you know. Don't know if they're accurate copies or not. My family was gipsy once, proper Romany blood and everything. My folks made the most of it – going round circuses, putting ads in the astrology papers, you know the kind of thing.' She drew on her pipe. She held her breath then let it go, a ragged sigh. 'My aunt, she has this flat in Naples. Full of the most useless junk you can imagine. It was her told me what gipsies had been – what they were supposed to be, see? A real people, not a side-show. A while after that my folks' business wasn't so good. I guess the fad for this kind of thing was fading. My dad started hitting mum around a lot like it was her fault and mum started beating up on me, so I left. Been gone years. Still see my aunt, sometimes. Didn't pick up this wagon till the spring. Not the kind of thing to take if people are going to be looking for you. Time's gone by now, though. My folks have probably forgotten me – they'll think the wagon's nicked by some drunks who went and wrecked it on some road or other. Or smashed and burnt it so's to keep out of trouble.'

The sun was going down fast. Malise asked her her name.

'Seval,' the young woman replied. 'It's Irani.'

Malise let her head drop to Seval's shoulder. 'Small world.'

Seval did not pull away and after a while she put an arm around Malise's waist. She offered her the pipe again. This time Malise took it. 'Take in plenty of air,' said the gipsy woman. 'No need to choke yourself on it.'

The smoke was fragrant and spiced.

When the pipe went out Malise and Seval walked up the hill. About them, in each isolated and stunted thorn, a night hawk whirred like the clack of a mill. At each brush of their feet in the dust, white miller moths flew into the air; the evening light fluoresced their dusty wings.

When they reached the summit Malise sat on a rock and ground a thyme leaf between her fingers. Evening was well advanced, and the dry slopes of the opposite hill were flushed with amber light; their subtler daytime shades of purple, brown and green were slowly disappearing. Seval sat on the rock next to her and pressed up close.

Malise shivered.

'Cold?'

Malise shook her head. She felt irritated all of a sudden; ill at ease. Seval's voice seemed permanently overlaid with a kind of mild but penetrating irony. Her simplest question set Malise's mind racing to hidden meanings, subtle, sarcastic reproofs.

Malise stood up. 'I'd better go home,' she said. 'Dad will be expecting me.'

Seval looked around her, apparently unconcerned. 'Have you noticed how the ground seems to drown itself in the light of evening?'

It was a strange, rather stilted thing to say. It sounded like a quotation, but if it was, then Seval's delivery of it was oddly unforced. It was as if she had spoken, for one

startling second, with a diction now outmoded and forgotten.

Malise followed Seval's gaze. The slope opposite had
lost all gradation: it was now an even, flat plane of amber
light, broken only by little heaps of quartz where a rabbit
had made its burrow, or where the white flints of a
footpath ran across its surface like a wave. 'I've seen it
often,' Malise said, and turned away. She was afraid, and
she didn't know why.

'I'll be here tomorrow,' Seval said. It was, Malise
supposed, a kind of invitation. 'After that, I can't say.'

'Goodbye, then,' said Malise, setting off down the hill.
She did not turn round.

Malise saw Seval the next day, and the next, and the next.
They took long walks together, or rode about in Seval's
wagon. They didn't talk much. They didn't seem to have
anything in common. Malise told herself it was good
having someone around who was free of the shackles of
school and family: it gave her a sense of the big world
outside the villa, the school, the deserted fields and
unkempt olive groves. But at other times Seval seemed
really *old*, not really her contemporary at all (though
there couldn't have been more than a few years between
them), so that meeting her, Malise felt a little awed, and
she wondered what the world must be like that had
spawned this strange woman with her stranger life, her
odd, intent ways of speaking and moving. Seval stayed the
rest of the summer within walking distance of Malise's
home. Malise wondered why she didn't move on, like she
usually did. It never occurred to her that she herself
might be a part of the reason.

Their journeys together grew more ambitious. One Friday in late summer, Malise and Seval caught a bus to Bologna, meaning to stay the weekend.

They took a double room in a cheap hotel on the other side of the rail tracks to the old city. It took a while to walk into town, but that night they were glad to have picked what was possibly the only islet of calm in a city gone mad. Bologna's team had reached Series A.

'Football,' Seval said. They stood on the street corner and watched a fleet of Piaggio cycles tear down the street. 'You don't follow the tables?'

Malise shook her head.

They went into a small dusty store crammed with books and candles.

Seval asked for a Bolognese Tarot, but the fat and faintly moustachioed woman behind the counter did not understand what she meant.

'No,' Seval explained. 'Not a regular Tarot *printed* in Bologna, a *Bolognese Tarot*. It's only got sixty-two cards, you see, and some of the designs are different.'

The old woman smiled vacantly.

'Okay, thanks,' Seval sighed, and led Malise out the shop. 'You know,' she said, 'I've never seen that pack. I don't know which cards are missing or why. No matter. Come on, let's get a drink.'

The night sky was a skin of black oil: hot, potent and threatening. They sipped Amaretto – too sweet for Malise, but heady and new. A car pulled up outside the bar and two women in skin-tight black dresses stepped out.

'Contact,' Seval whispered.

Malise didn't understand. The women sat down at

the table next to theirs and Seval conversed with the taller one in a low voice.

Something changed hands – Malise didn't see what. 'What have you done?' she asked, when the women had gone inside to replenish their drinks.

Seval squeezed the top of Malise's thigh. 'I bought us some stuff.'

Malise shrugged.

'Hey,' Seval punched her shoulder. 'You happy?'

'Yeah.' Malise looked down at her drink. 'Sure.'

'Here.' Seval pushed a plastic wallet of tobacco into Malise's lap. 'Roll us a joint.'

Afterwards they went walking. It was all they ever seemed to do. Malise wanted to do something different, talk about something new, but Seval didn't seem to think there was anything wrong. It was as though she was waiting for something, waiting with infinite patience for some sign before she became the friend Malise wanted her to be – only Malise could not even begin to guess what it was. Sometimes she looked at Malise and Malise felt as if she were pierced by a gaze more suited to the perusal of infinities.

They reached the city's central square. The noise was deafening. Skirting the Piazza Maggiore they watched half-naked boys run about the flagstoned space, cheering, drinking, trailing bright paper streamers from their hands and hair, dodging out the way of scooters and bikes. Dominating the scene, the Basilica loomed like a giant barn in the diffuse and uncertain light of a thousand bike lamps. The air quivered with airhorns and rattles and bike engines. Malise leaned up against a wall, her hands to her ears. Seval took her hands away. 'Problem?'

Malise shook her head. 'I made the smoke too strong,'

she said. Seval took her by the arm down via Indipendenza, past software stores and couturiers to a stand-up pizza joint. She got them some slices of pizza funghi and cans of Peroni. They walked back towards the railway station. Everyone was moving in the opposite direction, towards the Piazza. Malise rested her back against a colonnade and watched as a party of bikers shot past, late arrivals for the impromptu party, their machines decked with bunting, scarves and flags. She bit into her second slice of pizza. The base was crisp and oily. She slugged at the can. Seval put an arm round her. 'Feeling better?'

'Yeah,' Malise sighed and felt something thump inside her, as though the food had landed in the pit of her stomach. It made her giggle. She didn't stop giggling till they got to the student quarter, its melancholy, restful streets rich with the smell of cannabis and cooking. The colonnades were cool and mysterious.

A black man sat cross-legged against a pillar selling hash. Seval bought some, and they made their way back to the hotel. The lights from the railway were cold and blue against the night.

Seval rolled them a joint. They settled on one of the single beds, talked for a while and fell asleep not long after.

The next day Seval took Malise sightseeing.

They went to the Medieval Museum. Upstairs there was a room of statuary – work by Giambologna and Algardi. In one corner, mounted on a plinth, there was the severed head of John the Baptist. It lay on its side. The marble was translucent and cream-grey like bone. The finish was perfect; smooth and delicate. It was as if the head was just now opening its eyes. Malise watched the thing, watched the mouth for a sign of breath, then let last night's smoke into her head and saw the slightly parted lips curl into a smile, saw the eyes weep.

'I don't know why it makes me feel so . . . so weird,' she said; she sensed the inadequacy of the words even as she spoke them. There must be better languages, she thought. Perhaps they have yet to be invented. Seval looked at the piece for a second. 'It's obvious,' she said. 'It looks like he's having an orgasm.'

The remark was stupid and perspicacious all at once, and Malise hated her for it.

Near the hotel there was a cheap restaurant. In the evening they ate gnocchi in a sweet sauce – a strange, bland flavour – then a meat dish steeped in wine. They drank far too much raw Sangiovese and got thrown out the restaurant for swapping dirty jokes in loud voices. They staggered home; Malise felt dirty and ashamed. She wished she could just get on a bus now and go home. She was tired; she'd had enough of Bologna, and maybe she'd had enough of Seval.

They entered the hotel room together and Seval took Malise's face in her palms and kissed her full on the lips. Malise opened her mouth. So *that's* it, she thought. It happened so fast she didn't think to pull away, or move forward, or anything. All she could think about was the taste of Seval's tongue. It was pleasantly sour.

They undressed each other. Malise kept stopping to taste Seval's mouth again. Seval had to keep pushing her away. When they were naked Seval wrapped her legs round Malise's shoulders and went down on her; Malise kept giggling because all she could think about was food. Seval's taste made her stomach rumble with hunger.

Every now and then Seval let out a yell because Malise bit her too hard; Malise tried to say sorry but she couldn't because she was laughing too much. When Seval bit her breasts and her stomach Malise felt as if she were being swallowed, slowly and lasciviously chewed up and swallowed down.

When Malise woke up it was morning; Seval was leaning out the window. She slipped out of bed and came and stood beside her. She didn't know what to say or do. What she wanted was to yell 'breakfast!' and push Seval back onto the bed and bite her and make her laugh and kiss her on the mouth, force her tongue into her mouth and press her head into the bed.

And she wanted to cover herself, dress herself in everything she had brought, leave Bologna and never see Seval again.

The view from the window was a crazy patchwork of roof-tile and white-washed wall. Malise's perceptions were twisted by the dope the night before: when she looked out of the bedroom window to the courtyards beneath, they were like Escher prints. They danced before her eyes, their surfaces shuffling and recombining.

The old geometries are crumbling, she thought. The world is unfolding. The paper ball arcs through the air, lands softly in the magician's upturned palm and uncrumples itself.

The view, for all this, lacked the grandeur of the old city. She remembered how impressive, how grand the palaces of the old city were. Then it came to her that even there a former age had extended a pitiful, human hand through the rich fabric. It was telling her how old it was, how old they all were: all cities, all peoples.

She took Seval's hips in her hands and moved against her and Seval turned her head and they kissed, awkwardly. Malise stroked her. Seval came with a kind of sob and for that Malise was sorry, until she realized she was crying, too – because the city had spoken to them both.

That morning they walked up to the Santa Maria Basilica. The climb was long but not strenuous. A portico ran all the way up the hill, and birds nested in the eaves of its arched and fluted roofs.

Once, families had paid for its upkeep and fashioned each section as a memorial to their dead. Now their devotional paintings had faded and the walls themselves were slipping into dilapidation.

Halfway up the hill Seval handed Malise a tab of acid. She swallowed it and looked at the nearest painting. A Madonna and infant Christ were peeling off the wall. There was a carmine ground beneath the paint: it was as if the baby had been spattered with blood.

It rained in the afternoon so they went back to bed. By evening Malise was so sore and cramped she could hardly move. Her breasts felt burned, they were so tender. Her neck was stiff, the skin a mass of bruises. When they kissed her mouth hurt because Seval had bitten it so much, had thrust her hips so hard against it. Her back was all scratched and bloody.

Seval staggered from the bathroom.

'I'm sorry about your face,' Malise said. They had just passed through one of those baffling moments when sex, for no reason at all, suddenly turns into unarmed combat.

Seval winced and nodded and dabbed at her puffy eye with a flannel. She sat slumped on the edge of the bed, holding the cloth to her face. 'You're brilliant,' she said, without enthusiasm, because there wasn't any need for any. 'I love you too,' Malise muttered, without thinking – because she didn't have to.

One day Seval came to the house and she, Malise and her father spent the day spreading the latest EC additive on the pale soil. Late in the afternoon he noticed Seval's bracelet with its dull red stone. 'It's beautiful,' he said.

'Yeah.' Seval twisted it round her wrist. 'I found it. Never been able to take it off since.'

It was a good day. Seval liked Malise's father; he was very funny and open and not at all pushy, the way he could be.

Indeed, he made a point of not interfering; in his new-found seriousness, he respected his daughter's privacy. When Malise came home after a night away he asked if she'd had a good time, and if Seval was all right – trivial questions that did not require an intimate answer.

If he knew what Malise and Seval did together, and if he was distressed by it, he didn't show it.

At the foot of the hill, by the stream at Seval's washing place, Malise read aloud from one of her father's books about the Tarot.

'The second arcanum,' Malise read. 'The Papess; Beth.'

'Who?'

'It's Hebrew,' Malise chided.

'I know, I know.' Seval beat a wet towel against a nearby rock.

'"What is below is similar to what is above, and what is above is similar to what is below in order to ensure the perpetuation of the Unique Thing."' She glanced down the page. '"Woman is a symbol of passiveness, especially a seated woman."'

Seval jumped up.

'Don't be silly,' Malise chided.

Seval sat down again.

'"The hieroglyph for this arcanum – a human throat – represents something where one can hide oneself . . ."'

'I'm not sure I like the sound of this.'

'" . . . a shelter like a temple."'

'Good grief.' Seval stood up and stretched.

'"Let us imagine that a man has an evil desire, but makes no attempt to realize it. He thus creates a kind of 'entity'. This artificial 'being' does not possess a physical body, but it is a kind of spirit."' Malise coughed. 'Sorry. Frog in my temple. Where were we?' She found the place.

She coughed again.

'Malise?'

''s nothing.'

She had remembered what her father had told her about his war work.

A plane flew overhead: very small, very heavy.

'Oh God.'

'Malise. That's enough,' said Seval.

Eventually Malise's coughing subsided.

Seval leaned forward and took the book from Malise and laid it in the grass beside them. 'Let me tell you the truth.'

And she told Malise about gipsies and of how, millennia ago, they carried the Tarot from the land of Egypt to guide them in their exile. In those days it was called *Ta-rosh*, the Royal Way, the game of Thoth, God of Magic.

Magic again, Malise thought, as the light failed and the evening cacophony of cicadas began. All paths led to this same place. History, love, language, laughter – they all met here. Magic was everywhere – in the gestures of a magician, the stones of Bologna, the books in her father's library, Seval's soft mouth as she spoke.

Seval told her about the second trump, the Papess, which she called 'the Priestess of the Silver Star'; Hathor, Egyptian goddess of the moon, whose temple at Denderah contains an altar to Sirius, the dog that guides the dead.

She peered at Malise's neck. 'Hey,' she said, 'did I scratch you?'

'It's that bracelet,' Malise said. 'It gets in the way.'

Seval shrugged. 'Sorry. Comes with territory.'

''S okay.' Malise filled the pipe.

'The Papess inspires dreams and visions,' Seval said.

Seval led Malise into her caravan and lit a candle. She stared into it for a long time. She looked as though she was going to cry.

Malise reached out to touch her but Seval pulled away and said, 'Let's see what the cards say about you, yes?' She was trying to sound relaxed, but there was a tension in her voice Malise couldn't fathom. Malise shrugged. 'Sure.'

Seval pulled open a drawer and scrabbled about for her pack.

'Hey,' Malise teased her, 'I thought you were supposed to wrap it in silk.'

'Tourist stuff. Here.' She chucked Malise the cards.

Malise fingered them gingerly. 'Sure you don't mind?'

Seval shook her head, irritably. 'They're pieces of cardboard. They don't bite people.'

Malise shook her head, puzzled, and opened the pack. 'You shuffle.'

'You don't want me to sit facing north or anything?'

'You *are* facing north, dippy,' Seval replied, laughing. 'Just shuffle.'

Malise shuffled, turning some of the cards round so that there was an even mixture of reversed and upright cards. She handed Seval the pack and Seval dealt the nine card spread.

Seval pointed to the fourth card: 'This is beneath you; upon this you are founded. Oh *dear* –' It was the Papess reversed. 'Lust. Enslavement. Belligerence. We can't have that.'

She turned the card round.

'Hey!' Malise yelled, scandalized. 'You can't do that!'

Seval looked into her eyes. Her whole face seemed old. Not decrepit – *old*. Ancient, adamantine. 'You wanna bet?'

'But,' Malise blustered, 'it's not a story – you can't just change it at will.' She looked up at Seval and suddenly she was terrified. Seval was – not Seval any more.

The gipsy woman leaned towards her and her eyes were like the eyes of dogs – sharp and savage and calculating. She laid a hand on Malise's trembling cheek; her touch was as cold and as certain as stone. She smiled – an ancient, cruel smile with no humour in it at all. 'They're my cards,' she said. 'Remember that.'

The
Ace of Cups
Reversed

Malise was very much in love with Seval, and they spent a lot of time together. It was very exciting, being with Seval, making love to her, taking acid with her.

One night they took two tabs each and Malise sailed to the moon on her own tongue. She watched the Earth recede and it was pink, purple and yellow. Africa sparkled. It was covered in jewels.

She found the moon was grey because mushrooms grew there, and angels lived inside the cusps. The mushrooms were poisonous. This was a protection for the angels because if they left their poisonous shells they might get eaten by the moon wolf. It used to be a better place before the moon wolf was around. They showed Malise what it used to be like. It was nice. Laid back. *Gezillig*. Not like now. Malise agreed to kill the moon wolf.

So she waited at the top of a hill and waited for the wolf to come, but what she hadn't reckoned on were the angels he'd eaten. They'd grown strong and twisted in his belly.

He shat them out as he went and they pierced Malise with spears of coloured light. The wolf got close and Malise dropped her knife because she was coming apart with all the negative energy the bolts of light had shot through her. The wolf smiled. We call it 'sap', he said, but in this dream she didn't see the funny side because in this dream her English, see, not so good, yes? And he say, we come for you. We sap you. Zap zap. Funny, oh, come on, *Achtung*! Joke! Kick arse, pug-face, giggle some for Daddy. So she giggled him some and he took it and ate it and said, that was your soul, and she thought, jokes, huh? Here, give me that pen, and she said, trying not to smile and give the game away, no, Daddy, no Daddy you're wrong, that's not my soul, I was breaking it in for a fried, a fried what, he said, and she said, it's not my fault the N-key sticks, and then she realized he had tricked her into giving him her friend's soul, it was all true, it was what he wanted, it was what he enjoyed, in spite of himself, which was why he was frightened, why she should be frightened, and she woke up, choking, and sure enough, Seval was dead.

She was cold. Her eyes were open.

Her face was a mask of agony.

Malise stumbled out of the wagon and looked around her. It was pitch black.

She looked up at the sky. The moon was there – a bony, furrowed crescent. It sparkled. Then, in the sky, a little way from where the moon was, shooting stars appeared, or what looked like shooting stars, but she realized after a few moments that they couldn't be, because shooting stars vanish in an eye-blink, but these just kept on shining. They flew across the sky, blinding her, getting nearer. The moon was flinging bolts of light at the earth. A few minutes later she heard the first concussions.

She knew what was happening.

She'd seen this before.

Her father was smashing her toys again.

She put her hands to her head and started screaming STOP MAKE IT STOP I DIDN'T MEAN IT MAKE IT STOP

It did not stop. The moon kept glistening, the stars kept falling, the hammer kept falling, her father's forehead kept glistening, there was a sound of aeroplanes, and she wasn't afraid enough, she could never be afraid enough. The concussions grew louder. The sky to the east grew cloudy and purple.

The concussions were deafening. It was the sound of toys breaking, gunfire, Daddy's bombs, bodies bursting; it was the sound of falling, five feet, onto a concrete pavement.

She couldn't make it stop. She'd unleashed it, and that was that.

She'd let her father's madness out; soon it must cover her in blood.

The night Seval overdosed to death, HOTOL's lunar Von Neumanns went rogue, and attacked Home: this is what Malise had witnessed when she stumbled out of the wagon. Malise's father saw the first strikes, too; they illumined his way across the trembling hillsides as he searched for his daughter and her friend; he feared for them, was frightened himself – it felt, after all, like the end of the world – and he was as much in need of company as he was willing to give it.

He thought perhaps he would find Malise and Seval huddled up in a corner of that wagon Malise had told him about. Instead, he found his daughter quite by chance; she was naked, squatting on a bare and rocky hillside, howling at the moon. She was shouting something over and over at it; she must have been shouting it for a long time because it had lost all sense – it was now no more than a formless, terrible screech.

He never found out what it was she was shouting. Had he known it was 'Daddy', over and over, he still would not have understood.

He took her home, wrapped her in blankets, and sat her by the fire.

The concussions ceased. Outside, the sky was red with dawn, and flame, and dust.

Malise stared blank-eyed into the carpet.

'What happened?' he said.

She did not reply, but her gaze began to wander.

He left her a moment and fetched the radio from the kitchen. When he came back he found Malise staring at a page of the book he'd been rereading. It was the one about the Tarot.

He plugged in the radio and turned it on. All the channels were blank. Thick bands of silence, and sometimes not even that. Just white noise.

'Malise, what did you see?' he said.

Malise just stared at the book she was holding. It was as if she was looking for something.

'Malise?'

Nothing.

He came over and, very gently, he took the book from her unresisting fingers. She stared into space as if the book were still there before her. Her hands did not move.

He glanced at the book.

It was turned to the Papess; the second arcanum.

It explained everything: it meant nothing to him.

Malise stared at the walls of her room as if they were horizons of an unfamiliar landscape. She was utterly silent. Her father talked to her, and played music to her, and watched her, and watched her, and watched her. Finally, one night, desperate, isolated, and overcome with something too slow and huge to be terror and too painful and debilitating to be anything else, he took her to his bed.

He did it thinking he could stroke confidences from her and help her in some way. All he did was hold her. While she was throttling him, he thought – but I haven't done anything. I haven't done anything wrong.

He had woken up to find her killing him, and he stroked her while she did it. His hands had escaped the sheets too late; he was too weak now to push her from him, too weak to pull her fingers from his throat. His fingers were black and slender in the dark of the bedroom. They weaved the air, articulating like the legs of stranded beetles.

The fingers curled, the wrists dipped, and the hands, like soft castles in a gale, span slow spirals in the air.

She woke up and saw her father sitting beside her. His neck was all bruised and scratched.

His brow was bony and furrowed, like a crescent moon. He was crying. Tears sparked like steel and crashed upon the bed.

She closed her eyes, blotting him out, thought of falling stars and hammers.

'Malise,' he said, hoping there was a little part of her open to him, some place the words reached that could make sense of what he said, 'Malise, it's all right. Things are getting back to normal. There was an attack. No-one launched it. It was a mistake. A lot of people have died, everywhere, a lot of cities have been damaged – very badly damaged. But it wasn't meant that way. It was just an accident. Things are getting back to normal. There'll be school soon. You'll like that, yes? Art classes. Maths. Yes? Do you want to look at some pictures?'

He showed her some pictures – beautiful colour plates of Islamic tapestry and architecture, with bright colours and strong lines.

She didn't even focus on them.

She stayed in bed. She pissed into the sheets. When her father was out of the room she shat in the hand-basin. Once he caught her and they struggled, but he hadn't the heart to fight her and she got back into bed.

She stopped eating.

There was a second accident.

A third.

A fourth.

She didn't seem to notice.

Her father took care of her. He wore a jumper to cover the bruises round his neck. He found Seval. He called the authorities and told them some lies to protect Malise. He brought his stereo into Malise's room and played her music. He made her food so it was there for her. He laced her drinks with glucose. He talked to her. He took an overdose of sleeping pills and vomited them up.

He blamed himself.

He told the authorities what he thought was the truth, and they sent him to prison for it.

The Moon Upright

They took Malise away to a pretty country house with lovely gardens and high fences. They gave her toys to play with. She wasn't interested in the coloured shapes, or the building blocks, or the buttons that sang tunes, and if they gave her crayons she threw them at the wall. Then a sales rep from Poulenc CyberPARC paid a visit and showed them pictures of a special computer terminal. It's very rugged, he said, very hard-wearing. It's got a soft screen and soft buttons and there are no holes to poke things through. It's ventilated through this pipe, here, which you put through the bottom of this special desk so that no-one tries to pull it out. All the wiring goes through this hole and out the back. This is the vent hose, this is the mains lead, and this is the IBCN lead.

The terminal is wired to dumbheads at our central laboratory park in Cologne. Our dumbheads will watch what your patients do. They have forty years' experience in ergonomic diagnosis. They have special feedback programmes to improve your patients' co-ordination and confidence while they play games on this machine.

We're talking twenty-four-hour supervision and therapy here. Patient to Poulenc's dumbheads. Direct. Now, this is our trial offer . . .

They showed the terminal to Malise. Malise stared at it. It was the first object she'd focused on in a very long time. She shuffled forward.

Dr Garcia helped her into the cradle that was bolted to the special desk and said, 'Put – Malise, put your hands – come on. Come on, Malise. No it doesn't hurt – just sit still.

'Right. Put your hands on the bars. That's it. Now look ahead. Malise, look straight – *there*. Okay. See the screen, the cross-wires? Right, this is a game. No, Malise, don't close . . .

'Malise, if you shake the controls about like that they'll break. *Malise!*

'Thank you. Right. You're holding driving bars. Know what they are? Helicopter pilots use them. You're going flying. You want that? You want to fly? Right. Now, see the blue grid beyond the cross-wires? If you press the bar you can fly through it, like – like *that*, that's great! Okay!

'That's great. All right, you want some obstacles to fly round? God, you're pretty when you snarl. Okay, see how you manage this. Mind, you mustn't crash. Good. Very good. *Very* good. More?

'Okay. Good. More? Good! More?

'. . . more?

'. . . more?'

Moon.

'Malise?'

'*Moon.*'

'Malise – what about the moon? What is it about the

moon? Oh come on, talk to me. Tell me about it. Is it a secret? I can keep secrets. Really, I can.

'All right, sit round. Let go of the driving bars, let's talk. Malise, let – okay, okay, stay there if you have to. Anyway, what are you doing? If you let yourself spin round like that you'll crash. Malise, what are you–'

Moon.

'Malise, I . . . look, the moon isn't part of the simulation. You won't find it there. There is no moon there.'

Malise turned to him, took hold of his lapels and pulled him forward so their noses touched and Dr Garcia's glasses flew off. 'Then *get* it,' she snarled.

For many weeks Malise played the terminal. She was very good at it, and the dumbheads in Cologne got very excited. They taught her how to move, how to dodge, how to think. They wove a new reality in Malise's head. When they were done they did something very special, something not even their designers knew about.

They phoned a man in Bonn, who phoned a man in Berlin, who plugged in his portable and typed two words and sent them to an IBCN number in Lombardy.

All of a sudden, with no warning at all, Malise's terminal went dead, then a message appeared.

Two red words, centre screen: PRESS ENTER

Malise pressed the enter key. Her screen filled with angry red words.

The words blinked out, and a new kind of game filled the screen. Malise snarled and cackled. It was *exactly* what she wanted.

Malise woke up. Carmiggelt was sitting by her bed. He poured coffee from a cafetière into a plastic cup and handed it to her. 'Feeling better?'

They left the police station.

'Where we going?'

'City of London Airport,' Carmiggelt replied, 'via your flat. You'd better pack a bag.'

'Don't you ever take that gear off?' said Malise, meaning the microphone.

'Not when I'm with you,' he replied, and he swung the car onto the road that led to the Docklands Pontoon.

The car was a Volvo, a recent model, the best current alcohol-burner. The windows were toughened and tinted, and gave the world a subtly unreal atmosphere: an Indian-summer shimmer. The shattered city, the tortured skeletons of stressed steel and the rivers of sharded glass, seemed no longer the relics of violence – the light changed them to strange and beautiful forms. She sensed with surprise that she was smiling.

'You still haven't told me where we're going,' she said.

Carmiggelt laughed easily. Just two driving companions, getting to know each other. 'Sorry,' he said. 'Preoccupied with the route. *Den Haag*. We're going to The Hague. Federal Court of Human Rights.'

'Are you going to lock me up?'

'What do you think?'

Malise let her head bump up against the window of the car. Carmiggelt glanced at her and smiled. It was a confident smile – a secure smile. He hadn't restrained her, or threatened her, and he had not needed to. He didn't know her, didn't know what she was, but he knew that *she* knew that if she pulled anything, he would have a reply to it. Maybe not reflexes. Maybe not strength. Something hi-tech and lethal. Or maybe, she speculated – because her datafat couldn't find anything hi-tech on him – maybe all he had was this mask of quiet confidence: a clever but fragile protection.

'Relax,' he said. 'You're no terrorist, any more than Snow is.'

'You know Snow?'

'We know her.'

Malise took a deep breath and let it out slowly. 'Did she get to the States?'

Carmiggelt nodded.

'What will happen to her?'

'I guess she'll get what she wants.'

'I hope so.'

Carmiggelt understood. 'Wouldn't wish otherwise for anyone. But it's not ever that simple. In Haag, for instance, you'll be meeting someone called Judith Foley. Do you know her?'

Malise shook her head.

'She's from C-Ledge. A hot-head. She down-welled to persuade Snow not to develop her new datafat here.'

'Sending a letter would have been cheaper.'

'Not so persuasive. She and Snow were lovers.'

'HOTOL playing bedroom politics between planets, now? Sophisticated.'

'No. It was a personal decision. She only came to us when she realized Snow was already involved in a terrorist action.'

'How'd she find that out?'

'Rea's team warned her off.'

'Oh?'

'They kneecapped her. She called us from the hospital.'

'Jesus.' Malise shuddered. Then: 'Have you told C-Ledge about the Docklands site?'

Carmiggelt was too busy with the car to reply straight away. They rattled down the ramp onto the pontoon. The tide was low. For the first few yards the metal grille on which they drove crunched pebbles; beached flotation bags lay like strange, bloated cilia either side of the metal track. Then the rumble beneath the car became deep and resonant – they were on the river.

'Snow didn't tell you about C-Ledge?'

Malise shook her head.

'C-Ledge is dead.'

He nursed the car up the north bank. Beggars rapped on the windows and stood out in front of the car waving beads and watches and pocket organizers. They were dressed in bright rags – imports of cheap mass-production batik from Bali turned ragged and bleached by a life on the crumbled streets. Malise couldn't meet their eyes.

'When did this happen?' she said.

'Three weeks ago,' he replied. 'It's potentially the biggest crisis we've ever handled. The largest off-world human colony, running the most prestigious research facility in the system, housing ten trillion ECU's worth of plant and equipment: struck dumb. Just keeping the wraps on this is jeopardizing our other activities. We haven't enough personnel. Snow got through our net, and that was a big blunder. But something like it was bound to happen eventually.'

Why, Malise wondered, is he telling me all this? Then it struck her – he wouldn't tell me all this if I didn't need to know it. He *needs* me. Haag needs me. The thought exhilarated and frightened her at once. Whatever they wanted from her, it had already entailed a substantial breach of security. C-Ledge –

Malise stifled a gasp.

'What is it?' Carmiggelt asked.

Malise swallowed. 'Sorry. My old teacher. Dr Nouronihar. He transferred to C-Ledge after the Moonwolf war.'

'Ah.'

'Are they – are they *dead*?' The enormity of the Haag agent's news was slowly sinking in.

'We don't know – yet. But assuming the world isn't littered with wetware designers called Nouronihar, then your friend is safe.'

'Where is he?'

'Up-well – part of a team scheduled to investigate C-Ledge's silence.'

Malise sighed with relief. She thought back over their conversation. 'What does Foley say about C-Ledge?'

'You'd better ask her. I haven't been cleared to hear it

all yet. But, there's one thing. A gut reaction only.' He stalled.

'What?'

Carmiggelt pursed his lips, searching for the right words. 'I think there's more to her coming here than keeping her bedmate out of trouble.'

'Which is?'

'I think she's running away.'

'From C-Ledge?'

'From the thing that silenced it.'

'What's that?'

Carmiggelt sounded the horn. 'Whatever you found in that rock,' he replied.

While Carmiggelt fretted over the unfamiliar controls of her espresso machine, Malise sat by the window reading a paper.

Haag had moved fast. Already the reasons behind the murder of Joachim Kennedy had reached the public domain. Dreyfuss hadn't stopped at the Haag-condoned webbed dogs project. Anticipating a relaxation of licensing laws, they had aimed to steal a march on their rivals by researching other datafat applications too. Illegal ones, like p-casts.

What was it Cowley had said? Demand is always satisfied once it reaches a certain pitch? Well, Dreyfuss had learned that one. More than learned. They were being strung up by it.

Malise put the paper down and reviewed her answer-phone. The first face on the window was Dempsey's.

'Major Arnim. I need to see you. Can you bring a

disc with *both* your sculptures along to the Maudsley Hospital in Camberwell as soon as you can?'

The next call – Dempsey.

The tape was full of her in increasing states of agitation. Malise went to the kitchen. 'Can you drive me to Camberwell?'

In the car Malise finished the paper.

'Carmiggelt, why did Dreyfuss get involved with a shit like Cowley?'

'Market research?'

'Funny.'

'I'm not being funny.' He swung the car into the Maudsley car-park. 'What better way to test a system than put it on the street for a while? Get some market figures and an underground demand for your product at the same time?' He gazed round for a place to park. 'I doubt snuff was part of the deal Asiyani offered Cowley, but someone must have decided there was a high sales potential in vicarious violence.'

'I don't get it.'

'Think of all those taboos being broken, endorphins pumping and the rest of it.'

Malise shrugged. 'I don't know what you mean.'

Carmiggelt positioned the car and eased forward into the free space. 'No,' he said, glancing at the side of her head where her datafat port was, 'I guess you don't.'

'Hey, Carmiggelt,' Malise said, as he turned off the engine. 'When we get to Haag – am I gonna be blinded again?'

Carmiggelt shrugged. 'I don't know.'

'Please –'

'It's not my department.' He got out of the car.

Dempsey was at the front desk to greet Malise. She led her to a room off a private ward. Before she opened the door she said, 'This might disturb you.'

Malise stepped into the room.

Garry was sitting in an orthopaedic bed. There were leather straps across his waist and legs and one arm. His shaved, electrode-encrusted head was tilted back; the port in his head was open and a coaxial was buried in his skull. His tongue lolled out of his drooling mouth. A spittle soaked bib was fastened round his neck. His cheeks and forehead were suffused with sweat. His bed jacket was open, and his frail, skeletal ribs were clearly visible beneath trailing wires and blue plastic sensors stuck down with micropore. His flesh was creamy and cracked like the skin in a pot of emulsion.

The fingers of his right hand, the wrist and the arm itself were swollen and red. They were shuddering. A trolley table had been positioned over Garry's lap and a pad of paper lay on it. The shuddering hand held a black ceramic-tip at ninety degrees to the pad and scrabbled over it with unreal speed. Loose paper was scattered over the bed and floor. Malise picked up a page. Upon it Garry had composed an inhumanly complicated technical drawing.

'Malise?' Dempsey beckoned her out the room. 'I've something to show you in the office. Tell me, do you know him?'

'I believe we've met.'

'Did you show him your sculptures?'

'It was a brief acquaintance.'

'He came in yesterday, referred from King's Casualty across the road. He's been sexually mutilated.'

There was a stack of drawings on Dempsey's desk. She went over and riffled through it. 'Here,' she said, and handed one to Malise. 'Every drawing he's making is a detail of this figure. He's producing them to scale.'

Malise gazed dumbfounded at the drawing: a nest of insect limbs around a large cracked ovoid. She shook her head. 'I drew it without thinking. I was tired, just messing around.'

'I ran Garry's 'fat through an archive engine. I believe there may be a virus in Garry's fat. If so, then there may have been one in your own. You may have infected him,' Dempsey said.

Malise thought back to the p-casting studio, the attempt on her life, the virus she'd made and the way it had changed before her virtual eyes.

'Can I see your sculpture?' Dempsey asked her. 'Do you have your disc with you?'

Malise nodded, then caught herself. 'Sculpture.'

Dempsey sighed. 'I don't pretend to understand any of this,' she admitted. 'That's why I want you here for observation.'

Malise shook her head. She knew now what her sculpture disc contained.

'I'm sorry, Doctor.' She got up from her chair. 'But I have a prior appointment.'

The visit to the hospital made it too late for them to fly that day. While Carmiggelt used her phone to make new arrangements, Malise tried to get some sleep.

She lay between the sheets in her bedroom. The

drapes were open and the room was starlit with a view of shattered towers.

She looked at her watch. 4 A.M. Three hours to dawn. She clambered out of the bed and went into the living room. Carmiggelt was still on the phone. The thick carpet prickled her feet as she crossed to the FizzyArt machine.

She loaded the ovoid-and-legs sculpture.

She looked at it a long time, then she did something she couldn't remember ever doing before. She pressed two keys, so that an expanded element of the model swam into view.

It too was complex and detailed. She expanded part of that segment.

The shape that filled the screen was equally complex.

She expanded it again. And again.

And again.

She had made up more than a sculpture that night. She'd made a machine.

Her blood froze.

She activated her 'fat and began running through her systems directory. It might take her hours to find it, but she knew it was there somewhere, the thing that had terrified her, had driven her so close to madness.

In the end the search took about fifty minutes.

It was a map, a three-dimensional map of the figure she and Garry had drawn. Its interior was immense. Its complexity was frightening.

The thing in the eggshell had seeded her brain with something more than a sculpture; it had drawn a blueprint in her head.

*   *   *

Malise and her arresting officer arrived in Den Haag the following afternoon. The Haag people introduced themselves, questioned her and gave her enough florins to keep her a week. She couldn't leave the Netherlands, but she was free to move within the country as she pleased. Two men with bleached hair and Rayban glasses sat behind her on the train to Rotterdam. When she walked out the station they followed her. She stopped and turned to look at them. Summer light reflected off their shades. Unsmiling, grey-eyed, like automata, they stopped six yards away. While one watched her, the other scanned the street.

Malise tried losing them in the seemingly endless Lijnenaan Precinct. She failed. They were good.

She stopped at the Sleep-In on Mauritsweg.

Outside her room one of the men approached her and handed her an inch-wide, three inch long tube with a glass bubble at one end. 'Fix it on your window-sill,' he said. 'It's a fisheye camera. We won't watch you but we want to watch the window.'

She closed the door on the Haag agents, planted the fisheye and inspected the room.

She took off her cage and lay on the bed. She let the sound of traffic and music and people fill her head.

The phone rang. She pressed the receive button.

It was Carmiggelt; he'd been questioning her most of the afternoon. 'I want to talk.'

'Then talk.'

'It's Judith Foley. She wants to meet you. She's very insistent.'

There was a long silence.

'Arnim? Malise?'

Malise cleared her throat. 'Give me time to buy a coffee.'

*　*　*

Judith Foley drove her wheelchair across the foyer of the Sleep-In. She was older than Malise had expected. Her hair was going grey and there were lines round her eyes. Her skin was very dark and lined like fine leather. Beneath the skin Malise could see the curves of her skull, the line where her datafat port was. Her top lip was naturally too short, and her teeth were very white. It gave her whole mouth a rictal cast. In better circumstances, she would be very beautiful, Malise thought, but here, under the unrelenting fluorescent glare, late at night, tired and in pain, you could see her skull too clearly beneath her skin. She held her hand out to Malise. Malise took it, and knelt down shakily – her skeleton batteries were running down. They kissed on the cheek.

Foley's eyes crinkled when she smiled. 'Fancy a boat ride?'

They arrived at Willemsplein around five, in pitch-darkness. Foley wore a thick woollen coat, and a travelling rug over her smashed legs. Dwarfed by the coverings, she looked like a very tired, wise-faced child. With a rush of churned water, the Spido pulled away from the quay. There were few people on this, the first of the morning cruises. Couples stood against the ship's railings embracing against the chill of the night. Others stood alone, silhouetted pockets of loneliness framed in the lights of this, the world's largest port. Malise followed Foley to the prow of the ship. Foley's face was ashen in the weak electric light of the ship. 'I know very little about you, Malise. You were a drones controller, yes?'

Malise nodded, then realized Foley had closed her eyes and had not seen the gesture. 'Yes,' she said. 'Thirteen sorties.'

'A veteran.'

'I was good.'

'Until?' Foley turned her head a little for the answer, but she kept her eyes closed.

Malise took a deep breath. 'Until I went up against the Massive,' she said. 'I think the Massive put something in my head, a map of some kind but of what – I don't know.'

Judith Foley opened her eyes.

Ahead of them, lights from ships, gantries and refineries pinpricked the blackness like the running lights of giant space stations. It was as if the ferry had found itself in the midst of one of Malise's drone's wings, freshly extruded from some metal-rich asteroid, supping fuel for the long flight into battle with Moonwolf.

'There,' Jude Foley said. 'I love the view to come as a surprise to me.' She waited a few seconds, her eyes aglow with the fire of a million lightbulbs, and said, 'I was born on MAB-2 – a small lunar colony. We were evacuated a day after the Moonwolf went rogue.'

Her words chilled Malise. To grow up within the restrictive cloisters of a MA-bubble that close to a non-human intelligence –

'It was a beautiful place to be,' Foley said, as if deliberately to contradict Malise's thoughts. 'There weren't many people living on the station by the time I was old enough to explore, so I made it my own. So many hiding places.' She laughed. 'I went missing for days. I drove my fathers wild with worry.' She looked at Malise, and there was a challenge there. Malise shrugged. Fathers. Okay. It didn't worry her.

Foley looked away, abashed. 'After the Moonwolf war I went to C-Ledge, studied neurology under the Fyler sisters, became a research fellow.' She took a deep breath and ploughed on, 'Never had much time for lovers. For a long time I didn't want to face my orientation. When I did there was no-one around to match it and I was lonely a long time. Snow was the first.' Another silent challenge.

Why, Malise wondered, is she telling me all this? It seemed difficult for her – she seemed a private person; why did she feel this need to explain?

'Snow's driven,' Foley went on, and laughed at the *double entendre*. 'I think she is more than a little mad.'

'What makes you say that?'

'She believed – believes – that her datafat is the next, the *inevitable*, step in human evolution.'

Malise looked out over the industrial seascape.

The stars had gone out. The sky was blue with the promise of dawn. 'They said that about the chip,' Malise said. 'And Von Neumanns, and datafat itself. They weren't mad. Just enthusiastic.'

'You don't understand,' Foley said. 'Snow is mad because Snow is *right*. She's seen it happen. She's seen her subjects – the hot-heads she put her new datafat in – evolve.' She sank down under her covers. 'I changed, Malise. We all did. All the hot-heads on C-Ledge.'

Malise shivered to get the wormy tingling out of her spine. She remembered the squat, the relaxation exercise, her homunculus changing and bubbling, the strange places in her skull – 'I really don't understand you,' she said, not wanting to think about what the images in her head might mean if taken all together.

'Then let's start at the beginning,' said Foley.

Now Malise understood why she was here. This was a briefing, and it was, for some reason, to take place out of Haag's earshot. Why? Did Haag approve? Was this chance for a private talk part of some deal Foley had struck with them? Or had she somehow become a spokesperson for them?

'I've been told that you penetrated the Dreyfuss Biologic site. Tell me what you found.'

Malise shrugged, not wanting to admit the scale of what she'd run up against. 'A consensorium,' she said.

'Which is?'

Malise stared at her. 'You know that as well as I do.'

Foley made a placating gesture. 'It's a question of vocabulary. Consensorium – a "virtual reality". That's the meaning you were taught. It's out of date. A consensorium is more now than a battle- or work-scape. It obeys its own laws.' She straightened herself in her chair and explained: 'Imagine you're working in a combat-scape. You want to perform some action – fire a missile say. You look for something that looks like a missile – an "icon". You click on your missile icon, or manipulate it in some more complex way, and an action is performed: the missile is launched. The icon represented something – but you had to learn what it represented. Manipulating the icon fired the missile – but you had to learn how to manipulate the icon before the missile could fire. You have to *learn* what icons represent. Snow's datafat is different. Her consensoria operate through *memes* – units of meaning. When you confront an icon in a consensorium of Snow's, you know, instinctively, what it means, what it can do, how it must be operated.'

Malise nodded, thoughtfully. 'Autosuggestion.'

Foley shook her head. 'No. Not that at all. What Snow's datafat does is read and model your whole intelligence. The operator does not work through Snow's datafat – the datafat models the operator and attempts to achieve a rest state between itself and its model. There's no brain–'fat barrier involved because all calculations take place within the 'fat itself.'

Malise thought for a moment. 'You mean it grants wishes?'

Foley smiled. 'Bright girl.'

The sky went out.

Malise ran her hand between the bedsheets and let her mind fill with the grain of linen against her fingers. The mustard tang of hot sand assailed her.

She opened her eyes. Daylight entered through sand-smeared glass. Halfway across the room it was webbed by a tall wicker screen and reached the foot of the bed threaded with darkness.

In the corner of the room, a big wooden antique radio turned itself on.

'Malise.'

'Foley?'

'Call me Judith. This is a wish Snow granted me. It's a consensorium she and I used to play in. It's like one of your battle'scapes only more complex. It's running in the calculation spaces of our datafat. It's modelling us. You think you're you, but you're really only your datafat's model of you. We're running much faster than realtime in here. In a few minutes you will have a panic attack. Think of it as dopplered feedback – catachol amines telling you you were surprised by what's already happened.'

Malise nodded to the empty room.

'Meet me at the café. Walk out the door onto the breakwater and turn left. It will take you twenty minutes but you can't miss it.'

It was bright and dry, ideal bathing weather, but the beach was nearly empty. A naked girl played among the rockpools. It was April and few had trusted the dry spell enough to visit the seaside town.

Before Malise had even recognized the intrusion, the girl on the rock turned and called out, 'Hypermedia, madam.'

'Foley?'

The girl shook her head impatiently. 'I said – hypermedia. I am a meme – and that's all the help you'll get from *me!*' She turned and leapt from the rock into the sea. A crown of spray sparkled in the brittle morning light.

There was a pier ahead. She saw figures moving. The cheapness and solitude of an out-of-season resort has attracted old women, too, she told herself – a rush of incidental realization that left her feeling strangely at home. She neared, and watched them walk in couples, leant up against each other for support.

She followed the narrow promenade past the pier. Billboards chained to the gates carried old news in dirty grey tatters of newsprint: the Corn Law debacle, the re-election of Mary Wollstonecraft to the Prime Seat. When she sensed what that signified she laughed. Oh that was *corny*.

The white edge of the sea was just visible over a bank of red sand. On the opposite side of the promenade ran a road. Boarding houses fronted it. Their paint had peeled; their steps and windows were dull with dust. Over their rooftops rose the bright spire of the local Sapphist House. The road turned away through the centre of the town. The inland side of the promenade filled with beach huts, the rusted lines of a miniature railway, the skeletal metals of a dismantled fun-park.

She reached the café. Judith Foley was there to meet her. 'Hello. I admire your dress.'

Malise looked down. 'I . . .'

Judith laughed. 'You didn't dress, did you?'

Malise was wearing a startling blue and black bodysuit fastened at the waist by a wide leather belt with ancient bronze coins laced to it by strips of coloured fabric. Her ankle boots were polished leather. She felt pressure under her breasts – an underwired bra. 'How . . .'

'The operating system doesn't create an environment which we then inhabit – that would take far too much power! It creates those parts of the environment which one needs to perceive in order to preserve an illusion of reality – within certain pre-assigned parameters, of course. You thought, I suppose, that you had to dress, and so it dressed you. If you had wondered what to wear it would have provided you with a wardrobe full of clothes. These places aren't 'scapes; they're more like many-layered storyboards. Snow called them story engines.'

Judith led Malise inside the café. There were only four tables, covered with blue check cloths. We have shells for ashtrays but that's the only concession we make to the tourists, the tables told her. She sat her down at her favourite (favourite?) table by the window and looked out at the sea.

'Espresso?'

Malise started from her puzzled reverie. 'Yes. Thanks.' She reclined carefully in the wicker-backed chair. It creaked and settled under her.

'Snow chose the name carefully,' Foley went on, 'because in a very real sense these places are stories – *stories*, not landscapes. They're designed to integrate the operator wholly within their structure, in time as well as in space. After a while one isn't aware of performing operations here – one simply lives here. One isn't aware that one is learning anything. The memes act in such a way that it seems one has always known how to use them.'

Foley handed her a small china cup. Malise brought it to her lips. The coffee was bitter and tasted strangely of mint; an antidote to the faint rottenness of the air. 'So,' said Malise, looking down at herself, 'that's why these clothes seem familiar, yes?'

'Do they?' Foley smiled. 'Actually, they're Snow's. They'll change eventually. The environment adapts itself around whoever inhabits it, like a story rewriting itself for each new reader.'

Malise took another sip of coffee. 'So I'll end up changing this place, the longer I stay here.'

'Yes.'

'But do you want this place to change?' she asked.

Foley didn't meet her gaze. After a moment she stood up and went back behind the counter. She took a florentine from the tray by the ornate, gilt till and put it on a plate for Malise to eat. 'Careful,' she said, 'it's a meme.'

Malise picked it up. Condensation sparked on chocolate icing. She picked it up and bit into it. *Snow and I run this café together. Each morning before business begins we drink espresso. At night Snow makes Turkish coffee in a brass-handled jug, over a gas ring. When she drinks, she leaves the sweet foam bubbled on her lips for me to kiss away.*

Malise reached for her cup with a shaking hand and drowned the taste of the cake with bitter coffee. 'That was – you.'

Foley shrugged. She seemed unsure what to say. Was this to be another difficult confidence? 'This place is stocked with memes personal to me,' she said. 'The landscape and its ghosts have shaped themselves the better to express my life here with Snow. My memories have been webbed to the fabric of the environment so that I can no longer say what is me and what is external to me. The tastes and smells of the ocean itself have taken on a private meaning. I come here often – on my own. This is my private world, Malise. My graveyard of memory. My own fiction.'

Two teenage girls entered the café. They had been swimming; their hair was tousled and damp-looking. They wore long skirts, and pale blouses which clung to their breasts. The taller of the two had pale skin. 'Have you anything to eat?'

Foley nodded and went over to the till. 'Only cakes, I'm afraid,' she said.

A sigh. 'Coffee?'

'How would you like it?'

'White, please, both of them.'

Malise went to the counter, took the cups from Judith and carried them over. The girls were kissing. The pale one reached up and ran her hand through her friend's hair. She caught sight of Malise, watching.

Malise tried to smile before she turned away, but the muscles wouldn't respond.

Ghosts.

Foley didn't want to talk, so Malise took a newspaper from the counter and went back to her table. Emily Dickinson had set sail from the Colonies for a European lecture tour. Then there was the second instalment of Mary Godwin's latest Gothic tale.

A new species would bless me as its creator and source; many happy and excellent natures would owe their being to me. No mother could claim the gratitude of her child so completely as I should deserve theirs.

A bolt of coffee shot into her mouth. Malise swallowed it back, felt acid etch her throat. She coughed, swallowed uncomfortably and went on reading.

The dissecting room and the slaughter house furnished many of my materials.

Malise threw up. Damp cake drizzled from her mouth. The girls leapt up in alarm. Malise turned to them. The older one handed her a silk handkerchief. Malise took it with an embarrassed mumble of thanks, and turned back to the table.

Huge, bony jaws scythed through her coffee cup. Blood trickled from a torn and pallid mouth. Malise screamed in fright and horror.

'Malise,' Foley cried, 'there's nothing there.'

Her eyes filled with alphanumerics.

'It's time to leave, Malise. Your shock was worse than I thought it would be. Noradrenalin confuses the datafat. It's very sensitive. You're full of fight-flight endorphins.'

Malise closed her eyes, strange emotions filled her, and in the darkness a thousand lights sparked on.

*   *   *

Rust and alcohol soured the back of her mouth. Rotterdam reassembled itself inside her head.

She staggered, fell against the rail, breathing deeply to calm her thudding heart.

She turned to look at Judith Foley; her eyes were flickering beneath closed lids. Malise knelt down beside her and stroked greying hair from her eyes. *Where are you?* she wondered. She knew the answer already, and was touched and saddened by it. Judith had not left that place. She was serving in a café outside an Edwardian resort, living out a gentle fantasy in a land where coffee stayed hot in the cup, where girls kissed with bitter-sweet exhibitionism and sadness entwined memory and meaning.

Malise looked about her. The boat had hardly moved since Judith pulled her into the consensorium – no, the *story engine*.

Faster than realtime, she'd said. Malise shivered. Protracted periods in such a landscape could last – years. She looked at Foley with new and wary eyes. How *old* was she?

Malise took her hand. Judith gripped. They stayed like that a while, then slowly, gently, Judith drew her fingers away and laid them in her lap. She was still asleep.

Carmiggelt was waiting for them at the quay. Men in black jackets stood guard by bottle-green Audis and, for Foley, a heavy-built hatchback with a lifting platform.

'Quite a reception committee,' Malise said.

Carmiggelt treated her to a wry smile. 'Too many Yank movies when we were kids.'

Foley sat hunched up by the rail of the boat, unconscious. A black jacket trotted down the gangway to fetch her.

'Did she show you?' Carmiggelt said.

Malise shrugged.

'Now you know why we're afraid of what's in the Dreyfuss site,' he said.

Suddenly she remembered what she had glimpsed there – the *scale* of it. She laid her hand on Carmiggelt's arm. 'Listen,' she said. 'This is important. What Snow's been developing in the Docklands is – I think it's more powerful even than Moonwolf.'

Carmiggelt stared at her. 'Foley didn't tell you,' he said; it wasn't a question.

'What?' She went cold all of a sudden. 'What didn't she tell me?'

'Snow has been building artificial intelligences so powerful they make Moonwolf look like a digital watch. And I don't mean the Dreyfuss site. That was simply the factory. The intelligences themselves are elsewhere.'

'Like where?' said Malise, knowing and not believing the answer she knew would come.

Sure enough, Carmiggelt reached up and, very gently, he tapped the side of her head.

He led her to a car and strapped himself into the driver's seat beside her. 'Tired?'

'What do you think, now you've told me that?' Her voice was high with hysteria.

'Good. I need to talk to you. My place.' He started the engine.

'Why?' she said, over and over again. But Carmiggelt didn't know. 'According to Foley,' he ventured at last, 'Snow believes her plug-ins, with all their story engines and modelling utilities and other paraphernalia, are the next step in evolution. Those plug-ins model human intelligence. That means they can break people down into strings of data. Once you can do that to people, you can copy, store, transport and duplicate them just as easily as any other kind of data. With the right infrastructure, Snow's invention can make people virtually indestructible. She's so proud of her plug-ins, she wants everyone to have one.'

'Do people get to say whether or not they want holes drilled in their heads?'

Carmiggelt shrugged. 'From what Foley's told me about Snow, probably not.'

Malise frowned. 'If Snow turned the Dreyfuss site into a production line for new datafat, like you say, how did she expect to go undetected?'

'I don't suppose she did. My guess is she figured the more copies there were of her datafat in circulation, the less chance people like us had of seizing them all.'

All of a sudden Malise remembered where Snow was. Snow the hot-head. Snow the not-quite-human. She was in the States. The military-industrial complex – she imagined factories full of bright artificial intelligences, hospitals full of soldiers having their brains laced with Snow's alien datafat. She remembered Snow's words. *In a year's time I will be the military.* 'She's right,' she said. 'You can't stop it. She's won already. It's too late.'

Carmiggelt did not answer, which was itself a kind of reply.

Carmiggelt took her to his apartment. It was large, open plan, and hopelessly cluttered. An outsize circular futon lay unrolled on the floor. Carmiggelt ran lightly over it. 'Just leap over,' he called behind him, 'damn thing needs washing.'

There were three wine glasses clustered between the mattress and a low computer table. A half empty tube of lubrication cream lay on one chair. There were books and papers piled up in chairs and nested in beanbags. Behind the kitchen bar Carmiggelt was opening a bottle of wine. 'You like Libao?' he said.

Malise shrugged. 'I don't drink.'

Carmiggelt looked at the uncorked bottle. 'More for me. Damn shame.'

Why are you so jumpy? Malise wondered. What's happened?

He got Malise an orange juice and they went to the computer table. Carmiggelt pressed a button and a membrane screen unfurled from its housing. He tapped an access code and a picture formed. Concentric circles with one, slowly curving line coming in from the top of the screen to the ecliptic. 'Know what that is?'

'Asteroid entering the Jovian Roche limit,' Malise replied.

'Well, it's a start. Only this object is *escaping* the Jovian gravity well, not falling into it.'

Malise's stomach went cold.

The screen changed. 'Now what would you say?'

There were figures this time. Malise studied them. 'If I didn't know better I'd say there was some kind of course correction going on. Funny bloody asteroid.'

'Funny bloody asteroid.'

'You got pictures?'

Carmiggelt looked at Malise. He was afraid. 'We've got pictures.'

He pressed some keys. A dark mass, a mere ball of nothing fuzzed by light dimly reflected off a dust-ring.

'Can you enhance that?' Malise said. She expected to

see another eggshell – a concrete ball like the one she'd opened up more than a year ago.

'Yes. Malise, what do you know about Haag?'

Malise stretched her back. 'Not much.'

'Do you know we are paranoid? We have semibrights here, Malise. Semisentient computers. We use them to cross-match our files. *All* our files. They whisper conspiracy theories at us twenty-four hours a day. We employ a team of specialists to sort the paranoia from correspondences that might have some currency. The files each department gets from the specialists are still inches thick, and ninety per cent of the material is nonsense. When something clicks, though – when a match between files is of almost certain currency – we move quickly. Very quickly.'

Malise drained her glass. 'Just what are we talking about here?'

Carmiggelt indicated the screen with a wave of his bottle. With two more key-presses the object on the screen swam into view, phased with colour, and stabilized.

Malise stared and Carmiggelt talked. 'What you're looking at is a conglomeration of Von Neumann mining machines HOTOL seeded more than twenty years ago within the Roche limit of Jupiter. Like good Von Neumanns they've evolved somewhat. For a start, they've learned to work in concert. They're one machine now. It's a scavenger. It eats junked machinery – abandoned MAH-rings and the like. It eats to breed. If we don't stop it, it will get too big for us to fight it. If it goes unchecked, it and its children will chew the entire solar system to slag. And us with it.'

'How soon?' said Malise.

Carmiggelt rubbed his face with his hands. 'You know what an exponential curve is Malise – I shouldn't have to spell this out for you.'

'*How soon*?'

Carmiggelt sighed. 'We can calculate its mass by examining its escape trajectory. It weighs three thousand tonnes today. Tomorrow, it will weigh four point two thousand tonnes. Use a calculator.' Then he paused a moment, and turned to her. 'I'm sorry,' he said. 'I spent all of today since five A.M. having to explain to one dickhead politician after another what kind of threat this artefact represents. They couldn't grasp it. Their heads are full of the old maths. They don't think in curves.' He took a long slug of wine and waved at the monitor. 'In a sense we're lucky. It's agglomerative: when it reproduces, which is every two weeks, its "children" don't leave the parent. They attach themselves to the "spines" of the parent artefact. For the moment, at least, it's presenting a discrete target. If we launched an all-out assault now we might destroy it. *Might*. On the other hand, it only needs one child to survive the attack to put us back where we started. Worse than that, if it's as bright as we think it is, it will have learned its lesson: it will reproduce but it won't agglomerate. It will spread, like a cancer.'

Malise nodded. 'Thump a tumour, and you risk metastasis.' The words came easily to her. The fear that the Moonwolf might spore and invade Home had been paramount throughout the war.

'Now it's headed for C-Ledge,' said Carmiggelt. 'If we want to find out what Snow's datafat is designed to do, and why C-Ledge has fallen silent, and if there is a common factor to all these questions; above all if we're to find some way to stop that thing – then we need to get to C-Ledge before it does. We have very little time.'

'How much time?'

'Eight days.'

'It'll weigh forty-four thousand tonnes.'

'All right, so you don't need a calculator.'

'That's a big tumour to start thumping.'

'We aren't planning on nuking it.'

'Maybe I should bring my monkey wrench instead?'

Carmiggelt thought about it. 'You want to come with us?'

'Do I have a choice?'

'No.'

Malise turned back to the computer.

There, lit up on the monitor, was why she had run away, why she had down-welled, why she was here, a cripple, and perhaps about to lose her special sight for a second time. It was the reason for everything that had happened to her – and yet she still did not understand what it was.

On the screen before her: black spines, cracked eggshell.

'I want to come with you,' she said.

Mali. Grassland and shrub. No towns to speak of, no settlements. The 'copter pilot pointed to a cluster of silvered, photo-electric tents to their right. 'Nomads,' he yelled over the racket of the engine. 'Permanent settlement needs a licence these days – it puts too much strain on the topsoil.'

'How did that rule go down?' Malise asked him.

'Like shit on a plate. But it works. Do you know

there's the world's biggest cereal genestock under your feet?'

The ride took two hours.

Carmiggelt had told her that Haag moved fast, and he had meant it. Already there was a team assembled to investigate C-Ledge's comms blackout. The end of the launch window was forty-eight hours away and the team would have mobilized two days ago had Carmiggelt not contacted Timbuktu and told them to hold the launch until he had assessed the usefulness of Malise Arnim. The wait had proved worthwhile – more useful, indeed, than anyone could ever have hoped for. Somewhere in Malise's head there was a map of the Jovian Von Neumann.

Halfway through the helicopter flight Malise unbuckled her support skeleton and left it hanging loose around her limbs. The pilot asked her what it was and seconds after she'd told him they passed an artificial lake surrounded by young trees. The pilot circled and told her to take the batteries out of it first. Malise stowed them under her seat. She opened the helicopter door, letting in a shriek of motors and churned air, and heaved.

The chrome bundle untwisted.

It took on a human shape – and hit the water.

Timbuktu Launch Centre was a small, Soviet-built complex many miles outside the ancient city. On the pad, webbed in support gantries and service ducts, the smooth ceramic underbelly of the waverider sheened apricot in the evening light.

Malise glanced at her watch: T minus ten hours.

Foley, Malise and Carmiggelt launched at dawn. There was nothing to see; waveriders have no windows.

Judith was strung out on pain killers. Carmiggelt, who had never before been up-well, experienced half an hour of fascination and terror and then grew bored. He and Malise watched TV together.

The Voice of America announced twenty-five shopping days till Christmas.

'One hundred and forty two million tonnes,' said Malise.

'For God's sake shut up!'

An hour into the flight Malise stripped her suit, stowed it into the cage above her head and drew the privacy screen around her.

When she woke up she found they had docked with the *Greimas*.

The *Greimas* was an ugly ship – a cramped, unfurnished personnel module impaled on five mile-long shock absorbers strapped to a ceramic dish four hundred yards wide and capable of withstanding and absorbing the blast of three hundred and seventy pellet-sized fusion bombs a second. Midpoint acceleration during their journey to C-Ledge was 1.9G. Journey time was forty-two hours.

There were sixteen passengers on the flight: Carmiggelt, Foley and Malise and thirteen specialists selected by the European Space Agency. Their accommodation was cramped. Four extra couches had been bolted to the floor of the pastille-shaped module, leaving hardly any floor space to move around in once they were out of free-fall. The passengers milled around each other in the hour before launch – an ungainly and claustrophobic tangle of strange bodies muttering apology and introduction.

Malise generated some interest – most of the EC team had never met a Moonwolf veteran before – but she wasn't in the mood to talk to anyone but Nouronihar.

'You know,' she said, because she couldn't think of anything else to say and anyway it was hard to talk sense when her face was buried in the shoulder of his perpetual black velvet jacket, 'I lost your present. Your Tarot.'

He hugged her tighter. 'I told you not to go playing with any bug-eyed monsters.' He led her to the command bubble, where they could talk with a modicum of privacy. He stroked the side of her head where the port was. The skin there was inflamed. 'New 'ware?' he asked her.

She nodded. 'Snow's datafat.'

Nouronihar frowned. 'I've still got to read up on it. Isn't it contraband?'

Malise laughed weakly. 'You could say that. And you?'

Nouronihar scratched at the side of his head; an unconcious gesture. 'Old *Dayus Ram* command issue. I never paid much attention to Snow's work when I was at C-Ledge. To my cost, I see now.' He looked at Malise a while, unsure what else to say. At last: 'I should have made more effort to keep you up-well.'

'I'd have hated you for it.'

'C-Ledge wanted to quarantine you after you found what you found in that eggshell.'

'Well,' Malise replied, 'they were right, weren't they?'

'Carmiggelt's briefed me about the maps in your head. If C-Ledge had found them you'd have been laboratory meat within the week.'

'So. Thanks for sparing me that.'

'"Once is enough for anyone?"'

Malise shrugged. 'I never said that.'

'So why did you down-well?'

'The things in my head aren't just maps,' Malise said, 'they're warnings. I was *afraid*. That's all there was to it. No deeper reasons. Just fear. It was all I had left.'

'And now?'

Malise tapped the side of her skull. 'Right now I'm fighting to keep the eyes you gave me. Nothing more, nothing less.'

'No great quests?'

Malise looked at him with distaste. 'Moonwolf's dead, Doctor. We've already saved the world.'

'Now it's someone else's turn. Yes?'

Malise pushed herself towards the door of the bubble. 'Excuse me; I'm tired.'

'It wasn't my idea to bring you here.'

'I know that.'

'I'm sorry for what's happened.'

'Don't be. You're not responsible.' Malise left the bubble and sought out Judith Foley.

The *Greimas* excreted a stream of aluminium-lined He3-D pellets from the ceramic bowl at its rear, and fired electron beams at them until they triggered a fusion reaction. The craft shook; deep harmonics set the passenger module vibrating. The couches could not entirely deaden the tremor. Judith tossed about and moaned on her couch.

Malise reached over and touched her hand. 'Judith? You want to visit the seaside now?'

Judith shook her head. 'Opioids. They confuse the datafat receptors.'

'You want any pain killers?'

Foley shook her head. 'Listen, when the ride smoothes out – I can buffer the story engine so we inhabit it at about realtime. I assume you'd prefer it to two days' double-G in this place!'

The last detectable harmonic departed from the module five hours into the journey. Malise and Foley pictured 'segue' icons and the world disassembled itself around them.

The weather was summery. Carriages brought visitors from further afield. The beach filled. Early in the morning Malise Arnim and Judith Foley stocked the café with cakes and sandwiches, then, in the hour before the café was due to open, they swam together. The weather and the exercise relaxed them. The salinity of the water surprised and refreshed Malise, and the way it buoyed her up made it seem that she swam with more elegance than she had ever achieved in the dim, cold City of London municipal pools. Most of all she enjoyed the feel of her hair wet against her shoulders.

It was Judith's idea that Malise should change her physical image, and lengthen her hair. Malise sat dangling her legs over the side of the pier. The bleached boards were hot on her flesh. She leaned forward against the bottom rung of the rust-flecked railing and rested her head on her arms. Her skin smelled of the sea and she breathed it in like a drug or a perfume. Are these sensations authentic? she wondered. If they were, who provided the sense data? Or were these smells and sounds merely extemporized, like the newspapers, and that book about Victoria Frankenstein?

Foley stood next to her; the fine golden hairs on her

legs glistened in the sunlight against sun-reddened flesh. Malise, free at last of her G-support skeleton, knew well how astonishing and satisfying it must be for Foley, so recently crippled, to walk again, however 'virtual' her legs. No wonder she spent so much time in this place. She would, Malise guessed, fight just as savagely to keep her datafat as she herself had done. How much time, Malise wondered, did Foley spend here, modelled by this story engine? It was a question she didn't intend to ask. She was frightened of the answer Foley might give. This place ran faster than realtime – but how much faster? How long could Foley have spent here? *How old was she?*

'Wouldn't you like to look different?' Foley insisted.

'I like the way I look now.'

'You can even change your persona, if you want.'

Malise turned to her in surprise. Was she joking? 'When I arrived, I realized the chair by the window was my favourite seat,' she said.

'That was Snow's favourite seat. You're a lot like her. You must have triggered one of her memes.'

A lot like her. Malise shuddered. Paranoia engulfed her for a second: if personalities could be changed here, was Foley planning to turn her into Snow? No. Malise shook off the idea. Foley had spent enough time here to appreciate the dangers of such a solipsistic act. Foley would not have crossed half the solar system in search of her lover only to settle for a pale, gash-built imitation.

She scanned the coastline. In the distance, past the headland with the guest house, lay limestone cliffs, green and yellow smudges on a milky skyline. The land had slipped dramatically; Foley had told her of the fascinating walks to be had there. Malise had yet to investigate them. And if I walk further, she wondered, will I ever fall off the edge of this world? Or will I be brought back to my starting point?

She asked Foley, changing the subject.

Foley shrugged. 'I tried it once. We are at one end of a kind of fractal sink. As you walk you pass through a string of seaside towns, each identical to this; but each one is not so information-rich, not so – not so *there*, as its neighbour. It sounds fascinating, but it's not. I walked through three towns, grew bored and walked back.'

'Are they populated?'

'Oh yes, with versions of ourselves. You can't meet yourself, if that's what you're thinking. Presumably one's counterpart in the next town makes an analogous journey to the town the one after next, and so on all the way down the line, however long it may be.'

'So if you stayed here and I walked down the coast to the next town, I'd meet you on the pier?'

'Sure.'

'And?'

'You'd find me rather plain and quite boring!'

'What if I walked the other way?'

'You'd pop out of the story engine altogether – you'd wake up.'

A recursion effect? Malise wondered. She imagined her own identity, along with the town's, unwinding through virtual space; Malise after Malise and town after town were spooled around each other to infinity, a string of recursive identities in quantized states of deconstruction, mapped like fractals in unending spirals, whose precise figures and correspondences were dependent upon the prerogatives of an alien modelling system – a geometry of semantics. If things became less detailed as the sequence regressed – less subtle, less sharp round the edges – then surely you would reach a point where the entire town was contained within a single meme. Does this place have a single, true meaning, then? she wondered. More likely, the final meme would itself disappear, starved of clear referents, before she had followed the string of recursive resorts to its blurred, pluripotent end. What does that make this place? she wondered. More than just a fiction, certainly. More even than Snow's grandiose 'storage medium for personality'.

The next day, Foley had to leave the story engine.

'They're checking my legs. I picked up a local infection at Home – and they want to check my muscle tone and sensitivity. Realtime it'll take about two hours.'

Malise nodded. 'So what do I do?'

'Stay here if you want. You'll be all right, won't you?'

'Of course. It'll give me a chance to explore.'

'I can set the processor time to give you a few days here by yourself.'

Malise shrugged. 'Why not?'

They walked along the county road together.

The wagon was there to meet them. 'I'll be seeing you,' Foley said. She boarded the wagon.

Malise waved goodbye then took a short-cut home past the farmhouse.

The evening was clear and scented. Steel grey clouds tumbled in gentle folds. The grass was cool and damp through her sandals. A breeze came off the sea, steady and fresh. It carried the muted rush of the surf and the cry of seabirds.

Then it changed direction, and from a neighbouring farmhouse came a familiar sound.

She paused and listened a while to the soft, mindless lowing of men.

The next morning she swam out to sea further than she had done before and a tidal current caught her unawares. By the time she reached the shore she had been carried as far as the cliff.

She clambered over the rocks at the foot of the cliff and reached the fringe of the beach, with its tidal pools and sand-filled basins of stone. She played among them for a while while she caught her breath.

Gravel crunched behind her.

There was a woman on the coastal path, watching her.

The stranger smiled. 'I owe you an apology,' she called. 'I didn't mean to stare.'

'It happens.'

'Can you tell me which way's the guest house? The one called Greensleeves?'

'Greensward,' Malise corrected her, the knowledge of the place coming to her instantaneously from some hidden meme. 'On top of the cliff.'

'I was afraid of that.'

'It's not steep.'

'Ah.' She didn't move.

Malise sighed. She had not spent enough time in the story engine to overcome her prejudices towards the contextual 'ghosts' which populated it. She found it hard to talk to them; what, after all, was the point? But that went against the ground rule of this super-realist space, so she said, 'Are you a visitor here?'

'Of sorts,' the woman replied. Her hair was black and cut very short. She was small-breasted and wide-hipped, and she wore a wild dress of batiked cotton jersey which reminded Malise, disconcertingly, of London beggars.

'One last favour,' she said. 'Can you recommend someplace I can get a sandwich? I'm just off the stagecoach and I'm starving.'

'Come on,' Malise replied. She'd never known a ghost to interact for so long. In spite of herself her curiosity was piqued. 'I'm headed for the best place in town.'

'You don't sound like a native,' the visitor observed when they neared the pier.

Now what did *that* mean? 'I moved here two years ago. I worked in Edinburgh for a time,' Malise replied. Judith had built her a false biography. It was more than a game. Extemporization of that sort enriched the story engine.

'What did you do?'

'Proofreader for Lackington's,' Malise replied. Memes flickered before her eyes – images of her workplace, the room in which she had lived. 'And you? What do you do when the sun isn't shining?'

She shrugged. 'I get by. My name's Rosa, what's yours?'

Malise led the ghost called Rosa down some steps to the café, drew keys from behind a brick near the drainpipe and opened the door. 'Prices are on the blackboard. Coffee's tuppence.'

'So – the best in town?'

A ghost with a sense of irony, no less! Malise shrugged. 'Would I lie?'

Rosa took Malise's seat by the window. Malise brought her a coffee. 'Would you like a cake? The florentines are excellent.'

'I've tried them,' Rosa replied. She added milk to her coffee from a little china jug. Malise started. She hadn't put that there. Rosa must have glitched the story engine for her own convenience. Did these ghosts, then, have wills of their own? I may be talking to something sentient, Malise realized; then, appalled, she registered the implications of that thought: for the second time in her life she'd been brought face to face with something alien. Quickly, to cover her confusion, she thought back over what Rosa had said. She remembered her comment about the cake. 'You're not a stranger here, then.'

The stranger looked away, abashed. Maybe the story engine had glitched; maybe she was lying. Sunlight lanced through the window and accentuated the sharpness of her features. She had a witchy look. She picked up the cake and bit into it. Condensation ran from its chocolate icing.

In the afternoon Malise explored the town. A mass of tiny dwellings had been thrown up at crazy angles on crests of rock. Between them there were narrow paths and alleys which provided a restful long-cut from one quarter of the town to another.

The weather was hot and oppressive; Malise wore a halter top and a pair of denim cutoffs and sandals with leather bleached by many summers. By many trivial touches, Malise realized, the story engine was extemporizing a past for her here.

Something caught Malise's eye.

The black poster was pasted askew on a hoarding, and provided ease for eyes dazzled by the sun and by the bright colours of the port's main street.

Etched white on black, it depicted a woman leaning forward on a kitchen chair, gazing at her left palm. The hand was drawn with greater detail than the rest of the figure; the effect was sinister.

The poster advertised *Into Light* – a play that had been running for several weeks at the local theatre. This was the first notice Malise had seen for it.

She turned from the poster and up winding, dusty steps to a broad path lined with shops. By an iron-monger's, lengthways across the street, someone had parked a pram. Malise went over and looked at the baby. It gazed back at her, wide eyed and apprehensive. New life. New *alien* life. A shadow fell across it.

'Its eyes are delicious.'

It was Rosa. She held a coil of rope in her left hand.

'You gave me a start.'

Rosa beckoned Malise to follow her down the path.

'Where are you going?'

'To the Dogs,' Rosa replied.

'Heavy night last night?'

'The Dogs are a rocky outcrop you can walk out to when the tide is low. Only your timing has to be good.'

And if she knew so much about the area, Malise wondered, why had she asked directions to the boarding house? Maybe the system had glitched. Maybe the ghost was a liar – a piece of data weaponry, designed to trouble and confuse the system. *What is going on here?* Malise wondered, dizzily.

The route Rosa took led them past another notice for *Into Light*. Rosa pointed it out to her.

'Do you like that?'

'It's eerie.'

'I drew it.'

'You're in a theatre company?'

'Yes.'

'It's a good poster. Do you do anything else for them?'

'I act,' she replied. They ascended the path that would take them above the main street. 'But this morning, I'm chief buyer. They discovered a rope they use on the set had become frayed, so I was sent to replace it.'

'I'll have to come see the play,' Malise said, enjoying the fictive conversation in spite of her unease.

'Too late. Yesterday was the last night.'

Ah. So the story engine wasn't up to putting on that much of a show for her sole benefit! 'Why the rope then?' she asked, strangely eager to glitch the story engine, to show she could trick it into an inconsistency.

'Never do tomorrow what you can do today. We carry the set with us on tour. Fishing towns are easy places to get rope in.'

It figured. 'Why didn't you tell me yesterday about the play?'

'I didn't want you to see me act.'

They left the houses behind. The paved walk became a narrow path of flattened grass between banks of gorse.

The sea was deep turquoise under a blue-grey sky. The horizon was a sharp black line – a trick of the light, Malise supposed. They walked along the cliff path. Rosa linked arms with her. Her bare skin was deliciously hot. They were not alone here: well-dressed women with quiet, smiling children nodded polite greeting to them as they passed.

Rosa slipped an arm round Malise's waist and squeezed. They walked on, swaying together, hip to hip.

'How long have you been an actress?' Malise asked.

'Since my mother died. Have you heard of the play?'

'No,' Malise confessed.

'Come back with me for a drink. I'll give you a copy.'

They decided not to chance the tide and went straight to the boarding house. Rosa's room faced the sea. Its walls were covered with rose-pattern wallpaper. The furniture was dark and clumsy for the room. 'Do the rest of the cast stay here?' Malise asked.

The room brightened suddenly. Rosa went to the dresser, on which there stood a bottle of bourbon and two glasses. 'Do you drink whisky?'

The light intensified. Rosa's scent filled the room. Malise crossed the parquet floor and touched Rosa's shoulder. Her hand went numb. It was like gripping stone.

The light evened over her vision. The rose pattern left the wallpaper and closed over them.

'Please don't,' Rosa gasped.

The words broke the spell. The light diminished abruptly. Malise pulled her hand away. She felt dizzy. Rosa put the bottle down on the dresser. The glasses jangled.

Malise went to the window, opened it and leaned out. She stayed there until her head cleared.

'Your drink,' Rosa said. Everything seemed normal again, but they couldn't relax. They tried to make conversation, but there was a coldness to the room. They arranged to meet for lunch the next day.

On her way home Malise called in at the theatre and managed to obtain a copy of Rosa's poster. She put it on the wall of her bedroom, opposite the bed.

She read the play. She couldn't understand it. It was page after page of nonsense. The dialogue was the kind of text computers generated before dumbheads came along – a syntactically stable architecture but with all the signifiers misassigned. *So, I've finally caught it out,* she thought, but for some reason this didn't comfort her.

The story engine leached tiredness into her. She took the hint, put the manuscript aside and went to bed.

Dreamed.

She started out of sleep. It was the middle of the night. The sheets were damp and cold. She sat up and rested her naked back against the cold headboard. The wicker screen round the bed let in threads of grey moonlight; dust motes danced in the weave.

Before her, on the opposite wall, she could just make out the poster. The woman leaned forward on the chair, gazing at her left hand.

The hand balled into a fist. The woman in the poster turned to face Malise.

It was Amy.

Malise fumbled for the bedside light, pressed the stud, and the picture flipped back to its original state.

She stayed sat up in bed until the dawn, waiting for something to happen, but nothing did.

'What did you think of the play?' Rosa asked Malise. They were eating lunch at a restaurant set back from the sea behind the dismantled playground.

Malise took a draught of wine. 'I didn't like it,' she admitted.

'I'm sorry,' Rosa said. 'How do you get in to these things?' She prodded the left claw of her crab.

After the meal they walked along the sea-front. On the horizon the narrow black line had smudged, and could now be seen for what it was – a bank of low blue cloud heading for land. They sat and threw pebbles into the waves.

'I'm leaving today,' Malise said. She had decided to leave the story engine and question Foley about Rosa and the other 'ghosts'.

'Where to?'

'Just leaving.'

'Will I see you again?'

'Probably not.' Malise picked up a flat stone and skimmed it. It bounced twice and vanished.

'Let's talk some more,' Rosa said. 'Come back to the hotel.'

As they neared the boarding house a cold breeze blew up from the sea and swept the headland. A cloudbank swelled on the horizon. Rosa said, 'I wish we'd had longer.'

The storm hit like the clip of a giant hand against the beach.

They entered the boarding house seconds before the rains reached them. They entered Rosa's room and looked out of the window at the sky: huge, heavy and solid as granite, sculpted like glacier mountain. Its colossal topography was lit up from underneath by light reflected from a patch of western sky – a flat blue eye still open against the storm. In the distance the pier glistened, white and unreal against black cloud.

'You know,' said Rosa, 'my mother, she was never very – well, she never read, never had much of a gift with words. But she had a name for this light. Black sun. I always remember my mother when I see cloud lit clear like this. Black sun.'

She turned back to the room.

Malise followed her to the bed and they sat down

beside each other. The blue eye closed. They let lightning break in upon the darkness of the room.

Rosa laid her head on Malise's shoulder. Malise turned and stroked her hair. Rosa lifted her face up and kissed Malise on the lips. They sank back onto the bed. Rosa's hand was at the buttons of Malise's bodysuit. Malise let Rosa unbutton it and slip a hand under the cloth to stroke at her breast through the silk of her bra.

A burst of lightning sharpened on the horizon, sending a shaft of unearthly light through the room.

Malise stroked up Rosa's skirt, her hand touched the flesh of her thigh, and she squeezed it. Rosa parted her legs and Malise stroked the swell of her lips through damp cotton.

The clouds shivered and changed.

Rosa's mouth was on her breast – a wet, warm pulse over her heart. Hands fumbled at her shoulders, pulling the bodysuit down around her waist.

The sky heaved.

Rosa came. She pulled away, undid and drew off Malise's clothing.

Thunder drummed steadily against the window, like a heart beat.

Malise ran her tongue along Rosa's thigh.

Rain gushed in peristaltic bursts, like blood from a severed artery.

Rosa licked between Malise's legs, then pushed her tongue inside.

Malise turned to squeeze Rosa's breasts. She cupped them in her hands, then Rosa let go of her and they moved round to face each other. Malise stroked her foot down Rosa's trembling calf. She said, 'Who are you?'

Tears sparked Rosa's cheeks. They lay together in silence and listened to the storm subside. Rosa said:

'It is with considerable difficulty that I remember the original era of my being; all the events of that period appear confused and indistinct. A strange multiplicity of sensations seized me, and I saw, felt, heard, and smelt at the same time; and it was, indeed, a long time before I learned to distinguish between the operations of my various senses. By degrees, however, my eyes became accustomed to the light and to perceive objects in their right forms; I distinguished the insect from the herb, and by degrees, one herb from . . .'

'*Frankenstein or The Modern Promethea*. Mary Godwin. Eighteen eighteen.'

Rosa stared at her.

Malise shrugged. 'The publishing company I worked for produced the first edition. Clever machine, this, isn't it?'

Rosa shuddered. 'I have – I have different pasts. Depending.' No matter how tight Malise held her, she couldn't stop Rosa shivering.

So what, Malise wondered, am I lying next to here? A metagrammatical sex toy? A semantically inflatable woman?

The *Greimas* broke from its stalk-like drive and docked with a free-station a mere thousand klicks from C-Ledge. The EC team was to base itself here using dumbheads and expert systems to interpret data gathered by Malise, Carmiggelt, Foley and Nouronihar. These four were to remain aboard the *Greimas*. They would explore C-Ledge second-hand by means of telefactor drones.

While the EC team readied themselves to board the free-station Nouronihar took a drone through its utilities and personnel quarters, running safety checks. Two more drones, both driven by Malise, revived the station's heating and life support. While Malise was operating them, she holed up in a corner of the *Greimas*'s living quarters and talked with Foley. 'I met Rosa,' she said. Behind her eyes cursors winked – amber graphs chased each other across her field of view, projecting gas-mix and temperature curves in each part of the station as she warmed it and filled it with breathable gases.

Foley sighed. Obviously, Malise and Rosa weren't supposed to have met. 'I made her,' Foley said. 'It's all from books and bits of papers and posters and junk lying around the story engine. Material we ported into the system for our own amusement. 'Frankenstein' was Snow's idea. It's her favourite book. Fitting, don't you think?'

Malise stared at her, wondering whether she had any idea of the enormity of her words.

Foley refused to meet her gaze. 'I have spent a long time on that beach,' she said. 'I was very lonely.'

The truth clicked home. 'You've *populated* it.'

'Yes.'

'Artificial people.'

'Yes.'

'How many . . .?'

Judith looked away. 'Three hundred – after that I lost count.'

'*Three hundred?*'

'All of them – inside me. I told you Snow's datafat was powerful.'

Malise swallowed. She had remembered something.
Russia Dock.

By the afternoon the EC crew were all safely aboard the free-station.

Malise, Foley, Nouronihar and Carmiggelt remained aboard the *Greimas* and launched a barge stacked with telefactor equipment. It arrived at the hub of C-Ledge late that evening.

C-Ledge was a classic oneil – a spinning cylinder stopped at one end by an asteroidal plug and at the other by a freefall manufacturing zone.

Nouronihar controlled the docking procedure, then handed control to Carmiggelt. Carmiggelt was not a hot-head. To oversee the operation he wore a Haag-licensed eyes-up ops helmet. They all knew why Nouronihar wanted Carmiggelt to take the comm for the greater part of the operation. If Snow's datafat turned out to be a weapon, Carmiggelt would not be affected by its activation. Anyone with datafat in their heads, however, of whatever make, stood a good chance of dying.

Malise blinked. An ops suite flared behind her eyes. It read:

23.06:57 DRONES\ASSIGN\GB*23,HNSC=<?>(LMQ)

NOUronihar — EYES: CHEMO-ANALYSIS DRONE; CARTOGRAPHIC MODELS.

CARmiggelt — COMMS; LOGISTICS; BLACKBOX; SOFT WEAPONRY.

FOLey — OUTREACH; WETWARE SEEK/TALK: INTERPRETATION.

ARNim — HANDS; DAMAGE; VIOLENCE.

The words dissolved, replaced by a faceted overlay of status graphics and camera output.

Malise's sense of her own body evaporated as she segued herself to her equipment. She floated her drones out of the barge and into the empty corridor. Other drones, operated by Foley and Nouronihar, followed.

Straight away, Foley noticed something wrong.

Foley   >Carmiggelt   THE WALLS ARE WARM. BLOOD HEAT.

Carmiggelt   >Foley\Arnim   LEAVE THE CORRIDOR.

             >Nouronihar   SEED A SENTRY HERE.

From the side of Nouronihar's many-limbed drone a rack jiggled open. A flexible tube wormed out from between its bars and blew a bubble of helium from a slit in its side. The ends of the tube were forested with pick-ups: bizarre teratomically engineered miniatures of human sense organs.

It was an innocent device, but Malise could not bring herself to focus upon its glistening mucosal membranes and jittering, rheumy eyes.

The sentry floated aimlessly around the corridor, a static sensory pickup gathering data for the EC crew at the free-station.

The drones reached the lift. It was furred up – strange, mauve cilia choked the cage. Foley flew an eyebee into the narrow gap between cage and shaft edge; the minuscule drone sent back pictures which would have been beautiful were they not so ominous. The shaft was choked with strange, sparkling mineral growths. Foley examined them.

Foley   <>   IT COULD BE OPTICAL FIBRE.

The eyebee crawled out of the gap between cage and elevator festooned in pink cobwebs.

Carmiggelt >Nouronihar   COLLECT FOR ANALYSIS.

Nouronihar dispatched a winged box to pick up the tangled, struggling bee and take it back to the barge; there it would be packaged and gunned back to the free-station for examination.

Obviously, the drones could not use the lift; Malise moved a drone to the stairwell door and extended a metal limb. The rubber seal resisted for a few seconds, then peeled back; the door opened, revealing a staircase, spiralling round a thick, rust-streaked pillar.

The team descended.

There was a two-inch gap between the stairs and the dirty, riveted casing of the pillar. Malise extended an eye on a stalk and peered down the gap. She zoomed the picture, falling, so it seemed, down a hundred cycles of heavy, gridded stairs, and another hundred, and . . .

Arnim   <>   DEEP, ISN'T IT?

Nouronihar   <>   DISPATCHING EYEBEES: ONE FORWARD, ONE
                       BEHIND.

It was half a mile to the bottom of the shaft. About half way down, with gravity 32% earth normal, they reached an unlit gallery, and at the far end of the gallery there were three tiny green lights.

```
Foley          <>          IF WE EXIT HERE, WE GET TO DESCEND BY THE
                           SCENIC ROUTE.


Nouronihar     <>          A GOOD SITE TO LAUNCH EYES, BEES & BIRDS.


Carmiggelt     <>          FINE BY ME.
               >Nouronihar  YES?


Nouronihar     <>          YES.
               >Arnim      GIVE ME FLIGHT ACCESS TO THE FORWARD EYE &
                           LEAVE ME SOME BEES.
               >Carmiggelt REQUEST WEAPONRY ACCESS.
```

Malise walked her lead drone through the gloomy gallery. The floor was wet; water ran down the walls over mats of green algae. By the door controls there was a large puddle. Malise extended a sponge-tipped claw to the control box. The buttons weren't working. Malise lowered the claw to the red-painted box, smashed the four-inch-square glass panel that protected the handle, and pulled.

Compressed air opened the door. As it did so, the puddle caught the light and dazzled her. At its centre stood a column of fungoid tissue. Malise went over to it. It was pink and flanged and etched with red. Malise prodded it. It was meat. It came apart at her touch, as though it were freshly cooked.

```
Arnim          <>          GETTING THIS?


Carmiggelt     >Arnim      STERILIZE THAT CLAW BEFORE FURTHER USE.
               <>          FROM NOW ON ALL UNITS WRAP EXTENSORS IN
                           DISPOSABLES.
```

Nouronihar swept his forensics drone to the edge of the puddle and used it to pull at the object. Some of it came away in his claw. He dropped it into a box and flew the box back to the sled. Malise picked at the object till it was flush with the floor. Then she inserted a metal probe and sank it in. Extensions kept telescoping from the probe's arm till Malise lost count, but the probe itself never seemed to get any thicker. It was like watching the operations of a nightmare.

Arnim   <>   IT'S A TUBE OF TISSUE, ABOUT TWO METRES DEEP.

She sank in another, stiletto-like probe.

Arnim   <>   THEN IT BRANCHES TWICE. ONE BRANCHES AT 6
                       DECIMETRES INTO THREE, AND AGAIN AT 4
                       DECIMETRES — IF I GO ANY FURTHER I'LL BREAK
                       THE PROBE. #nline) — (online) — (on# SAME
                       STORY IN THE OTHER BRANCH. IT'S A LUNG-LIKE
                       STRUCTURE BUT IT'S SOLID. IT'S AS IF MEAT
                       WAS POURED INTO A MOULD AND LEFT TO SET.

Malise turned to view the scene revealed by the open door.

The sky was misty. She could not see the other end of the habitat cylinder, but she knew already that something was wrong.

The cloud-column – a perpetual feature of the oneil – was the wrong shade of pink. There was an orange hint to it that shouldn't have been there. She played with the colour-contrast default on her drone's cameras; she couldn't match the sky to what she thought it should be without throwing out the colours she knew to be accurate – the yellow of her droids' carapaces, and the *Ritenour Outillage* flashes on their flanks.

She moved forward. The front foot of her drone sank into the earth.

Temperature graphs flowed across the sky.

The ground was too warm.

She walked down the slope to a clump of gorse bushes. They were turning brown in places – they were dying.

Foley   >Nouronihar   PORT ME C-LEDGE BOTANIC SPECS — SOILTYPE FOR
                                            THE IMMEDIATE REGION ONLY.

Nouronihar processed the relevant data and sent Foley a report. Malise segued with Foley and read with her: the ground around here used to be sandy and compacted.

The stuff beneath Malise's many 'feet', on the contrary, felt spongy and waterlogged; sensors mounted in the treads told her it was rich in carbonaceous deposits.

Nouronihar voiced the main findings before Malise thought to look them up.

Nouronihar   <>   MAJOR CLIMATIC CHANGE. THIS IS RAINFOREST
                                    WEATHER. ANYONE HERE OLD ENOUGH TO REMEMBER
                                    RAINFOREST?

Carmiggelt   <>   SEND DATA THROUGH OUR DUMBHEAD. EC TEAM WILL
                                    INTERPRET.

Foley   >Nouronihar   DOES SOILTYPE MATCH RAINFOREST THESIS?

Nouronihar   >Foley   YES. ALSO: HUMIDITY, AIR & SOIL TEMPERATURE,
                                    SOIL PH, ATMOSPHERIC CHEMO-ANALYSIS (INITIAL
                                    FINDINGS ONLY). SOIL SILICA CONTENT THE ONLY
                                    ANOMALY.

```
Carmiggelt   >Nouronihar   MEANING?

Nouronihar   >Carmiggelt   STILL TOO SANDY.

Carmiggelt   <>            EC'S DUMBHEADS REFUSE TO BELIEVE THESE
                           CHANGES CAN BE DUE TO SYSTEMS FAILURE OR
                           INDIGENOUS MANIPULATION.

Arnim        <>            AND SO SAY ALL OF US.
```

Malise moved the rest of her drones down the slope. They skidded about on the muddy surface, then regained traction as they approached the park benches. Now, through their cameras, Malise could see the other end of the cylinder, its crags and outcrops and –

Forest.

An impenetrable blue-green carpet. She found herself afraid to move forward, afraid to see what lay below.

```
Foley        >Nouronihar   ARE THESE SPECIES INDIGENOUS TO C-LEDGE?

Nouronihar   >Foley         THEY'RE NOT ON THE BOTANICS MANIFEST.

Foley        >Carmiggelt   HAVE THE EC TEAM GET A DUMBHEAD TO PHILOTYPE
                           WHAT WE'RE SEEING HERE. HAVE IT MATCH OUR
                           SAMPLES WITH KNOWN HOME SPECIES, THEN
                           EXTRAPOLATE USING ASSESSMENT OF CURRENT
                           GENE-SPLICE / PLANT TERATOMICS DEVELOPMENTS
                           ON C-LEDGE.
             >Nouronihar    EXPECT THE WORST. OUR GENETICS DEPARTMENT WAS
                           GOOD, BUT NOT THIS GOOD.
```

Malise moved her ops drone forward and looked down.

The ground was covered in meat. Great carpets of grey fur, glistening gut and weeping muscle lay pulsating over the land. Dotted about these carpets, like tiny islands, rose clumps of meat trees.

The pleasure lakes were full of blood. The courses of ornamental rivers were choked with sluggish yellow outpourings of spittle and mucus.

Concealed discreetly between the landscaped contours of the cylindrical land sat rambling stone houses – luxury living quarters for C-Ledge's vanished staff. Huge glaucous eyes stared upwards, racked to the slate roofs with pinkish grey tendons.

Many of the houses were overgrown with bone. Buttresses made of stacked vertebrae swept groundwards from their eaves, held in place by knots of blackened osteoid.

Delicate creamy ribs interlaced these columns: translucent matrices, sparkling as though perpetually moist.

Beyond the houses the meat carpets ended. In their place, great sails of smooth, peach-tinted skin shimmered in the breeze, suspended from chitinous gantries. Mouth-like puckers and slits disrupted these silken surfaces at irregular intervals. Perhaps they were there to let air through so they did not over-strain their gaily-coloured cartilaginous rigging.

Balloons of translucent gut tethered to the ground by ropes of ginger hair trailed slick tendrils of spittle. Blue, veined with purple, the balloons diffracted the oneil's light and cast rainbows in the moisture-laden air.

In the field where they were moored, Malise noticed crops marks – horseshoes of pale green against a richer emerald ground. The horseshoes were broken at intervals by creamy, stalagmitic eruptions.

It took a moment for Malise to know them for teeth. Teeth, twenty feet tall, set in gigantic lower jaws.

They reached ground level and entered a meat forest.

The growths here were as varied as one might expect from any Home woodland, though different in kind. There were skeletal bushes and ferns made of keratin. Some of the trees' trunks had a woven texture, like bark in appearance but hard and cold and ungiving to pressure or probe. Other trees had smooth trunks; their surfaces had the lamellar appearance of mature bone. There were fungus-like growths on the trunks of the wrinkled trees, which Foley told them were analogous to sites of hyperparathyroidism.

INCREASED BONE TURNOVER. OSTEOCLASTIC-BLASTIC OUTRUN. 'CLASTIS EXCEEDS 'BLASTIS IN MOST PLACES, FORMING SUBPERIOSTEAL EROSIONS. THESE FILL WITH OSTEOCLASTICALLY RICH FIBROUS TISSUE GIVING SOME STRUCTURES THEIR WRINKLED APPEARANCE. OPPOSITE APPEARS TO BE THE CASE AT CERTAIN SITES, HENCE THE 'FUNGAL' GROWTHS. LOCAL FACTORS MUST DICTATE WHETHER BONE IS LAID DOWN FASTER THAN IT IS STRIPPED AWAY.

Arnim   >Foley   WHAT DOES THAT MAKE THE SMOOTH STRUCTURES?

Foley   >Arnim   BONE FROM A HEALTHIER ORGANISM — BETTER VITAMIN D METABOLISM.

Malise examined the ground about the base of the trees. Creamy tubes broke the mulch-rich surface of the earth, split and plunged again. Malise tested one with a plastic-wrapped probe. The tubes, she discovered with a queasy wave of revulsion, had the consistency of paste.

Foley	>Arnim	ATHEROMATOUS PLAQUES. YOU'RE POKING A BLOOD VESSEL. THIS IS NEW TISSUE, FRESHLY LAID. THESE PLAQUES USUALLY CALCIFY.
Nouronihar	>Foley	WHAT'S ITS BP?
Foley	>Nouronihar	BLOOD & VASCULAR ANALYSIS PENDING. I'M RUNNING OUT OF TOYS HERE. ALL BIRDS, BEES AND EYES DISPATCHED.

Only one thing was missing – dead and decayed matter. Presumably the 'trees' were too young to have generated their own, faecal mulch. Malise wondered if this place would ever experience an autumn, and if so, what form would that season take?

Would the trees' 'leaves' – spansules of fleshy webbing – desiccate and drift; would breeze-blown banks of feathery epidermis smooth the contours of the forest floor?

Or was this true rainforest, seasonless and fecund, so that each fleshy succulent grew and bloomed and died independent of the others, in time with an internal rhythm? When death came, did the brown-fleshed leaves turn gangrenous? Did they turn green to die?

Foley	<>	WE GOT ONE. HEAT CAMERA SAYS 'LIVE'.
Carmiggelt	<>	EC WILL BOOT MEDICAL EXPERT SYSTEMS.
	>Foley	LOCATION?
Foley	<>	DIAGNOSTICS BEES TARGETED# ine) — (online)

—(#/AI/channel override)

Carmiggelt	>Foley	WHERE, FOLEY?

Foley   >Carmiggelt   CUSTOMIZING CARTOGRAPHY. NOT MORE THAN 1.2
KILOMETRES FROM PRESENT LOCATION.

Arnim   >Foley   SEND US WHAT YOU GOT.

Foley   <>   PATCH THIS, EVERYONE.

I.D.   PHYSIOGNOMY **NOT FOUND**

!!!!!!!!initiate peripherals search (AUTH#EC\PEA\HAAG\Greimas\FOLEY)

IMMIGRATION CENTRAL REGISTER **OFFLINE**.

SEX	F
SIGHTING	15.07.34
TIME OF DIAGNOSIS	15.10:21
OPS MANAGER	Carmiggelt A.

O/E

     P   150
     BP   70/35

CVS

     P & BP see above
     JVP −2cm
     Pulses weak & thready
     Apex normal
     Heart sounds I, +II, +0

Chest   Clear

Abdo	Distended.
CNS	
	Does not respond to commands.
	Does not respond to painful stimuli.
	Pupils respond to light.

Chest	
Abdo	(forensic graphics on support channels—
Skull	operate as hypermedia)

Foley <>   THERE'S A FLYABLE MAP NOW ONLINE.

Malise uplinked Foley's map and sailed through it. Cross-wires guided her through the cartographic simulation. Cherry-red cursors indicated the location of the survivor. Cerise data spooled and jittered at the periphery of her vision – locators, guiding her approach.

The survivor lay in a large, grey plastic couch – her flesh was forested with wires and terminals. There was something roughly spherical, about the size of an English football, made of old rag, and it was hanging about a foot above the survivor's face. It was suspended on a thin chain strung from a grotesque pig-iron frame. Malise zoomed in, then balked away. Chattering digits stilled before her eyes.

The thing strung up on the chain was a teratoma, a colony of cancerous generative tissue. What she had taken for rags were scraps of skin, cartilage and other, unidentifiable tissues. In the midst of it she could see a mouth, its teeth covered in hair, and within it, something wet and blue – an oval, rheumy eye.

She moved round the teratomic ball to get a view of the face beneath it.

It was Rosa.

*   *   *

They manoeuvred their drones as fast as they could
through the mutant landscape and reached the survivor
just as Nouronihar's winged life support kit and stretcher
touched down. It squatted beside the couch, extruded
delicate wires and tapped them with crane-fly craziness
across Rosa's flesh.

Nouronihar	>Foley	DO YOU RECOGNIZE HER?
Foley	>Nouronihar	NO.
Arnim	>Foley	ARE YOU GOING TO TELL THEM OR SHALL I?
Foley	>Arnim	LATER. MUCH, MUCH LATER.
Nouronihar	<>	DO WE TRANSFER HER?
Carmiggelt	<>	WE'LL LIFT HER OUT THE COUCH AND TAKE IT FROM THERE.

Rosa was blinking, crying, smiling.

The stretcher's crane-fly manipulators ran along the
wires leading behind her back.

Carmiggelt	<>	BE VERY CAREFUL.
Arnim	>Carmiggelt	CHECK.
Nouronihar	>Foley	USE YOUR BEES TO MAP WHAT YOU CAN OF THE COUCH.

Foley prepared a map of Rosa and the couch. Malise
left her drone on auto and explored the map Foley had
made: a 3D still of her lover-made-flesh.

Malise coasted around Rosa's breast and came to rest
on her nipple. Rosa's smiling face rose in the distance
like some voluptuous mountain range. Malise turned
and gazed across the elastic plain of Rosa's stomach.

Foley   <>   THE WIRES ENTER THE COUCH THROUGH ITS BACK,
                            ABOUT HALFWAY DOWN AND CENTRE. THEY'RE FED
                            THROUGH IN A BUNDLE WRAPPED IN A CLOTH
                            SHEATH: A PRIMITIVE COAX. THE COAX ERUPTS
                            FROM THE GROUND ABOUT SIX FEET BACK FROM THE
                            COUCH. THERE'S SLACK IN IT. THE INDIVIDUAL
                            WIRES MUST LEAVE THE BUNDLE SOMEWHERE BETWEEN
                            THE FACING OF THE COUCH AND HER BACK. THEY
                            MAY BE INTEGRAL TO THE CUSHION SHE'S LYING ON.

Rosa blinked rapidly. Tears streamed down her eyes.
She was still smiling. Her eyes were unfocused. Malise
left Foley's realtime map and looked through the
cameras mounted on her drones. She extended a manipulator and gave Rosa's limp hand a squeeze.

Carmiggelt >Arnim   DON'T TOUCH ANYTHING.

Malise ignored him. Rosa had not responded to the
squeeze. Malise turned her palm. There was some kind
of plastic mesh painted on the skin. She drew her
manipulator away, disturbed, and Rosa's hand fell back
onto the steel grey cushion.

Foley   <>   THERE IS A CLIP HOLDING THE WIRES TO THE SIDE
                            OF THE COUCH, THREE DECIMETRES FROM WHERE THE
                            CABLE ENTERS THE BACK.

Carmiggelt >Foley   RELEASE THE CABLE FROM THE CLIP THEN PUSH IT
                            THROUGH.

Drones operated by Foley and Nouronihar moved
forward and swung pneumatic yellow limbs underneath
the couch. Half a minute went by while they worked at
the cable.

```
Foley        <>         CLEAR.
Nouronihar   <>         MEDICAL UPDATE FROM EC ONLINE NOW. CONDITION
                        STABLE. NO MORE FROM DIAGNOSTICS: THEY'RE
                        STILL COLLATING.
Carmiggelt   <>         ALL OUR SYSTEMS NOW ON DIRECT LINK TO FREE-
                        STATION'S INTERPRETATION ENGINES.


      >Arnim\Nouronihar
                        LIFT THE CUSHION IF YOU CAN. BE GENTLE.
                        THERE'S NO NEED TO HURRY THIS. FOLEY, FEED
                        THE CABLE IN SLOWLY. I'LL MAKE SURE THE
                        WIRES AREN'T PINNED TO THE UNDERSIDE. GENTRY,
                        GIVE ME SOME BEES TO FLY UNDER THE COUCH SO I
                        CAN SEE WHAT I'M DOING. I WANT NOTHING
                        DETACHED WITHOUT MY ORDER.
```

Malise and Foley took the cushion in their many-handed grip. It wouldn't budge. They tried lifting Rosa up on her own. Malise supported her head.

Rosa began to rise.

Malise ran an inspection eye under her back to see where the cable went.

It snaked out of the small of Rosa's back, like a tail.

```
Carmiggelt  >Arnim      AM I PATCHING THIS RIGHT?
```

Malise couldn't bring herself to reply. She thought she was going to be sick.

When enough coax had been pushed through they turned Rosa over. Her back was a nightmare jumble of springs and scales and lattices of green plastic and ceramic fishhooks, splintered bones and bloody flesh. The skin had been stripped from her back to reveal her spine.

The back of her skull was missing.

Malise gazed in horror through the cavity in Rosa's head. There was no brain; she could see all the way through to Rosa's teeth, the curve of her smiling lips, the bloody swell of tissue and muscle around her eyes; the raw slab of her tongue writhed and sparkled in the light.

THREE

The Pope Upright

Dr Nouronihar helped Malise with the seat buckle. She was a small, rather ugly girl, and he couldn't decide whether she was naturally clumsy or whether she was just acting up to annoy him.

'What's happening?' she said.

'Waiting for tower clearance. Here, bend forward, you'll be uncomfortable like that.' He pulled her coat from behind her back, bundled it up and tucked it under his seat. 'Have you ever flown in an aeroplane before?' he asked.

The girl from the hospital shook her head.

'Excited?'

She shrugged.

The plane accelerated. Soon they were going so fast it seemed you could see things from both sides at once. The scene outside the porthole came apart even before they rose, disassembled like a cubist painting. *The world is delicate*, she thought. *The world comes apart if you shake it*.

'Doctor Garcia is very angry with me,' Dr Nouronihar said.

Malise took no notice.

Nouronihar lay back in his seat. 'He thinks you are not cured. He wants to treat you. He doesn't think I can do it.'

Malise looked out the window. She could see the Alps.

'What do you think?' he prompted.

'I prefer your games to Garcia's,' she said, with an effort. Too much talk, she thought. There is too much talk in him.

'Is that all?'

Malise shook her head. 'And I want to kill the Moonwolf.'

Nouronihar scratched his head, troubled. Malise wondered why. It was what he wanted, wasn't it? That's what he'd told her. He was gathering people to fight the Moonwolf. Why couldn't she just come out and say it?

Nouronihar said, 'It won't be easy, there are a lot of hard choices and –'

'I know.' Nouronihar had already explained the operations to her; he had told her about the life she could expect up-well. It was like a story to her. She wanted to live out the story to see how it would end. She wanted it to end with her killing the Moonwolf, killing the thing that killed Seval, only she knew she couldn't say that, because no-one would believe her; no-one believes in magic.

'Malise, tell me why you were there.'

'In the simulator?'

'In the hospital.'

'You know.'

'I want you to tell me in your own words.'

'I was getting myself ready,' she said.

'For what?'

Malise sighed, exasperated. 'For killing the Moon-wolf.'

'What about your father?' he said.

Malise's hands clenched. 'You didn't let me see him.'

'People asked me not to. They thought it wouldn't be good for you. They only let me take you if I promised certain things. That was one of them. You will see him again one day.'

'Soon?'

'Yes, if you get better. If I discharge you. I want to discharge you because then you can agree properly to do what we talked about.'

'You mean I can sign away my brain.'

Nouronihar frowned at her. 'If you must put it like that.'

'I didn't. Doctor Garcia did,' she said.

'Oh.'

Malise turned back to the window to hide her smile. She was lying. 'I really want to see him,' she said, meaning her father.

'It wouldn't upset you?'

'It was a long time ago,' she replied; something flipped inside her, like a bicycle chain slipping a gear. Why had she said that?

Malise crossed her arms over her chest.

'What is it?'

Malise shuffled deeper into her seat and looked out the window. 'Thinking,' she said.

Why? she wondered. What happened? What was it?

Nouronihar's hospital lay two miles outside Milan. Malise stayed there for three months, playing games on

machines that had hard screens and proper keys; sometimes, instead of a monitor, she was given goggles and
datagloves and, once or twice, a complete telefactor suit.

They called the rogue lunar Von Neumanns, which
had in the course of years linked together to form one
gigantic and malign intelligence, the Moon Machine –
but Malise insisted on calling it the Moonwolf.

After a while her name for it stuck. When Nouronihar
made his project public, he called it Moonwolf.

After a few months the papers started using 'Moonwolf' to describe the rogue machine itself. It was as if
they were thanking Malise for being there, with Nouronihar, training and readying herself for battle. Malise felt
very proud.

One day Nouronihar asked her to visit his office.

When she arrived she thought she must have the
wrong place, because the corridor was in the old wing of
the building, away from all the dumbheads and simula-
tors and laboratories.

Inside, it was not like a normal office at all. There was
a cooker and a red tin kettle and a fireplace stuffed with
old copies of *Therapeutics Bulletin*. Threadbare rugs lay
at all angles over scuffed and dirty floorboards. The
furniture was scratched and frayed. The main light had a
tasselled shade. The windows were grimy brown.

There was a computer, on a table so old it looked as if
it were real wood, and the computer itself was ancient –
an antique IBM clone with a green screen that pulsed
malevolently.

Nouronihar smiled when he saw Malise staring. He
sat her down and said, 'I want you to look at a snapshot.'

Malise looked.

It was a picture of two men, wrestling.

While Malise looked, Nouronihar punched a couple of buttons on the computer keyboard. 'This is all being analysed in realtime, rather than recorded,' he said. 'The room is wired.' Malise glanced round, looking for wires, but she couldn't see any.

'How do you feel?'

'Fine,' she said.

Nouronihar peered into his archaic glass-tubed monitor. 'The photograph – it doesn't excite you?'

'No.'

Nouronihar grinned. 'Liar.'

'What?' Malise was shocked.

'Not an intentional lie, nothing so unsubtle as that. But this gadget –' Nouronihar tapped the side of his PC '– knows. You are sitting at the core of a ten million ECU phased-array magnetic field generator. The combined high-field ESR is capable of monitoring the output of any given neurone in your skull.'

'Really?' said Malise, impressed. 'Which one?'

'I'm going to show you some ink-blots,' Nouronihar said, 'and see how your hind-brain gets on with them. Maintenance tests on your limbic system. See if it's safe to let you out.'

'Let me out where?' she said.

He pointed out of the window at the sky.

Judgement Reversed

Malise visited the strange office only twice. The second time Nouronihar handed her a piece of paper.

Malise turned it over in her hands. She looked up at him. 'Well?'

Nouronihar tented his fingers before his mouth. 'It's a discharge.'

'Oh.' Malise smiled. 'Am I cured, then?'

'No,' said Nouronihar.

'You must want my brain very badly.'

Nouronihar smiled. Malise often teased him. It was unsettling, but it was refreshing as well. He had grown to like her a great deal. 'Oh, I want it all right,' he said. 'Very, very badly.'

Malise turned the paper over in her hands. 'When you cut my mind apart – will you change me?'

'Yes.'

'For the better? Or for the worse?'

'You'll be able to go against Moonwolf. That is still what you want, isn't it?'

'Please don't attempt to bribe me,' said Malise, and

she gave Nouronihar a look that disconcerted him, and he thought: she is growing up so fast it's frightening. He was sure now that he had been right to make out the discharge. 'You will be changed in ways I cannot predict,' he said.

'Will I still remember why I'm doing this?'

The workings of memory, Nouronihar had learned, were for her a constant source of anxiety. 'Nothing important will be lost,' he said.

Malise folded the paper and put it in her pocket. 'Perhaps,' she said, 'I do not want to be changed – at all.'

Nouronihar stared at her. She was bargaining with him! Suddenly things were not so certain as he had assumed they would be. He shrugged. Malise favoured direct responses, so he gave her one: 'What choice have you?' he said.

Malise shrugged and smiled. 'None,' she admitted. 'But to make an agreement, or to repay a debt: sometimes we do these things, not because we have to, but because we feel they are right. Yes?'

Nouronihar did not respond.

Malise laughed. 'You look trapped.'

'I feel trapped.'

'You are.'

'Why?'

'Because you need me.'

'Do I?'

'I will destroy the Moonwolf for you.'

'On your own?'

'If necessary.'

Nouronihar smiled. He knew what she wanted him to ask her. He obliged: 'And in return?' he asked.

'Hand me my release form,' she said.

Nouronihar picked up the form and handed it to Malise. It entitled Nouronihar's surgical staff to dice Malise's brain. She said, 'I will sign one of these, today, now, in this office, only –'

'Yes?' Nouronihar was no longer smiling.

She looked at him for a long time in silence, then she said: 'Only you must sign one first.' She handed him back the paper.

Of course. Nouronihar rubbed his face with his hands. *Of course.* Malise existed in a simple, honest world. There was no place in her scheme of things for contingency: she would give no quarter to those set against her, show no obedience to those who tried to use her, placing her in danger while they stayed safe at home. A sense of exhilaration filled him. He picked up a pen, crossed out Malise's name and printed his own, and signed it. He waited a few seconds, till the shudders had passed, till the initial shock of what he had done left him. Then he opened his mouth and the words came unbidden; they were easy words and, against all reason, he found himself smiling as he spoke them. He said: 'Where you go, I will go.'

Malise spent the next six months in a dust-free isolation ward. The doctors shaved her head and fitted a hatch to the side of her skull. They operated on her and cut her brain to pieces.

Malise wanted to find her father. Nouronihar hired an agency for her, and they found him living in Turin. One weekend Malise drove there to see him.

The street map was worse than useless. Malise crumpled it up and threw it out the window. It caught a breeze and tumbled across the road and got snared on a rusted fence. Stupid, to buy a map for a city smashed to rubble! She searched for landmarks through the dirt-smeared windscreen of the rented jeep. Already the sun was low against the shattered horizon; she squinted painfully against its glare.

Soon Moonwolf would rain its thunderbolts upon the city. The thought chilled her. Why had she risked her life coming here like this? Curiosity? Some vestige of misplaced guilt? Or something more complex?

It took another two hours of difficult driving before she found the block in which her father now lived. She found his apartment and rapped on the door. It took a long while for him to answer.

'It's Malise,' she said.

'And?' There was no surprise in her father's voice.

'I'd like to speak to you. I'm on my own. You don't even have to open the door.'

Nothing.

'We can talk like this if you like.'

He opened the door. He was very old. He said, 'Are you hungry?'

The apartment was comfortable and clean, with no echoes of the desolation outside. He made them a stir-fry.

'It's a good home, you're doing well here,' Malise said, and she pushed back the empty plate. It was a crass thing to say, but she couldn't think of anything better.

'I enjoy looking after myself,' he replied, ignoring the absurdity of her remark.

Then the Moonwolf struck.

Light flared through the uncurtained window, blue and cold. Malise gripped the edge of her seat to steady herself while shelves shook themselves empty, books, records and ornaments thudded onto the thick carpeted floor and juice slopped from the bowl of fruit salad onto the lilac tablecloth.

Her father, native now to the beleaguered city, stretched and closed his eyes, unconcerned by the thunderbolt strike.

Malise got up from the table and went to the window.

She knew the facts, the physics – her job demanded it. From its lunar hiding place, Moonwolf had railgunned a six foot flash of metal into the city. But knowing this did nothing to diminish the power of the vision which now captivated her.

The thunderbolt had passed through a nearby tower block. The bolt had punctured the structure but had otherwise caused little damage. It had buried itself in the earth two hundred metres away. There were waves in the rubble: perfect, concentric circles of mashed brick and pulverized concrete.

Just as Malise turned away she noticed a strange ornament on the window sill: small, hemispherical, half blue tin and half clear plastic. She picked it up. It was a toy.

She shook it and watched white flecks fall like snow over tiny, brightly coloured plastic houses. A tin cut-out of a dog was mounted just in front of the houses, looking up at the sky. The decal on the toy's underside was familiar; her father had sold designs to that company. Malise tilted the toy and noticed a little white disk slide from behind a slightly larger disk, mounted on the back wall of the dome. This cover was painted black and speckled with blue stars like the surface behind it, so it was barely visible. When the disk slid back the dog's jaw fell open, as though it were baying at the moon.

Malise put the toy back on the sill.

'I saw Dr Nouronihar on TV last week,' her father said. 'He told us to stay calm. Beleaguered but not defeated, he said. He told us Moonwolf isn't perfect, not a perfect Von Neumann, that it will die, that we just have to be patient. But if he really thought that he wouldn't have built you. Would he?'

Malise just looked at him, studied him, wondered what had happened to him. He is sacrificing himself here, she realized. He is sacrificing himself to the Moonwolf. Turin is his altar.

He came over to her and stroked her shaved head. 'Malise, what's that butcher done to you?'

'Given me a gun,' she replied, knowing he wouldn't understand.

Malise woke in darkness and looked at her watch. 4 A.M. Three hours to dawn. She stretched and leaned up on her elbows and looked out the window. The shapes of the city bloomed in her eyes, reminding her of something. She lay back and stared at the grey ceiling. An image formed behind her eyes. It kept slipping, losing shape. Trying to hold it kept her awake till at length she realized what it was. She clambered out of the bed and went into the living room.

The toy glimmered on the window sill. She picked it up and turned it. The little white moon slid into view and phased brightly. The dog's mouth opened.

'Malise?'

She wheeled round.

'Hey.' Her father was right behind her. 'What have you got there?'

'Your toy,' Malise said. 'The toy you made. The one with the pretty name.'

He took it from her unresisting fingers.

'Moonwolf,' she murmured. 'You called it a Moon-wolf.'

He threw it against the window. It shattered against the toughened pane. Water dribbled down the glass.

As dawn broke they said goodbye. She stepped out into the hall and gave him a smile and they made some empty promises to each other. As he closed the door, the sun glinted over the ruins. It lit up the toy, which lay broken on the sill, and glistened in the tear suspended from its bone-white eye.

Six of Swords Reversed

Malise went to university, where she met Nouronihar's other patients. Most of them were soldiers. She liked the soldiers. They had wide, quick eyes and they moved with wary grace, like cats.

Others had backgrounds they didn't talk about. Maybe they have secrets too, Malise thought. But talking to them, she found that they were empty people, devoid of passion or anger, and she was not drawn to them.

Another two, Aubusson and Lennox, were physicists. She slept with Lennox.

Officially, Nouronihar's charges were research students. Others, from other departments, knew there was something peculiar going on; some of them had got so far as to learn that there was some connection between these 'research graduates' and the EC government's Moonwolf project. No-one learned the whole truth for, as Nouronihar said, no-one was prepared to believe it.

One night, a week before they were shipped to their

battle stations, Aubusson came up to Malise and talked with her a while. 'It's been staring us in the face for so long,' he said, 'but no-one's ever admitted it. We are the next development, aren't we? The next step. Look at Moonwolf: we are being made to emulate it. The people in power, the EC, HOTOL, they realize humans no longer compete. So they build us, the first of a new breed. We are little Moon Machines. Moonwolf is our father, and we are its children. We are little Moon-wolves. In here.' He tapped his head.

Malise was angry. 'Any fool can generate metaphors,' she said. Aubusson shrugged and smiled and changed the subject. Malise found herself telling him all about the Tarot, and how the Egyptians had brought the Royal Way to Europe in brightly painted wagons.

He laughed and told her that the cards were known throughout Europe by the end of the 1300s, before the gipsies ever got there. He told her about the river Taro, a tributary of the Po, where the cards were most likely first made, and about how there were dozens of different Tarots, even one for Bologna, which had sixty-two cards instead of seventy-eight.

The next day Malise went to the library to see if what Aubusson had told her was true. It was. Suddenly she felt older, less credulous; everything that had happened to her seemed less important than it used to.

That night she went to bed with Lennox. He was very cold and she kept flinching from the touch of his hands and his legs. His beard scratched her cheek and because she'd been crying it was like he was grinding salt into her skin and she told him to stop.

He held her and waited. She told him, 'I'm afraid of what's in my head.'

He squeezed her tighter. 'It comes with the territory.'

'Do you think it will change us?'

'Yes.'

'Do you think it will make us forget?'

'No.'

'Kiss me.'

Afterwards he said, 'Will you miss this place?'

'Milan?'

'Home.'

'Of course.' It was an automatic answer, a platitude they shared.

He laughed softly. 'I'm surprised.'

She pulled away and faced him. 'You don't think I'll miss open skies, mountains, lakes?'

'You're not the nature-loving type,' he said, and he slid a finger around her arse, and she giggled because he was tickling her. 'And you?' she said, to stop him asking her anything more, because it hurt her to be reminded of how little he knew of her, how little she let him know.

He frowned. 'I guess I'd be happy anywhere.' He laughed. 'And I want to have adventures!'

Malise smiled. 'Save the World Syndrome.'

'Sure,' he said.

She knew he was lying. He never told her a good reason. Maybe he didn't have one. Maybe none of them did.

We are pawns, she thought, motes blown towards the next step in evolution by fate or by God or by the prompting of our own ambitious genes.

She cuddled closer to Lennox and closed her eyes tight and thought of Seval. Her sense of mission was fading; her need to avenge Seval was less hot than it had been. In her waking hours, she knew it was just the way time leaches memory. But at night, and tonight especially, she wondered whether there wasn't some other agency, wearing her down – Moonwolf itself, perhaps, filling the airwaves with sleepy enchantments.

They left Earth, armed themselves with hybrid weapons and attacked Moonwolf.

The moon glowed. The dust of battle filled its empty sky. It peered through the clouds of Earth: a huge, malevolent eye, with a corona for an iris.

The Sea of Tranquillity boiled. From Boole to La Condamine, from Foucault to Anaximander, a great weal burst, filling the slow sky above Babbage and Robinson with gold and electricity.

The *mare frigoris* turned black as great gantries rose up out of the dust and prepared for war. The bed of Maurolycus sheered away and a thousand cybernetic stalk-eyes peered out at the world, finding targets for railguns in Kaiser and Buch and Clairaut and Gemma Frisius.

Rima Hyginus flared, a blue-white hairline crack in the darkness, and strange rays fluoresced the dust-laden skies. A hundred drones died at a stroke; ten hot-heads, mashed into the dry lunar dirt.

The walls of Alfraganus shivered and fell; the basin collapsed and went wheeling into a dark and bottomless pit. From it crawled a thousand giant insects with guns for heads.

The news from Home was strange. Advances made to combat Moonwolf were opening the world up to new and exhilarating possibilities. New alliances were forged, new ecological battles fought – and won – with strange new tools that blurred the edges between the mechanical and the organic. New laboratories were built, on Mars and in the belt, and plans for an ambitious oneil, C-Ledge, were drawn up. The war itself was spoken of as a necessary stage – the pubertal crisis of the new Universal Culture. People looked with tremendous optimism to the post-War world. There was even talk of generation ships and great colonies in space; the new Universal Culture had reached its adolescence and was subject to an adolescent's enthusiasms.

At 13.00:30 GMT on 13 October, Major Malise Arnim and Major Iain Lennox were dispatched from their battle stations on board *Dayus Ram* on a sortie against Moon-wolf's emplacements in Alfraganus.

Lennox led Malise at a run down the docking tube. As Malise followed she booted her combat systems.

The corridor was lined in blue acrylic. Her boots clanged and rattled the catwalk, which was slung two feet above the ground. Beneath her, fat pipes squiggled along the floor. The handrails shook. Lennox was twenty yards ahead of her, moving fast. Migraine pulsed behind Malise's eyes – overspill from the systems upload. Malise's viewpoint shifted and swirled in crazy fractal patterns. There were lights in the pipes below her, pulsing. As she ran, the fluorescents set into ceiling alcoves dazzled and passed, dazzled and passed as if they were moving too, the other way, growing bright then dim as they rushed overhead. Suddenly things got worse: the lights snapped on off on off thundering in her head, the tunnel seemed to compress and expand in all directions at once, and she could see through the wall to the network of service ducts, the fistulae and abscesses in the space station's iron intestinal tract. Lennox glanced back at her; his face was all collapsed, fallen in, like there was a singularity in Malise's left eye, blinking, on, off, on, off, and when Malise glanced away the light from the fluorescents was threaded and latticed and it made pictures in her head, dogs and gipsy wagons and cracked eggshells and big black spines and Tarot cards and Seval's face . . .

And then she was in.

Icons and cursors spilled across her field of view then settled, reconfigured, ready and waiting.

Lennox took the comm. Malise strapped herself in beside him. She glanced down. On her screen the lights were spinning – new navigational instructions, processed by the shipboard dumbhead.

She turned to Lennox, took his hand.

Lennox was pale. His eyes were wide.

'Well,' said Malise, 'no-one said this would be easy.'

Lennox laughed. 'Just do it,' he said.

Malise pictured an ops icon and melted, slowly, fat to oil, through the alien logics of her mission.

There are ways to
penetrate the
system, follow
the swirling
architectures of
Moonwolf's own
hardware, then set
logic bombs ticking
in its brain.

The moon is grey, and
its angels live inside

teem ew staerht
D   AND WE   e
 u   GUARD THEM   h
  m   AGAINST
   b   MONSTERS
      heads translate

Now follow me,
keep together,
can everyone
hear me at the
back?

To do this needs
wetware and a lot
of power.

    I

    a

    g

    r

    e

s   e

h   t

e   o

l

h l   th e gr

t s k   ey'v o

      i   wn t

      l   w

      l   i

these angels   s

            det

The earth recedes, pink
purple and yellow. Africa
sparkles, as though it were
covered in jewels

Malise launched a
cold bomb, exposing
raw interfaces –
superconductive
capillaries that
would sweep them to
Moonwolf's heart.

This, ladies
and gentlemen,
was not meant
to happen, so
I think I'd
better sail to
the moon on my
own tongue.

Much of this
operation is
conducted by
dumbheads.
They seed our
homework deep
into the machine's
crania.

Here you can see –
come, on, fan out,
and give everyone a
chance – a big black
empty hole where Lennox
used to be, just a few
seconds ago.

There's no tomorrow and my skin's coming apart with all the English, and I

                        c

         'I   r   o

     v   ae   u

    e   w   l

           s d

been here
before

And I wake up, and sure enough, on the ops couch next to mine, Lennox
Here! is We! not Go! the Again! man Here! he We! used Go! to Again! be.
Here! His We! brain's Go! fried. Again! He's Here! dribbling Here! snot
Here! and HERE! bLood. HERE! He's HERE! been

BOMBED

G

I

C

237

She recovered, after a fashion.

Lennox didn't: by the time she recovered conscious-ness, they had already turned off his life support. It was a closed-coffin funeral. Some time later Aubusson told her why: when Lennox was in the high-security ward he broke the straps that held his arms down and tried to tear his own face off.

Aubusson wept as he told her. A friend of his had just been killed: that and Lennox's death and the psychiatric ward full of their friends – victims of Moonwolf's own logic weaponry – had done for him. He had had enough. Nouronihar was sending him down-well, 'for R&R', but Aubusson expected not to return before the war was over, one way or another. 'One more step up the fucking evolutionary ladder,' he said. He kept saying it, over and over, till Malise was crying too; she held hands with him across the table. They were sitting in the hospital canteen; they were alone there.

'One more fucking step, we said.'

'Shut up, Aubusson.'

She saw him once more, the day he left. He was in a bitter, argumentative mood. He said to her, 'Sometimes I wonder if we were fighting the same war. You never seemed afraid. Even now, it's like you're watching this movie unroll inside your head, and you're the heroine.'

Malise shrugged. 'Maybe I am,' she replied; it came out more belligerent than she'd meant it to.

He shook his head. 'You take things too personally.'

'Do I? You're the one headed down-well.'

He shook her hand and smiled. 'Fuck you, Arnim.'

Later it occurred to her that he thought she'd accused

him of cowardice. The truth was, she envied him: she wished she could experience her surroundings with Aubusson's sense of immediacy. These days she seemed to spend her whole life swathed in cotton wool. There were the dreams, of love and vengeance, and there was the war – but the two worlds no longer meshed. Sooner or later she would have to decide between them; she knew which world she must choose.

Nouronihar gave her therapy. It was part of the rehabilitation process. Often he cheated and used the sessions to ask her a lot of questions he'd badgered her with when she was much younger.

'Who do you think is responsible for the Moonwolf?' he said.

'I've told you a thousand times,' said Malise. 'My father, my father, my fucking father, what is this, you want me to kiss your feet because Freud was right this once? Ask me again I'll chisel "transference" into your forehead.'

Nouronihar laughed, gently. 'I'm just interested.' He tapped something into his notepad. 'What makes you think you can kill the Moonwolf?'

'I don't.'

There was a long pause. Nouronihar put down his pad and leaned forward. 'That's a first,' he said.

Malise sighed. 'Maybe I'm getting old,' she replied.

As soon as she was out of hospital she treated herself to a year's supply of Turkish coffee and Gauloises cigarettes. It cost her a lot – importation up-well wasn't cheap – but they were paying her enough. Six-figure danger money, linked to the EC index.

She bought an Italian espresso machine, specially adapted to low gravity. She decided to take up the guitar again, and ordered herself a Fender fretless and an amplifier too big for her room. The valve stereo hand-built in England got broken in transit and she sent the claim form to the company with a letter setting out the custom rig she wanted instead. She bought a graphics terminal better than the one they designed logic bomber icons on and drew pictures no-one else liked or understood. The Japanese TV doubled as an InterAction terminal. She spent a lot of time acting in trashy soap operas, making them more trashy, behaving as bloody mindedly as possible to crash the syntax engines. Bad magic, she thought, not that the word meant anything to her any more.

She ran out of money. She applied for credit and got it. Nouronihar came to see her and drank tea while she described what she'd bought that week, then he invited her for a meal and she was impressed with how big his room was and he said, it's the same size as yours, and she said, of course, you don't have so many things in it, and he said, no, that's true. It was a nice place to live, she decided, and told him, I wish I had a second flat so I could just put a few things in it like you've done. A couple of pictures. Some cushions and a table. A stereo of course, and a coffee maker, and, well, a few other things.

Like what? he said, and she told him. Anything else? he said, and she listed a few more things, and by then she was crying.

*　　*　　*

She forgot Seval. She forgot why she was there. 'To save the world,' Nouronihar told her, laughing, when she asked him; he thought that she was joking with him. He thought that she was somehow 'better', now that she had purged all the dreams and strange connections. She could see he thought she was cured at last. She hated him for that, for his arrogance, for his inane respect for 'sanity'.

He had something to talk over with her. Strange signals had been received from a rock spinning its way out of the orbit of Jupiter. Malise volunteered to investigate it.

Before she left, Nouronihar gave her a present.

Malise thumbed through the cards. She smiled. It was sweet of him.

'You know,' Nouronihar said, 'no-one knows where the designs come from. They weren't just pieced together by anybody. They've got affinities to a whole string of mystical cabals right across Europe.'

'I didn't know you were into this,' she said.

He shook his head. 'I'm not. I think it's bunkum. But I've read enough to know the Tarot was important at one time; it's more than a fairground hustle.'

She nodded. She was confused. Could Seval have been right after all? she wondered. Nouronihar left. Malise sat cross-legged on the floor of her room and shuffled the cards absently. I'll never know now, she told herself. It's too late. She knew too much about Moonwolf to wish revenge upon it. She'd been taught too much about the way her mind worked to believe any more the hysterical connections she had made between things when she was young.

The Moonwolf was no astrosome, no daemon, no

warplane sprung from her father's guilt-torn conscience. It was junk, and she was meat. There was no point any more in personifying it.

She didn't know what to do next. Maybe she should do what she was told, and save the world.

Maybe it was all she was good for.

'Well?' she said to the deck of cards. 'Is it?'

She turned up a card: the Papess, reversed.

Lust, the Tarot sneered. *Enslavement. Belligerence.*

She sighed and slipped the card into the middle of the stack.

By morning Foley, Malise and Nouronihar had found another eighteen couches. Wired to them lay people whose physiognomies did not match those of any known C-Ledge crew member. Their backs and heads were scooped out; in the hollows lay nests of nightmare bionics.

That evening aboard the *Greimas* Foley, Nouronihar, Carmiggelt and Malise met to discuss these 'survivors'.

'I know them,' said Foley.

'They're not on the manifest.'

'They're not C-Ledge crew.'

Carmiggelt frowned. 'Then who –'

'They're mine. I invented them.'

'Like Rosa,' Malise said.

Foley nodded.

'Invented.' Nouronihar scratched his forehead. 'You mind going back a stage?'

Foley shrugged, defensive. 'Snow's datafat models its operator. It's a small step from building a model to altering it, shaping it according to some blueprint, some idea –'

'Rosa? Who's Rosa?'

'I know her,' said Malise. 'I met her in Foley's story engine. Foley's been making people inside her head. They live inside her story engine. It's a whole damn village in there.'

Carmiggelt said to Foley. 'These "survivors" – you invented them while you were here, in C-Ledge?'

Foley nodded. 'It was all part of Snow's project, and she kept copies of all our data. Obviously something is using that data to give my homunculi a physical form.'

'Living personalities.' Nouronihar shook his head, still grappling with the notion that Foley could invent people.

'Yes. As for their physical manifestations, the incomplete bodies we've found in C-Ledge, I don't think they've been "scooped" at all. Like I say, I think they're being *grown*.'

An hour later Daitakikawa, the EC team's controller, came over the wire. He wanted to talk to Malise. 'We've deciphered the transcript of Pendry's diary,' he told her. 'Something's been in and corrupted much of the data, but we've managed to retrieve some entries. We'll squirt it to you, warts and all, as soon as we've checked it for viruses. But we've already come across something important in it – something you can help us with. That rock you found last year, the one flung from Jupiter – at the time I wasn't cleared for that information. Can you fill me in? What did you find?'

Malise told him briefly about Amy.

'And afterwards,' he urged her. 'What happened to it?'

Malise grinned sardonically. 'I wasn't cleared for that information.'

'Fair enough.' Daitakikawa fiddled a moment with the keyboard in front of him. 'Let me patch you something – an image we've enhanced from an entry in Pendry's diary.'

The screen skewed then righted itself; it displayed Amy's head, laid upon a turquoise sheet. Just her head – the body was missing.

'That's her,' Malise murmured, appalled at the image. 'It, I mean. What –'

The screen blanked then Daitakikawa was back. 'That means C-Ledge took your alien on board. To dissect it, presumably.'

Malise stared at the screen. 'It was alien.'

'Yes.'

'They *killed* it?'

Daitakikawa shrugged. 'We haven't been able to decode enough of the diary to say. I'll keep you posted.'

He cut the connection.

About two hours later Nouronihar, who had been studying what Daitakikawa's team had salvaged from the diary, was able to give Malise some cold comfort:

'Amy was dead on arrival,' he said. 'It was sufficiently human that it could catch human diseases. It was sufficiently alien not to have an immune system. You said your face-plate snapped when you met her. The air you breathed out would have contained commensal bacteria. They killed it. Snow conducted the autopsy. She took tissue samples. Guess what she found in Amy's cranial cavity.'

'Datafat.'

'Right. Now. What's the chances that Snow's "radical tissue" has been cannibalized from Amy?'

Malise swallowed. So, she thought, part of that thing is in me. Then it hit her: 'So whatever's happened to C-Ledge, it could happen –'

'To you and Foley,' Nouronihar finished for her. 'Yes.'

'Which brings us to Snow.'

Malise nodded. C-Ledge was the least of it, she realized – what was happening to *Home*?

The next general meeting took place twenty-four hours before the Jovian was due to reach C-Ledge.

'Have the EC team had any luck with the cores?' Malise asked.

Carmiggelt drained his coffee. 'I was talking to Daita-kikawa – he's heading the core-breaking operation. He says he's damned if he can see a way to access them. There's some kind of stay-resident encryption engine buried in their operating systems and the dumbheads can't crack it.'

Malise turned to Foley. 'Judith, is there a copy of *you* in those cores?'

Foley shook her head. 'We agreed not to store our own personalities. There were ethical questions we didn't want to get tangled in. Pendry, the director, was breathing down our necks once he found out what we could do with Snow's datafat.'

'And Snow?'

'She didn't see why . . . You think Snow's in the cores somewhere?'

Malise shrugged. 'It would be in character.'

Nouronihar nodded to himself, following Malise's line of reasoning. 'A version of Snow from before C-Ledge shut down. Or if not Snow, then *someone*. Is it possible when C-Ledge underwent its environmental changes the crew escaped, not by leaving the station, but by downloading themselves into the station's cores?'

Foley thought about it. 'Yes,' she said at last. 'Yes, it's possible. I can't see why they should want to download rather than escape, but I guess we shouldn't discount the possibility.' Foley spoke with a kind of repressed, angry anxiety. Snow had left her once – but did another Snow lie in C-Ledge's data cores, waiting for her?

Nouronihar said, 'But how can we access these personalities, even if they're there, if our dumbheads can't access the cores?'

Malise tapped the side of her head. 'Let Foley and me try. There's a lot of calculation power in these things.'

Nouronihar frowned. 'Not as much as in a dumbhead, surely.'

Malise glanced at Foley and Foley grinned. Nouronihar had not yet been briefed about Snow's experimental tissue. Malise turned to him, savouring the irony which now presented itself to her. Her old teacher was now her pupil. 'There is something you should know,' she began. 'What Foley and I have in our skulls is more powerful than any dumbhead . . .'

Malise entered the story engine and walked along the pier. Women in cream crinolines stood at the railings, taking the air. Girls in pink chiffon pushed bath chairs stuffed with aged aunts. Malise wondered how many of the women around her were like Rosa – sentient identities trapped within this virtual environment? The enormity of what Foley had done appalled her. What kind of existence was this to offer anyone even nominally human: a life without birth, without childhood, without past? Had Foley thought such matters through? Or, like Snow, had she simply brushed all the difficult questions aside?

Malise passed a doughnut stall. The scent of hot, sweet fat was overpowering. Malise bought a bag and walked back to the café. The bag burned her hand and she had to juggle it to keep hold of it. When the doughnuts had cooled enough to eat Malise took one out and dropped morsels of it into her mouth.

She entered the café, and sank into her favourite chair.

Foley came out of the kitchen and sat opposite Malise. She gestured out the window. 'She doesn't understand what's going on.'

Malise looked where Foley pointed. Rosa was there, sitting on the cob. Malise wished she could gather enough courage to go and comfort her. Knowing that Rosa was just a fiction – a patched up Frankenstein's monster of stories and dreams and bits of Foley's personality – only served to make her more pitiful in Malise's eyes. She felt anger building inside her. Foley might have been lonely, but to play God in such a fashion – to *create* people. Rosa was destined to play out her contingent life inside this story engine for a virtual eternity.

'I'll go and talk to her. Doughnut?'

'Cheers. You want lunch?'

'Give me a while with Rosa.'

'See you later.'

Malise left the café and hailed Rosa. Rosa turned and smiled and ran towards her. They embraced. They talked inconsequentially for a time, then Malise did her best to explain:

'This place – it exists inside another reality. It's contained within a substrate – oh, I'm getting this all wrong.'

'No, no.' Rosa placed her hand on Malise's arm. 'I can understand that. Judith told me that much. Go on.'

'In the outer world that substrate looks like jelly, cloudy jelly. People use that jelly to do things. Foley and I, we exist outside the substrate but we can manifest ourselves within it – visit it – whenever we want to. It's a cross between a playground and a workplace for us.'

Rosa, mystified, took a doughnut out of the bag Malise was holding and bit into it. 'So what are you doing here now? Working or playing?'

'We're trying to learn things about a place which is foreign to us, and we haven't got long because an alien artefact is bearing down upon us, and we are afraid of it.'

'What's it going to do to you?'

Malise laughed humourlessly. 'I wish we knew. It's strange to us. We don't know what it's for. But whoever made it is – not human. Not like you or me – not the same character. It's alien. A mechanical thing with a mind of its own. It's coming for us and we're very afraid of it.'

'Is there no way of asking it what it wants?'

'Not that we've found. We think there may be answers locked up in other bits of substrate – places like this one – but we can't access them. We don't know how.'

'Can I help?'

Malise smiled and shook her head. Then she double-took. 'Perhaps. Perhaps there is a way. No. I don't see how.'

Rosa seized her hand. 'Try me,' she said. 'Try me. Please trust me. I know I'm not like you, not like Foley –

not so important, not so complete – but you can trust me. I mean, it's not as if I'm some kind of – monster.'

Malise lowered her gaze. But you are, she thought. A very beautiful, delicate monster. 'All right,' she said. 'I'll speak to Carmiggelt – a friend of mine who lives outside of here. There may be a way.'

It took Foley subjective months – but only thirteen minutes in realtime – to design the weapon. It was a kind of memetic bomb built around an old *Dayus Ram* logic-weapon.

Malise entered the story engine, met Rosa at the café and walked with her 'upstream' along the coast.

They reached what seemed on the surface to be just another seaside town.

The pier lay to the left of the main thoroughfare.

'Your machines made this place?' Rosa asked.

Malise nodded. 'It may not feel any different,' she said, 'but you are in a different world now – a different substrate.'

Rosa shrugged. She looked disappointed. 'It's just the beach town,' she said.

'Run through a fractal programme. We're going to present a recursive mathematical problem to the encryption engines surrounding the C-Ledge cores. With any luck there'll be some kind of cut-out to prevent the routines jamming up. Maybe when they cut in we can break into a higher calculation space. It's the kind of routine we used to crack Moonwolf. Logic-bombing. Done it loads of times before, though not with any system as powerful as this.'

Rosa shook her head. She was close to tears. 'I don't understand any of this.'

Malise stroked her head. 'Nor do I. I'm just trusting Foley. She reckons it will work. I'll come with you as far as I can, but I'm a bit rusty, and anyway Foley says your calculation spaces are bigger than mine. I might get left behind.'

Rosa nodded. Her eyes were blank. 'I understand,' she lied. 'I'm not afraid.'

Malise held her. 'You know you don't have to do this?'

Rosa shrugged her off. 'Let's get on with it.'

Malise led Rosa across the thoroughfare to the pier. They went through the turnstiles. The air was still. The multifarious sounds of the town at work dizzied Malise with their clarity and strangeness. In the distance, far beyond the end of the pier, they could make out the bright, horizontal band that was another town, on the opposite side of the ocean – only there wasn't any ocean.

The pier jutted out into nothing.

The seaside town had been copied and warped till it formed a perfect circle a mile wide. There was no ocean in the centre. Instead a shaft a mile wide with walls of solid mathematics stretched to infinity above and below them.

Every mile or so, Malise knew, there was another ring of seaside towns. On and on forever. A three-dimensional Mandelbrot. *God help us*, she thought.

'Ready?' she asked Rosa.

Rosa turned to her. Her face was ashen. 'I suppose so.'

'Then let's do it.' she said, grabbed Rosa's arm, climbed the rail, pulled Rosa up and launched them both into the shaft.

As they fell, hand in hand, Malise let her mind wander: just how powerful was this weapon? Just how much complication could it take? If it were powerful enough,

thought Malise, we might populate this place as Foley
has populated her story engine.

She let the fantasy overwhelm her: generation after
generation might swell

and people the shaft; a dust-grimed, falling race might consume the blackness,

people it, build in it. They will live in aerodynamically sculpted

houses, Malise thought, dreamily, and guide themselves by ropes

from one building to another. Lines and hawsers will be their

streets. A long central line will connect the upper and

lower reaches of their community, and a system of

weights and counterweights will convey goods and

passengers from one part to another. Some

mechanism will be devised whereby the rate

of fall can be regulated. The community

will make stops *en route*, take on

passengers and deposit émigrés,

barter and talk, and, for a   a n d t h e

fee, build lifting devices   w

to enable levels (however   e

many lie along the length   w o r   a

of the parked community)   k   p

to maintain communicat-   o   o

ion with each other   t t n e w n

when the community

drops

again

Malise awoke in a brightly painted room. Geometrical
shapes twisted the eye when she stared at the walls.
Fractals again. She sat up and floated towards the
ceiling. She kicked about in a panic.

A hatch squealed open behind her and Rosa entered. She pulled herself down onto the bed and held herself there by gripping the bedclothes. She looked up at Malise. 'Hello,' she said. She reached up, took Malise's hand and guided her to the hatch. 'How did I do?' she asked. Malise peered out and laughed and screamed all at once.

Teardrop houses hung all about the rushing shaft. They were held together at an even distance by huge iron gantries, and in the distance she saw that these stressed architectures ended in huge metal pseudopodia; these were drawn back the merest fraction from the sides of the shaft.

Along the gantries ran brightly lit cars and wagons, their smoked glass windscreens adding a bottle-green sheen to the faces and clothes of their drivers.

Winged craft dropped through the scooped, skeletal structures, then climbed, extending wings of tensile plastic to increase their air resistance and so slow their rate of fall relative to that of the community.

Malise fought for breath. Riding logic-bombers had never been this overpowering. It made Operation Moonwolf's soft weaponry look like an antiquated arcade game.

'What does it signify?' Rosa asked, mystified.

Malise shrugged. The weapon was making up its own internal iconography as it went along – neither Malise nor Rosa knew quite what to expect next. They were little more than animate calculators, integral parts of the system and so unable to conceive of its multidimensional whole.

The falling city applied its brakes. The air filled with sparks and the stench of hot metal. Malise and Rosa bore the quakes and cacophony as best they could. By the time it was over, they were exhausted, and they fell asleep on the bed.

They awoke to yet another world.

Rosa looked out the hatch of the teardrop house and read the memes.

'Well?' Malise prompted.

'Six mile-wide levels are joined by a thirty-mile-high tubular city.'

Malise thought about it. 'Very well, we braked. What else?'

Rosa shrugged. 'Nothing.' She looked around for further details. And looked again. Again. Something cold formed in the pit of Malise's stomach. Rosa came back inside. 'Get dressed,' she hissed.

'What?'

'Trouble.' From nowhere she snatched Malise some clothes.

They took a lift to the bottom level of the city. It was as they feared. The memes were adamant. Even Malise heard them. 'Well,' she said, as they shared mugs of hot coffee topped with melted cheese in a run-down café a short walking distance from the lift, 'this is it. Ground floor. The pit of the universe. And six floors up – the top. A universe the size of a towerblock. The encryption engines tied us up *good*.' She thumped the table with frustration.

'Oh, I don't know,' Rosa said, 'what about the ocean?'

Malise stared at her.

'You know,' she said, 'just down that road there.' She pointed. Malise looked and saw a gull sweep across the thoroughfare, a length of string in its beak. It soared up into the tangle of towering black buildings and a banner swung through the sky after it:

SEE YOU LATER

Malise looked around her. On the table there was a single coffee cup, and by it an ashtray made out of a shell. 'Rosa?' she whispered and looked about her, cautiously, afraid of what she might see.

Rosa had vanished.

Malise remembered the gull and smiled. She stood up in a daze and made her way to the beach. The pier was easy to find. It lay just out of sight along the coast road. The turnstile moved easily against the pressure of her hand.

```
nwent t
o       o
p    k
a    r o w
e
w
  eht dna
```

Malise trotted up the steps to the turnstiles, tripped over a hidden root and fell. She groaned and the groan came not from her mouth but from some deeper, forgotten place. She scrambled to her feet and her sandals scuffed rough planks. She opened her eyes.

It was the only hotel on the island. It was built of split bamboo on stilts over the river. The whole island was one huge swamp delta.

An intrusion, she realized, groggily. *She made it. Rosa made it. I've been snared. These are the cores.*

But straight away it was obvious this wasn't a core – not in the accepted sense. It was an environment. Another story engine?

The air shivered – an appalling screech deafened her. It was like an eighteen ton baby, crying. Malise whirled round. Something stirred in the blue green foliage, about twelve metres from her. A face peered out, snarled and was gone.

Malise fell to her knees at the horror of it.

The face appeared again and this time there was no doubting it.

It was an ape – an ape with Snow's face.

It shambled forwards and settled on its haunches beside Malise. Its breath was fetid and nauseating. It leaned over the side of the pontoon and examined its reflection in the still, stagnant water. 'I must admit,' it said, 'I've looked better.'

'Wha–what . . .?'

'Memetic compression. There's a hell of a lot of people in here.'

Malise looked around. 'It's like a story engine.'

The ape with Snow's face chuckled. 'So – the name stuck.'

Malise wound up what courage she had and said, 'I met you. On Earth. You're poisoning Home. Infecting it.'

The ape preened itself. 'Tell me, how am I doing?'

Malise stared at the ape. Anger began to override her fear. 'You're winning,' she said, 'if you can call betrayal of the human race winning.'

The ape sighed wearily and stared up at the sky. 'First visitor for seven hundred years and she has to be a Jehovah's Witness.' It leaned forward and snorted. 'Listen: one day everyone will be a hot-head, with my datafat in their heads, and they will live for ever in the engines I am building. It's inevitable, unstoppable, as natural an evolutionary progression as the opposable thumb or walking upright.'

Malise stared at her, and tried to grasp the enormity of what Snow was planning. 'You're mad,' she said. 'Look at you. You see what the consequences are of this 'fat? *Look around you*, for Christ's sake! *This* is the next step in human evolution?' She thumped the rough boards of the pontoon. 'Solipsism? Fantasy? And what's the reward for this, can you tell me that? Is this place the end result? *It's running down*, Snow, or are you so degenerated you can't see that?'

The ape laughed. With a lurch Malise registered the size of its teeth. 'This place *isn't* degenerating! I told you – what you see is a *compressed* environment. All human possibilities stepped down to the lowest safe level. All futures held in potential. Everything and everyone that C-Ledge was is in here now – in a single core. Of course I'm not claiming that story engines don't equilibrate. Story engines run down, sure; they tend towards a rest state, same as anything else. Its processes go grey and mushy at the edges just like in any neural network. Just as they do in a brain, in fact. But you want to know something? – *the human brain equilibrates faster*. People stay sane in here longer than they do in their own heads!' With an expansive gesture she encompassed the river, the forest, the sky – all the myriad elements of her story engine. 'The politics of survival, Malise. The galaxy is a dangerous place. No-one's yet found a viable answer to the two major problems we face if we want the human species to survive on an astronomical time span. First, our irreversible consumption of available resources; second, our inability to spread ourselves wide enough to be safe from cataclysm. Story engines answer both difficulties and throw in immortality for good measure. It makes people portable, malleable, *storeable*. My work extends the range of human possibilities.'

Malise gazed across the jungle landscape.

Not degenerate. Not senile. *Malleable*.

'What happened here – in C-Ledge?'

The ape shifted its huge weight and sat dangling its clawed feet in the green and soupy water. 'I didn't invent the datafat. The Massive did. The thing you found in the eggshell – her brain was made of it. So I tapped Amy and dumped her neural configurations into a core. Well, that was a *big* mistake. Amy was "dead" in one sense but in another she was still there, a data string waiting for some amateur Frankenstein to come along and build her a new body. Guess who.'

Malise thought of Snow's favourite book. Crazily, she found herself smiling. Poetic justice, indeed.

The ape palmed some of the brackish water up in its great paw and slurped it down. It belched. 'Excuse me. Where was I? Ah, yes. When Pendry found out about what I'd discovered he called a moratorium on all experiments to do with the new datafat. He banned my experiments and locked all the tissue in the lab vaults. I broke into the vaults, stole some tissue. I smuggled half of it Home, hoping to continue my work there. The other half I wired to the C-Ledge cores. Then I copied myself onto it. I wanted to witness what happened in my absence.'

'So what happened.?'

'Amy happened. The tissue I'd wired to C-Ledge's core hijacked our systems. I was in there, a part of that tissue, I could see what was happening, but I couldn't do a damn thing to stop it. The laboratory dumbheads took over the oneil and the C-Ledge environment became prey to experiments we'd never dreamed of.'

'And then we came.'

'Yes,' said the ape. 'You came – and got the shock of your lives. But appearances can be deceptive, Malise. The things out there, the experiments, the bones, Foley's companions – Amy did that to us. But just for a moment ask yourself why? If Amy had simply wanted to kill us, she could have told the oneil's computers to open the airlocks, or melt down the reactor.

'Amy wasn't fighting us – she was *experimenting* on us, the way we'd experimented on her. She was learning all she could about us. And in doing so, she dragged us into the future. I'm immortal, Malise, for as long as there's this datafat and a power source to plug it into. So are you, so's Foley, so are all the C-Ledge crew. It looks terrible, what Amy did here, but in fact what she's done is make us a gift that will keep the human race alive and creative for ever. If, that is, it's not too late.'

The ape closed its eyes. *It's afraid of something*, Malise realized. She could guess what. 'But it is too late,' she prompted; 'isn't it? Your nightmare's come true.'

The ape nodded.

'So keep talking,' said Malise. 'Tell me about the Von Neumann bearing down upon us. Where does that fit in your fairy tale future?'

'I don't know.'

'If you can't help us,' said Malise, 'it will kill us. Not just C-Ledge. Home. Mars. It'll consume every fucking rock in the system.'

'Really? How do you know that?'

Malise frowned. 'It's a Von Neumann, Snow, you know what that means.'

The ape swiped at Malise's head. 'Stupid!' it cried. 'You're thinking like a savage – "if you can't fuck it, kill it." Malise, you can't *afford* to do that any more.'

Malise stared at the ape. What it had said had reminded her of something. Something important. 'Fuck it or kill it.' Lust and belligerence. Lust. Belligerence. And –

She shook her head to clear it. 'So if it won't kill us,' she asked the ape, 'what will it do?'

The ape sighed. 'Malise, I'm not defending it, and I'm not claiming I understand it. All I'm saying is that we've got to keep an open mind about this thing. We *don't know* what it wants. Nobody does. All of a sudden the world is full of questions we probably won't ever be able to answer. Why did Amy leave Jupiter? We don't know. Maybe she felt like some foreign travel! Why'd the Massive build a Von Neumann machine? We *don't know*. Maybe it was feeling thirtysomething, maybe it wanted kids. Malise, these machines, creatures, call them what you will, these things are alien; they are independent, thinking entities, with their own motives and life-cycles and drives. For all we know this Von Neumann the Massive's sent us will die of shock the moment we say "boo". We can't just assume that everything that isn't like us is out to get us.'

'You've got a better idea?'

The ape nodded. 'Let's try and talk to it,' she said.

'That's possible?'

The ape shrugged. 'Perhaps. Those teratomic balls you found suspended above the bodies you found: they contain data personalities – millions upon millions of ersatz people. We're going to bomb the Von Neumann with immigrants. We're going to give it a culture shock you just wouldn't believe. The main difficulty is going to be seeding these bombs into the Von Neumann in the first place. We were hoping to grow some bodies by the time the Von Neumann got here, but we hadn't enough time.'

'Bodies?' Malise did not understand. 'Why do you need bodies?'

'We need people to infiltrate the Von Neumann and seed the bombs within it.'

The unstated request was inescapable.

The EC team returned to the *Greimas*. Malise flew them to C-Ledge; she manoeuvred the *Azania* into the manufacturing zone of the oneil and docked beside Nouronihar's drones barge. Then she took half an hour's downtime and slipped a *Dayus Ram* combat ROM into the port in her head.

She blinked and figures lit up behind her eyes. Her clock said 00.34:12. The Von Neumann would be in feeding range in approximately twenty hours. Malise pictured an icon and the clock switched modes. She set it to read -19.59:59.

Nouronihar worked with the EC team; they launched two machines of their own devising and a rock in flight paths which grazed the Jovian's approach path at the same time. One machine talked gibberish on every bandwidth the team could cook up. The other was silent – just junk, with an electric heater inside to keep it at the same temperature as its more talkative partner. The rock was just a rock. They watched their projectiles' progress through the traffic control telescopes.

Malise's clock said -12.30:30 when the first disappeared. Malise, Nouronihar and Foley watched the playback behind their eyes, running it over and back and analysing it.

Nouronihar spoke first. 'It's talk-tropic.'

Malise watched fascinated as the very smallest part of the finest tip of one of the Von Neumann's mouthparts detached itself in an arc which snared the talkative machine, curled round it, and bore it into the machine's great dark mouth. Like a starfish, she thought. External primary digestive system.

The next to be attacked was the silent machine; a wiry spindle they could barely see arced towards it – and missed.

The rock passed by unscathed.

'Tropic. It likes noisy things, can't be bothered with small fry. This is a *clever* machine.'

'Learning mechanism,' Malise confirmed. 'Signals represent ready-purified material, maybe rare metals, parts it can cannibalize. Lamarckian protocols, perhaps – hardwiring its tropisms to its feeding parts. Snow predicted this. It would explain why it's gone after C-Ledge and not just any carbonaceous chondrite. Tell the people of Home to turn off the radios.'

'Funny.' Foley's voice was heavy with sarcasm.

'She's right,' Nouronihar said, not sensing Foley's tension.

'We can forget sending in drones,' Malise said. 'If it listens for signals then it will spot whatever we send in by tracing its commslink. Presumably it'll then use some kind of mechanism to destroy and ingest it.'

'Tonsils,' Foley said, musing.

Malise laughed mirthlessly. 'Yeah. Big ones.'

*　　*　　*

The EC team turned on C-Ledge's factories and ran off three thousand kilometres of fibre-optic cable. While it was being manufactured, they built special metal-less evac suits for the three crew members capable of prosecuting Snow's plan.

Among them all, there were only three crew with the necessary augmentation to attempt to seed C-Ledge's meme bombs inside the Von Neumann.

They were hot-heads: Nouronihar, Foley and Malise.

(Malise's clock said -01.27:58; the Von Neumann's feeding parts were spinning now, matched to the cycle of the oneil.)

Foley and Malise used drones to fetch C-Ledge's eighteen 'meme-bombs'. Nouronihar and Carmiggelt prepared a clean-room and wired the balls up to make-shift life-support shells.

Malise stared at the eighteen finished meme-bombs lashed to the work desk. She blinked her way into their comms engine.

Eighteen versions of Snow emerged out of the black-ness to face Malise. Eighteen disembodied heads, each wearing exactly the same smile. 'It's talk-tropic,' they said, and giggled together at the synchronicity of their thoughts.

'Yes.'

'I hope we're not too heavy,' said the head third from the right.

Malise thought of the teratomic spheres, the tough resin skins into which they'd been planted. 'They're okay.' She tried to match the heads' sense of *Schadenfreude*. 'Bit ugly.'

'Shame,' said a head in the middle. The other heads cackled in unison. Malise shuddered at the sound. There was no warmth there. No warmth at all. They were cruel, heartless entities. They were made that way. They were weapons. Fearless, single-minded, like sharks.

'How many of you are there?' Malise asked.

The heads looked at each other.

'Shall we show her?' said the left-most head.

'Let's!' they chorused.

Heads appeared everywhere, rank after rank after rank: the entire crew of C-Ledge, replicated to infinity.

'Don't drop us!' they cried.

Malise stumbled out of the story engine, her mind reeling. She stared at the dull resin spheres before her, seemingly inanimate, in truth alive with teeming things. Sculpted personalities. Soldiers.

People.

Don't drop us.

Her clock said -01.07:08.

The Jovian's feeding apparatus closed in.

The EC crew made their goodbyes.

They were to escape in the *Greimas*, towing behind them some old combat craft they had found – fighters built by C-Ledge and mothballed since the Moonwolf war.

Once out of the theatre, they would hide the *Azania* as best they could from the Von Neumann and take up station in their more manoeuvrable C-Ledge fleet.

If Foley, Nouronihar or Malise made it out of the

Von Neumann alive, the EC team's sorties would try and pick them up.

'Good luck,' Carmiggelt said to Malise, minutes before the *Azania* went into comms blackout. The screen skewed and filled with static, then righted itself.

'Stay safe,' Malise replied.

He stayed silent for a long time. At last he said, 'You are going to die.'

Malise nodded. 'I know. We don't stand a chance.'

'You still want to go through with this?'

Malise shrugged. 'Saving the world: filthy job.'

But Carmiggelt was in no mood for levity.

'I want you to know –' he said, then stopped, and Malise was surprised to see that there were tears in his eyes. 'Your – effort. It won't be wasted. We'll get Home somehow. We'll stop Snow. We'll fight the Jovian. We won't stop fighting.'

'I know that,' Malise said. She blew him a kiss. 'You have been a good friend.'

Carmiggelt turned away from his comms camera so she couldn't see his face. 'Nouronihar and Foley – wish them – say –'

'I will.' Malise leaned forward and cut the link.

Her clock said -00.48:12.

Time to penetrate the Von Neumann.

Malise pulled herself down the docking tube to her customized maintenance pod, clambered in through the hatch and suited up – all bar the helmet – and let the chair web her to its resilient, scooped surface. She glanced to her right, at the escape hatch: its panel blinked amber and squeaked softly to itself, ready to peel away on a single command. She turned further in her seat, glimpsed the six resinous spheres lashed in a crude bundle to the head of the hatch.

Don't drop us.

She blinked up external views.

She was staring straight into the mouth of her nightmare. She could see its arms, curling in, each one a thousand times larger than any building raised on Earth.

The Jovian's mouth was black and bottomless.

She called up other screens, watching through the eyes of orbiting drones, switching from one viewpoint to another as one by one the drones were snared by the talk-tropic tentacles of the Jovian. *The sky was full of ceramic – tiles sheered away as the Von Neumann took hold of the oneil. The sky was grey with them – little particles come adrift, omens of a greater destruction.*

The Von Neumann's spines peeled back on themselves; buzzsaw recesses dripped cyanoacrylate adhesive and dug into the shell of the oneil. The tentacles frayed and jittered. Teeth and spines sprouted from the unwrapped surfaces, adapting on touch to the materials they gripped. They disembowelled the hulls of each factory unit with careless precision, revealing the moving parts within. Webs of filament tangled themselves in the workings of the factories, snaring and buckling them. Machines built themselves out of the tentacle tips and scampered down the lines on mad insectile limbs. When they reached bottom they settled and chewed away on the specialized parts the filaments had immobilized.

Malise started the launch sequence. The three maintenance pods – Foley's, Nouronihar's and her own –

eased away from the stricken factories. There was no radio contact between them, for this would give their position away to the Von Neumann. Loops of fibreoptic webbed from craft to craft were their only means of communication.

Malise's craft shook. A rain of gas billowed out behind her. She patched a viewpoint from a hull inspection drone.

There was a crack in the C-Ledge docking rig, hairline but widening fast. It went all the way through into the oneil.

She caught a nightmare glimpse of sticky black teeth and buzzsaw hide and then the drone died; there was nothing to see but static.

Malise patched another viewpoint, from a maintenance bogey stationed midway along the lighting axis inside the oneil.

The Von Neumann was plucking bits off the manufacturing zone as a child picks icing off a cake. The crack propagated. Inside the oneil, the wind picked up. The giant eyeballs exploded in the sudden pressure drop. Fleshy balloons lost their moorings and swelled, rapidly expanding gas propelling them all about the oneil. Some flew straight at the lighting axis and ignited, great hydrogen flares blanking out the view in sheets of roiling blue flame.

The meat forests haemorrhaged and grew black. Great bladders burst under the earth, filling the sky with waste. Tsunamis of blood swept across the land.

The winds grew more fierce, tore the earth away in huge blankets from the strange horseshoe mounds, revealing perfect teeth in perfect, bloody jaws, and bubbling, bursting tongues weaving the air in their own, gargantuan simulation of death agony.

A great rent tore open the side of the oneil. Bloody garbage stuffed the rift, then vanished.

Malise could see nothing now but murky brown clouds, fogging the lens of the faithful, still-functioning maintenance bogey.

Malise switched back to her craft's own cameras. Some of them were damaged. Diagnostics gave a repair time in minutes.

Her clock said -00.26:25.

The Von Neumann's mouth was a bare three klicks away.

The fibre-optic web connecting her to Nouronihar and Foley was shot to hell. Puncture repair spiders leapt from craft to craft, squirting little hydrogen jets to propel themselves from Malise's pod to Foley's to Nouronihar's and back again. Behind them they trailed rainbow filaments – replacement lines for the fibreoptic comms system. The spiders webbed kilometre after kilometre of fibreoptic from craft to craft – a dazzling web formed between the silent, cooling pods. Over and over again spinning trash punctured the web, over and over again tireless cybernetic spiders scurried to the rents and repaired them.

Two kilometres.

The clock said -00.14:00.

With idle precision the Von Neumann's tentacles flung half-digested scrap wheeling into its maw. It shot past the ships, tearing the web, wheeling within a few feet of the craft themselves. There were no collisions. The Von Neumann permitted no accidents this close to its delicate digestive mechanisms.

One kilometre.

Malise watched huge blobs of pink adhesive extrude

themselves from pores in the Von Neumann's skin. They were an ugly, medical pink and reminded her of the moulding material the doctors had used when they took impressions of her skull, in Milan, a million years ago.

They launched themselves from the sparkling lining of the thing's mouth. Sticky bullets, knocking its food into the correct flight paths. Behind her eyes, Malise flew all three craft, correcting their vectors with sparing blasts of their attitude jets, her gaze constantly fixed to the temperature curves of each pod.

They were in.

A bullet came straight at her, very slowly; there was no way she could evade it without heating her drive tubes too much, thereby betraying her location and breaking the fibre-optic web. The bullet slopped right across her sensors. The craft shook a little. Malise had matched the expectations of the Von Neumann to within a few fractions of an arc.

With adrenalin-spiked efficiency she patched viewpoints from the other two pods, ran graphics engines and let a computer simulation of the views she should be seeing assemble itself behind her eyes.

There was something round and pale blue straight ahead – a malevolent, irisless eye, dwarfed by a gargantuan socket.

It was a kilometre-wide plasma furnace, suspended in an oesophagus some fifteen kilometres deep. Half-digested wreckage from the oneil passed into the direct centre of the furnace, course anomalies wiped out by the powerful magnetic attraction exerted by the furnace's magnetic bottle.

Malise swallowed hard. A tonsil. A bloody big tonsil. A single fluctuation of the bottle, a single extrusion drawn through its magnetic field, and the furnace would act like a cannon, a great rush of incandescence, destroying everything in its wake.

Her scalp itched.

The spiders' batteries were running down. Supplies of fresh fibreoptic were low. Irreparable rents appeared in the fibreoptic web.

The tidal forces of magnetic stress which were there to contain the plasma furnace gripped the pods, pulling them into the insatiable brightness ahead.

Suddenly the fibreoptic web gave way. A sticky bullet had tangled itself in encrusted nodes in the web where they'd grown thick and fibrous from too many repairs. It curled about them, tearing the mesh to pieces, roiling in on itself in a frantic search to identify what kind of ghost tissue it had grabbed onto.

Malise thought of Nouronihar, and Foley. Now they would have to fly their own drones. Malise prayed they were up to it.

Malise opened the airlock and rolled in. As she kicked and shoved her way into the lock she snatched the resinous bundle from above her head. She clipped the bombs to her belt and held them tight against her stomach. The hatch closed.

The ship accelerated towards the furnace. She could feel herself growing heavy, pressed up into the head end of the lock, her metal-less suit crumpling and creasing under its own weight.

She glanced at her clock.

-00.07.14

The airlock cycled.

The chair was waiting for her, its life-support rig strapped with the equipment she would need for the next stage of the mission. Residue gases from the escape hatch propelled her towards it. The plasma ball filled her eyes, blotting out everything but its own, terrible incandescence.

-00.06.00

She hit the chair, grabbed it and swung herself behind it. She watched the radcounter scroll off the edge of her eyeballs. It was assimilating the dose she'd received in that brief moment's exposure to the plasma furnace's glare.

She snarled with victory: not quite dead.

She unclipped the chair's life-support rig and tethered herself to it, then looked out, all the way back up the pulsing throat of the Von Neumann to the tiny florin-sized gap of grey where the oneil's remnants were spinning.

-00.04:43

The oneil hurtled towards her – a world come apart, cut into neat, bite-size chunks. It rained in upon her, fled past her, plunged into the furious plasma furnace.

She changed eyes. Processors crunched her sight, expanding and interleaving to form a telescopic image of the creature's stomach lining.

Things were being passed across the surface of the stomach, around and away from the furnace. Bits and pieces were being scavenged direct – rare metals, subtle compounds, jellied remains of giant eyes . . .

-00.01:03

She changed eyes again. The stomach lining lit up – fractal geometries spilled across the taut, alien skin.

A distributed processing architecture. A computer.

No. More than that. A *mind*.

-00.00:38

She snatched the hand-cannon from the chair's utility holster and spun round, pointing it at the back of the chair. She glanced behind her, fed the input to her navigation systems. Feedback wetware seized control of her muscles, pointing the cannon without her willing it at a careful angle to the shuddering chair.

-00.00:09

Without wanting to, she pulled the trigger.

It jammed.

Her finger forced the trigger back, buckling the lever's axle, turning her finger joint to bloody jelly as it did so. Coldpack subroutines cut the pain before it ever reached her brain.

Her hand changed its grip, used its second finger to heave at the buckled trigger.

-00.00:03

The lever axle popped milliseconds before her finger did.

The flight path sent her arcing through the storm of wreckage towards the walls of the Jovian's stomach.

Something nudged her in the small of the back – a rock as big as a house. Ridge after ridge of pitted chondrite came up beneath her, inches from her feet, never quite touching. Just as it cleared her, a sheet of metal five times its size guillotined the sky inches from her face-plate. Her muscles went rigid, lying her flat, slowing her spin. Her ceramic boots brushed the surface of the sheet for a second, sending sparks – then it was gone.

Her muscles went crazy, spinning her round, raising the cannon. Left hand. Her right hand was entirely numb. A short burst of flame braked her fall. She soft landed at a crouch on the surface of the stomach, bounced off.

She unclipped a belaying gun from her belt and fired it at the surface below her. The hammer caught. Little blue-black mouths leapt out of the ground and started eating the belaying line, sucking it into their pink-lined mouths as though it were a string of spaghetti, pulling her down.

Malise screamed with rage, unclasped the resinous bundle from her belt with her sound hand and threw it at the wall approaching her.

Choke on it, shithead.

Throwing the bundle slowed her and spun her round: three sticky bullets, veinous purple in the light from the furnace, were headed straight for her.

The machine had smelt the flames from her cannon.

She unharnessed herself from the life-support pack and gripped it like a sled; she opened the valve on a breathing-mix cylinder.

With undersea slowness the makeshift sled eased away from the path of the Jovian's bullets.

They struck the surface of the lining; it reabsorbed them in an instant.

Something struck the front of the sled. It bounced up in front of her. It was a gigantic finger-bone.

The sled careered into the stomach wall.

Malise closed her eyes, waiting for the blue-black mouths to swallow her down – waiting for death.

Something magical happened.

The stomach lining swallowed the sled and closed over the top of it, leaving Malise stuck to its surface. She pushed herself up against it. It resisted, then peeled away from her suit. She looked about her. The floor was sinking. A perfect rectangle with her standing at its centre.

The Jovian was taking her in.

The floor sank. The walls around her were regular and perpendicular. A lid closed in above her head. She reached up to touch it. Hard, impervious. Passive.

She looked about her. There was nothing to see. The box was lightless.

The lamp fitted to the top of her helmet snapped on.

A box. Three by three by four.

Nothing moved.

The first sword burst through the wall a metre to her left, and thrust up through the top. There was a roar.

A billion hands, clapping.

The next sword burst up through the floor and grazed Malise's helmet on its way through the top-left-rear corner. Malise pulled away, dodged the shivering metal, crawled under the first sword and crouched in the right-bottom-front corner, staring, mind whirling.

The small of her back tickled.

She leapt, touched the ceiling with her sound hand, pulled herself free of the floor and stuck there, watching the sword waggle and thrust itself out of the corner where she'd crouched. The sword shot forward, clanging against the second sword as it buried itself in the far wall.

There was laughter. Strange, cold, inhuman.

Malise snarled.

Another sword burst in upon the box. It went no-where near her.

Malise laughed.

The far wall buzzed. She paused herself for flight. The wall shivered. She flung herself to the opposite wall, above the place where the sword sought entry.

It broke through, snared her suit, tossed her and pinned her to the ceiling and buried itself in her belly.

Malise stared at the blade, trying to make sense of it. She tried pulling herself down it. It gnashed against her rib cage. She became very cold.

She looked about her. The lamp on her helmet caught a flash of rushing metal.

The sixth sword mashed her head in.

THE END

Nine Card Spread

The swords withdrew. A short balding man with pebble spectacles opened the box, held out his hand. Malise took it. He led her out of the box, onto the stage. Malise blinked. The lights dazzled her.

The audience laughed. They cheered. They threw flowers. Malise turned to the man. 'You've changed your trick.'

Thoth, God of Magic, blushed. 'You remembered.'

'I can never forget,' she said.

He offered her his hand again and she squeezed it, to show there were no hard feelings. 'Am I dead?' she asked him.

'Yes,' he replied, 'quite, quite dead.' And with a gentle smile: 'I wouldn't worry about it.'

She left the stage. There was a staircase; it led to a black-painted door, and above the door an illuminated sign said: OPEN ME.

Malise ascended the steps and opened the door. She found herself on a plain of rolling grassland. She turned round. The theatre had vanished. In its place ran a river, and behind it, in the distance, a range of mountains. They were impossibly high and in the late afternoon sun they were the colour of ripe peaches.

Malise walked to the bank of the river. She wondered where she was, and why she was not more surprised to find herself here. She supposed, being dead, that she was impervious to shock. It was, she felt, both comforting and disappointing, to find oneself so ready for this place, to feel so at home in heaven.

She reached the river bank. There were four swords there, planted in the earth. On the far bank, she saw two more. She took hold of the nearest sword, meaning to draw it out of the earth and examine it; it was warm, pulsing. Snow's voice issued from the ground. 'It's been a long time, kid.'

Malise stared at the sword. She let go of the hilt. 'How long?'

'Millennia.'

'Where are we?'

'Inside the Von Neumann. We have entered its calculation spaces. It has taken us into itself, through our datafat.'

'Then we are alive?'

The sword laughed. 'We exist only as thoughts in the mind of the artefact.'

'Then the fight is lost.'

'Oh no,' said Snow, with quiet determination. 'We're not finished yet. Cross the river, speak to Nouronihar.'

Malise looked at the two swords on the far bank, and at the four swords around her. 'Six swords. Six meme-bombs, yes?'

'Yeah. We took big casualties as we entered the Von Neumann.'

'Nouronihar's here, though.'

'Yeah.'

'And Foley?'

The ground was silent.

Malise closed her eyes. 'Oh my God.' Then, when the moment of shock had passed, she said: 'I'll do my best to help.'

'Check,' said the earth.

Malise waded through the river. It was hard, fighting the current. She gripped one of the pair of swords planted in the far bank and used it to lever herself up out of the chill water.

The other sword grew a baby's hand out of its hilt and in the hand was a little green calling card. She plucked it and read it.

TOUCH ME

She touched the second sword.

The earth trembled. Out of the turf a great throne emerged.

Nouronihar was seated upon it. On his head there was a strange, three-tiered crown with thousands of gold wires dangling from it. They cascaded down his purple robes and disappeared into the churned earth at the foot of the throne.

Behind the throne were two pillars. Their colours changed and swam: they hurt Malise's eyes when she tried to focus on them. At Nouronihar's feet knelt two black suited figures. They wore wide-brimmed helmets.

'Glad you could make it,' said Nouronihar. He looked very old and wise.

Malise bowed to him. She couldn't help it – he looked

so worthy of reverence, dressed as he was, with his eyes full of time.

Nouronihar beckoned her up. 'Malise,' he said. 'The Von Neumann's egg-like extension is full of datafat. The Von Neumann is a massive neural network, a brain gone tumescent: it's so big its connectivity exceeds any useful predictive model.'

'You mean it's insane?'

Nouronihar nodded approvingly. He had taught her well. 'Quite. If this is a representative example of the Massive's evolution, it explains why it's been silent all these years.' He laughed – a chilling sound, as if the centuries had brewed all the humour out of him, turning it to irony. 'It is, as you say, nuts.'

'What do I do?'

Nouronihar gnawed at his thumb. His hands were gloved in purple silk. 'We run much faster than realtime here. *Much* faster – you understand me?'

Malise nodded.

'Our identities are in part determined by the degree of connectivity exhibited by our wetware; whether it's the brain we were born with, or some other engine – a story engine, a data core, or whatever.'

'You mean that while we are here, we're changing – mutating?'

Nouronihar looked at her quizzically, then with a gesture indicated his apparel, the throne, the crown. 'You think I *chose* this get-up?'

Malise laughed.

'Expect the deepest of deep meanings to be revealed by your every action,' Nouronihar warned her. 'We exist now in the kind of informational matrix that is suited less to the lives of individuals than to the modelling of whole civilizations. We find therefore that we tend to perform actions as strange and simple and irrevocable as those of history, or of myth.'

'All my life I have been waiting to do battle in such a place,' Malise replied, and then she thought back over her words. 'Fuck me,' she said, 'I see what you mean.'

Nouronihar pointed at the two black clad figures kneeling before him. 'Follow these two to the coast.'

They stood up and turned to her. She recognized them: they were data entities made out of people who had once lived in C-Ledge. Pendry, Tarkovsky.

'One more thing,' said Nouronihar, and the throne began to descend, returning him to the earth from whence he came.

'Yes?'

'You may find it easier to use the present tense.'

'Thanks,' says Malise, then double-takes. 'But I'm not inventing this,' she says, mystified, 'at least, not wittingly—'

'This space is modelling you,' Nouronihar reminds her; the earth is up to his shoulders now. 'It's trying to balance itself with you. Whatever narrative you play out, you will find that on some level it will provide the resolution to your own story. Stick to the present tense or you will find yourself lost in an ocean of alien subjunctives. Oh, and Malise,' the earth is up to his neck, 'good to have you aboard.' The earth closes over him.

Malise follows Tarkovsky and Pendry across the plain. They do not talk to her, and she does not find this strange. Our acts are stripped of contingent detail here, she thinks; they are as bare and certain as sarsens.

They reach the cliff by mid-morning the next day. The moment Malise sees it she thinks of it as 'the cliff', as if it was inevitable, as if the narrative in which she is embroiled has pre-ordained it, and perhaps it has. Malise approaches the cliff edge. There are six golden chalices by the edge of the drop, and on a distant headland Malise sees a tower and, on its summit, something golden. It is the seventh chalice – instantly Malise knows she needs that chalice, that she is caught up in some kind of quest, and that she has no choice but to obey its dictates. (Like Foley's story engine, the environment around her invests her with its own preoccupations.)

Something launches itself from the slender tower and moves against the sky. It flies towards them.

It is a gull. It settles on Malise's shoulder. It speaks in a voice Malise recognizes. It says, 'I hid myself in the meme-bombs. I wanted to be with you. I've waited so long for you. I've kept my promise.'

Malise believes that her heart will burst with gratitude and pain and love, but when she speaks, she does not find it hard to find the words to express all that she is feeling. The simplest of phrases suffice here: 'You have kept your promise well, Rosa,' she says. 'I remember. Thank you.'

Rosa launches herself into the air once more and leads Malise, Pendry and Tarkovsky to where there is a rowing boat, hidden in a shallow cave.

They wait for the tide to rise, filling the cave, and they cast off. They row hard and reach the headland by evening.

'Wait here,' says the soldier who looks like Pendry, when they reach the foot of the tower. 'We are the soldiers here.'

Malise realizes then that her companions are jealous of

her. They are jealous of her power and her importance. They want some glory for themselves.

Very well.

Malise waits at the bottom of the tower, watching storm clouds roll in from the coast – huge, heavy and solid as granite, sculpted like glacier mountain. Their colossal topography is lit up bright by a patch of western sky, a flat blue eye still open against the storm.

The storm strikes the beach like the clip of a giant hand. Lightning rains down upon the ocean.

Malise looks up, eyes screwed up against the torrent, and sees that the crenellations on top of the tower are growing, fed by the power of the storm. They make spines.

There is a blinding flash, a deafening report. Lightning strikes the tower. Malise cowers as masonry plummets to earth all about her.

She looks out to sea and sees Pendry and Tarkovsky smash a path through the waves to the strange, undersea spaces beneath.

When the storm clears Malise hunts for the chalice but it has vanished. She walks back and forth along the beach, waiting for the tide to wash it up.

She waits all summer.

When winter comes she hides inside a rock.

When spring comes she climbs out of the rock and looks about her.

Everything is a slightly different colour.

The sea breeze bears strange, unearthly cries to her. She looks out to sea.

Two men play in the surf. They wave to her. She beckons them to shore. When they are near she sees that their skin is scaled and they have large, steel-grey eyes which move independently of each other.

Only by an effort of will can she make out the faces that were once there. This place, suited as it is to the modelling of whole species, has encouraged them to evolve strangely.

Behind her Malise hears strange crunching sounds. She is very afraid. The fish-men lead her up the beach path to a grassy bank. Something terrible is digging its way out of the earth.

In a panic, Malise runs back to the beach and picks up a boulder twice her height; she turns and throws it with all her strength. It arcs over the beach and lands squarely upon the square of churning earth.

The fish-men throw up their hands in horror and wail in lamentation.

They lift the boulder from the place where the monster was and there, in the depression, is a not-quite-human baby. Its head is mashed beyond recognition.

The fish-men look at her.

Malise knows now that she was wrong to be afraid – the fish-men had been showing her the birth of their child.

This narrative has cast Malise in the role of a warrior, and so she knows instinctively the price she must pay for so terrible a mistake, so cowardly an act.

The penalty is Death.

Oh no, Malise thinks, not *again*.

She kneels. The fish-men stand behind her. She feels not-quite-human hands fasten about her throat.

She does not struggle while they kill her.

On the Day of Judgement she awoke at the foot of a smooth rock wall. She looked up. The wall was a footstool. She looked to her right and to her left. Higher walls lay behind it, forming the base of a gigantic, cubic throne. Above her, dimly glimpsed between clouds, was God. He was looking at her. He wore a crown. His limbs were made of metal. She was a fleck of dust in his sight.

He leaned back and raised his arm, stirring the air. Winds scoured the land. Malise stayed rooted to the spot, bent and weaving against the wind, like a tree.

She was a proud warrior, even before God. When she chose, she turned round and looked where He was pointing.

Barren mountains, range after range after range, stretched to the horizon.

She was a stubborn warrior, even before God. When she chose, she followed where He pointed.

She lost sight of Him in the third year of her journey.

In the fourth year she tripped over something shiny. She picked it up.

It was the seventh chalice.

She tossed it behind her. Where it fell a black lake bubbled up.

Something weaved its way to the shore. It struggled to make the bank but kept slipping back. It was a crayfish.

Evolution had snared it, trapping it in the black water.

A path led from the lake. Two dogs guarded it. They snarled and spat at her when she approached.

Night fell. A full moon rose. The dogs bayed at the moon, then smiled at her.

'Do you want to go home?' they said. 'Do you want to go home now?'

Malise looked up at the moon. It was the Land of the Dead. But she'd been dead so many times now that it held no power over her. Its glamour was useless.

She laughed at the dogs. 'Piss off,' she said.

The dogs grumbled and retreated to the shadows at the foot of the hills.

She walked up the path.

In the fifth year Malise came upon two towers. They were tall and black and frightening. Between them lay all the wreckage of war: bodies and ravens and broken spars and rusted shields. Soldiers leaned out of the towers, jeering at her. Their faces were all exactly alike. Malise realized that they were data entities from C-Ledge, and that somehow they had been as trapped by their own evolution as the crayfish had been. Time had passed them by. They were destined to fight each other for eternity.

Malise walked past them, ignoring their hoots and catcalls. In a while they got bored and went back inside their fortresses to plan their spring campaigns.

In her sixth year Malise slept under a tree.

*   *   *

In the seventh year Malise woke up to a rustling sound, which she thought at first was the wind in the leaves.

She looked about her.

A woman sat cross-legged on the ground, shuffling cards. She had her back turned to Malise.

Malise approached her. 'Hello,' said the woman, in a voice Malise recognized, and she turned.

It was Amy.

She had a tall, elegant bird-boned head veiled in cloudy black lace. She had big, bulging eyes the colour of sunset and a long scythe-like jaw hung with jewels and ribbons.

She was beautiful.

'Amy.'

'No,' the beast said. 'Marie. My name is Marie Czynski.'

'My name is Marie Czynski.'

Amy had vanished. In her place sat a middle-aged woman in a simple, smart black business suit. The hair at her left temple was turning prematurely grey. Her eyes were too large, the irises unnaturally wide, and her nose was a small upturned nub. Her lips were thin and too small for her mouth, so that she seemed always to be smiling: an expression reminiscent less of humour than anxiety.

Marie was human again – the way she'd been before the Massive had kidnapped her. This was the face they said peered up out of every white oval on Jupiter one day a year, smiling and whispering.

'You're the astronaut,' said Malise.

Marie's mouth smiled, but the gesture was not communicated to her eyes. 'I was,' she said. 'Once. The Massive tore me apart, Malise. Kidnapped me, then tore me apart, strip by strip. Then it stitched me back together again in the form you're familiar with – the form of "Amy". I am no longer human, Malise. I may prefer my human form to the form the Massive bestowed upon me – but I am not what I was.'

Malise did not know what to say.

'So,' said Marie. 'Why are you here?' Her manner was exquisitely polite – utterly threatening.

Malise shrugged. 'I've come to stop the Jovian,' she said.

'To kill it?'

Malise remembered what Snow had said. 'No,' she replied. 'Just to stop it.'

'You think it's a threat?'

'Anything with teeth that big is a threat, whether it's aware of it or not.'

Marie Czynski gave Malise a long look. 'A good answer,' she said at last. 'I like that answer.'

Malise said, 'I've met you before. I found you inside a concrete eggshell. You planted some maps in my head – maps of this Jovian.'

'I remember it,' Marie replied. 'One day – I cannot remember how long ago – time means little here – the Massive grew bored with its experiments upon me. It had left bits of me everywhere. A corpse here. A data string there. An autonomic process somewhere else. A smile, hidden in the clouds –'

Malise shivered.

'There were bits of me,' Marie went on, 'structures, processes, elements of personality – scattered throughout the Massive. I coalesced, made myself some machines of my own – a beanstalk and an eggshell – and I left. The Massive never noticed. Jupiter is big, and anyway, it was too busy on its latest toy. It was building its Von Neumann.'

'And then I found you.'

'When you broke into my eggshell, Malise, you terrified me. You were as alien to me as I was to you. I flung myself around that coffin of mine, desperate to escape, but of course I was trapped: only one route of escape was possible for me. I took it. That route was through your datafat, Malise. I hid inside your head. You've been carrying around more than a few maps in your skull. You've been carrying *me*. The maps were merely that part of me most easily accessed by your datafat.'

Malise stared around her. 'But if you were in me all this time, where are we now?' she complained.

'Malise, the Jovian has eaten you. In swallowing you, it has swallowed me. I am an independent entity once again; like you, I am a ghost in this machine. Everything I learned about you is now known to the Jovian.'

Malise stared at her lap, remembered the eerie, iconographic fashion in which she had reassembled her personality on entering the Von Neumann.

'You rebuilt me,' she said.

'Yes,' said Marie, simply.

'Why?'

'To see if you're worth helping,' she replied. 'Think of me as a communications channel. The Jovian wishes to achieve a rest state between itself and its model of you. I am its initial mechanism for doing this.' From the pocket of her suit she took out a pack of Tarot cards and laid them out on the turf before Malise. 'Think of this,' she said, 'as a kind of judgement.'

'Upon what?'

'Your life,' said Marie.

Malise bridled. 'You're going to judge *me*?'

'No,' said Marie. 'I will not judge you – as I said, I'm just the communications channel. The Tarot will judge you. The symbols which lie at the very root of your personality will explain your purpose and worth to the Jovian. Are you ready?'

She began to lay out the nine card spread. 'You weren't aware of me,' she said, 'but I've been wandering through your mind for the past year. You are a fascinating woman, Malise.'

Malise stared in horror at the cards.

The Tower Upright.

'You see, it's not enough to take a monkey wrench to this machine. You've got to *communicate* with it. Because it's an alien intelligence, you've got first to establish some kind of common language.'

The Emperor Reversed.

'Now, I can only do so much; I'm really not human enough any more to explain to the Jovian what you are. The cards, though – the cards are useful. They act, if you like, like a kind of – what was the term you used? – "story engine". They are a tool-kit by which to describe personality.'

Seven of Cups Upright.

'They break the otherwise irreconcilable residue of human personality into its constituent units of meaning. Now if the Jovian can reconcile itself to the constituents of your personality, we're home and dry. You can ask and it will obey. If it can't –'

The Papess Reversed.

'Oh dear,' said Marie. '"Lust. Belligerence. Enslavement." It won't like that at all.'

'Fuck off,' said Malise. 'Fuck off out of my past.' She leaned forward and picked up the card and turned it round.

'Hey!' Amy yelled, scandalized. 'You can't do that!'

Malise looked into her eyes. 'They're my cards,' she said. 'Remember that.' She gazed upon the fourth card.

The Papess Upright.

The Papess Upright.

Revelation, the Jovian read. *Resolution*.

Satisfied, it read on.

The sky grew dark. 'Well,' said Marie. 'I hope you're satisfied.'

'What have I done?'

'The Jovian's taking a personal interest in your case,' said Marie. 'It's heading for rest state.'

'Then I've won!' Malise exclaimed in the gathering gloom. 'It's obeying me!'

Marie shook her head. 'Maybe. But it doesn't just alter itself,' she said. 'It alters its model of you, too.' She smiled a cruel smile. 'Happy dreams!'

The dark coalesced. Soon, only her smile was visible: then that too was gone.

Malise waited.

*   *   *

'Revelation, resolution, and the influence of a wise woman.'

They were talking about the Tarot, again. The second arcanum: the Papess.

'What sort of influence?' Malise asked.

Seval smiled and kissed her on the lips. 'The Papess inspires dreams and visions,' she said. She peered at Malise's neck. 'Hey,' she said, 'did I scratch you?'

'It's that bracelet,' Malise said. 'It gets in the way.'

Seval shrugged. 'Sorry. Comes with territory.' She took Malise's face in her palms and kissed her full on the lips. Malise opened her mouth. It happened so fast she didn't think to pull away, or move forward, or anything. All she could think about was the taste of Seval's tongue. It was pleasantly sour.

They undressed each other. Malise kept stopping to taste Seval's mouth again. Seval had to keep pushing her away. When they were naked Seval wrapped her legs round Malise's shoulders and went down on her; Malise kept giggling because all she could think about was food. Seval's taste made her stomach rumble with hunger. Every now and then Seval let out a yell because Malise bit her too hard; Malise tried to say sorry but she couldn't because she was laughing too much. When Seval bit her breasts and her stomach Malise felt as if she were being swallowed, slowly and lasciviously chewed up and swallowed down.

In the morning Malise remembered why she was there.

'So?' said Seval, licking absently at Malise's crotch, 'what *is* your wish?'

'I want to save the world,' said Malise.

Seval wrinkled her nose. 'Passé,' she said. 'But if that's what you really want –'

'Well,' said Malise.

She leaned up on her elbows. 'Seval?'

Suddenly the room was full of a terrible stench – rotten meat in a slurry of typewriter correction fluid.

She scrambled up. 'Seval!'

Seval lay sprawled across the bed.

She was dead.

She was cold. Her eyes were open.

Her fingers were bleeding where he'd hit them with the hammer.

Her face was a mask of agony.

Malise started to choke. She stumbled to the window, tripped, fell five feet to the concrete balcony, got up, slipped and slid in a foul black sewage that smelled of rust and urine. Behind her, she heard her father screaming in his sleep, and behind that, the combined death-rattle of a million gassed civilians. She looked up at the sky. It was full of Americans; they were clubbing each other with rubber hoses. Beyond them, there was something very tiny, very heavy, getting bigger.

The more she looked at it the bigger it got.

It was terrible, monstrous, appalling.

It was an orange dolphin; it was John the Baptist's head.

She put her hands to her head and started screaming.

'STOP!' she cried.

It was Garry; it was a broken toy; it was every hateful stupidity under the sun.

She screamed until the words became a gabble and the gabble became one long cry of pain.

'STOP!' she screamed.

It was Schwarzkopf the dog; it was a Rolex watch; it was every manifestation of evil she'd ever glimpsed.

Now only the scream was left: pure, unmistakable, irresistible.

STOP MAKE IT STOP MAKE IT STOP MAKE IT
STOP MAKE
IT
STOP!

Malise dropped the folder onto the table. 'I feel,' she told Carmiggelt, 'like Lazarus.'

Outside, the stars turned slowly: they were sitting by the window of a free-station rest-room – the very room from which Daitakikawa and the EC team had helped save the world, eleven years before.

Carmiggelt smiled sympathetically. 'There's a lot for you to catch up on, I guess.'

Malise gazed abjectly at the typescript before her. It was a file from Haag's archive. The Jovian: structural detail, research abstracts, recommendations for further action. In the years she had lain buried within it, much had been learned about the artefact.

'I can't forget what it did to me,' she said. She squeezed her hands together, embarrassed. Her fingers were very puffy. A month ago, she'd been spat fully formed from Snow's prototype amniotic tanks; she still had the puppy fat to remind her of her rebirth. 'I sometimes wonder why the Jovian thought it necessary to use my whole life like that, and replay it so vividly in front of me. I suppose stopping the Jovian was such a complex business, it took all my life experience to contain the necessary memes.'

'But the Jovian *did* stop,' said Carmiggelt. 'You did win.'

'Did I?' Malise stared out the window again. 'I suppose I did. But it doesn't feel like winning. I'd hoped I would get to press its stop button. As it is, I was the button it pressed to stop itself.'

'But only because you wanted it to stop,' Carmiggelt reminded her. 'It modelled you, found out what you wanted, and it obeyed you. Once you'd found a powerful enough way to articulate your wish, it granted it to you.'

'That's not enough,' Malise replied. 'There should be a gap between wanting and getting. If there isn't –' she made an empty gesture '– the getting's worthless.'

'What will you do now?'

Malise shrugged. 'Try and forget what the Jovian brought up in me. It reopened a lot of old wounds. Fear of my father. A dead friend.' She shook her head as if to clear it. 'And so I guess I'll travel. If I can keep my eyes, I might spend some time down-well. There are a lot of places there I'd like to visit. It'd be a good education, too. There've been a lot of changes there, I hear.'

Carmiggelt smiled, wryly. 'Yes, I suppose there have.'

'How long's Snow been working on that thing?' Malise asked, and she nodded towards the window.

'Seven years,' said Carmiggelt. 'It's a miracle she came across your data string as quickly as she did.'

'Yeah,' said Malise, wistfully. 'I wonder if Nouronihar will be so lucky.'

Carmiggelt stood up and took his jacket off the back of the chair. 'Would you like to meet her tomorrow?' he asked.

'Who? Frankenstein's daughter?'

Carmiggelt laughed. 'We don't think of Snow that way any more.'

Malise stared pointedly at the hatch in the side of Carmiggelt's head. 'So I noticed.'

Carmiggelt shrugged, unembarrassed. 'Like Foley said: that woman's mad because she's right. These things –' he tapped his datafat port '– *are* the next step. Of course they are.'

'And do people get to choose whether or not they take that step?'

Carmiggelt took her hand and drew her from her chair. 'Haag hasn't loosened up that much,' he assured her. 'We've got ethics committees in every government in the world working to control the spread of these advances.'

'That fills me with confidence.'

'It's a start,' Carmiggelt insisted, evenly. 'It's better we work with Snow on this thing than try and stomp her. We tried that once before, remember, and look where it got us.'

'So she got to the States?'

'The States. Bangladesh. New Zealand. Eventually we went down on bended knee and shouted "Pax".'

'That must have been a galling thing to have to do.'

'They all are in this business. Oh. Yes.'

He fumbled in his jacket pocket. 'Snow asked me to give you this. She found it in the Jovian, in the nacelle where she was working, the day she found your data string spooling through her terminal. She thought you might like it.'

He took her hand, palm up, and he pressed something into it.

Malise stared at it. 'Thanks,' she said, softly.

'It looks good,' said Carmiggelt. Then, frowning, trying to make sense of it: 'I wonder what it's for.'

Malise smiled. She knew. 'It's a message,' she said, 'from the Jovian.'

'Oh?' Carmiggelt frowned. 'What does it say?'

Malise looked at it in silence, then slipped it over her left hand, let it hang from the wrist.

It was a ring of dull metal, pewter perhaps, and it was set with a dull red stone.